KU-741-685

What if there was a
child who could draw
maps that showed the
crossing points between
the worlds?

This book is dedicated to the FACCINI family Emily, Ben, Francesco, Delfina and Bay

HODDER CHILDREN'S BOOKS

First published in Great Britain in 2023 by
Hodder & Stoughton Limited. This paperback
edition first published in 2024

1 3 5 7 9 10 8 6 4 2

Text and illustrations copyright
© Cressida Cowell, 2023

The moral right of the author has been asserted.

All characters and events in this publication,
other than those clearly in the public domain,
are fictitious and any resemblance to real
persons, living or dead, is purely coincidental.

All rights reserved.
No part of this publication may be reproduced,
stored in a retrieval system, or transmitted, in
any form or by any means, without the prior
permission in writing of the publisher, nor be
otherwise circulated in any form of binding or
cover other than that in which it is published
and without a similar condition including this
condition being imposed on the subsequent
purchaser.

A CIP catalogue record for this book
is available from the British Library.

ISBN 978 1 444 96824 8

Printed and bound in Great Britain by
Clays Ltd, Elcograf S.p.A

The paper and board used in this book are
made from wood from responsible sources.

FSC
MIX
Paper | Supporting
responsible forestry
www.fsc.org FSC® C104740

Hodder Children's Books
An imprint of
Hachette Children's Group
Part of Hodder & Stoughton Limited
Carmelite House
50 Victoria Embankment
London EC4Y 0DZ

An Hachette UK Company
www.hachette.co.uk

www.hachettechildrens.co.uk

To Isabel

Which Way Round the Galaxy

written and illustrated by

CRESSIDA COWELL

hodder

This is a story with four heroes.
Who will be your favourite?

K2 O'Hero

Creative, brave
but a little unsure
of himself

Izzabird
O'Hero

Disobedient, cheeky,
means well

Theo Smith

Clever, kind, inventive and cool

Mabel Smith

Shy, thoughtful, Wonderful with animals

And there's a baby...
Annipeck
O'Hero-Smith

... and a little robot called Puck

TABLETOP MOUNTAINS
Everlasting Rings
Which Way
Snowshark Migrations
The Witch's 'X'
Which Way
Snow whirls
K 22

Prologue
by
Horizabel the Grimm

I am the Story Maker.

My name is Horizabel Delft, also known as 'the Grimm', orphan, bounty hunter, and the finest Starcrosser in the universe.

I keep the peace for the Universal Government. Which is a big job.

Because the universe is mind-bogglingly, ear-bubblingly, gobsmackingly huge.

But long ago in the distant past, a Magical human with a special Gift drew an Alternative Atlas of the universe, showing the exact location of the Which Way portals, where you can step between the worlds in a fraction of an instant, and save so much time and expense on space travel.

We call this 'Starcrossing'.

Only the very special ones, law-makers and bounty hunters like me, hold a precious copy of that original Alternative Atlas, and we fly through the universe, making sure no illegal Atlases are used, eliminating those who travel through the Which Ways without our permission, keeping the peace between the worlds.

We are very cool. We have great wings that help us cross the vast space-distances, we have no families to burden us, and we have successfully kept the peace in the galaxies for a wonderfully long time.

But now, for the first time in thousands of years, a descendant of the original Atlas-Maker has been born, a boy called K2, who has that same, truly extraordinary, Atlas Gift – and his Gift is EVEN MORE POWERFUL than his ancestor's.

The CHILD-WITH-THE-ATLAS-GIFT is now in hiding, with the rest of his family, who I strongly suspect may ALL have similarly strange and unusual Gifts . . . *and that makes them very dangerous.*

The baby, Annipeck, for instance, has the Gift of Magic-That-Works-On-Plastic, and that has never been seen before in the universe.

But we do not know what the other three children's Magical Gifts are yet.

What are those Gifts going to be?

Their Gifts could be ANYTHING, my mind is *reeling* with the perilous possibilities . . .

At the moment the boy and his family are

hiding in the House of the O'Hero-Smiths, on Planet Earth, and *I* cannot get to them, because K2's tricksome aunts have closed all the Which Ways that lead there so clam-fast shut that even the smallest of spirits could not slip through the cracks.

They can go OUT.

But no one *else* can GET IN.

And this is a very good thing, because . . .

Dangerous, DANGEROUS people want to get hold of the child and the family and their unusual and powerful Gifts, and the family is not safe, either from those dangerous people, or, I have to admit . . . from *me*. Because I know I ought to get rid of them, for the security of the universe.

(Please do not blame me. That is, after all, my job.)

So the children themselves, their entire family, their home galaxy, and way, way beyond, are in desperate, urgent peril.

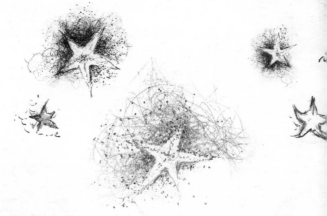

Let us meet one of those bad people, and you will see what I mean . . .

Hold tight. Grip firmly on to the feathers on the back of my neck, for we are going a long, long way across the universe to a world known as Blink 22.

Hold your breath.
We're going in . . .

Blink 22

Chapter 1
Death in the Prophecy

Once upon a galaxy, far, far away, there was a lonely
sun on the edge of an alien milky way that had
one shining frozen star a-wandering around
it. On that bright particular star, this forbidden frozen
planet, known as Blink 22, all was cold as ice, but it was ice
mixed with a freezing FIRE. There were flames embedded
within the glaciers, embers glowing steadily in the heart
of each snowflake, massive bonfires raging underneath the
great fields of permafrost. The fire-ice covered most of the
landmasses, but there was the odd oasis built on strange
tabletop ice constructions that stood above the freezing
floes, steaming and bubbling and brimming with life.

Over the entire fire-frozen planet, the burning ice
floats howled and cracked and the wind raged so wild and
lonesome your thoughts would freeze the moment they
left your head. The only bright spot was the rainbow rings
arching across the daytime sky, never-changing, offering a
hope of something better, but otherwise, there was nothing,
nothing, for as far as the eye could see.

But wait . . ..

A single figure making its way across the endless desert
of fire-ice, a great robot called THE EXCORIATOR with

a robot
called →
THE EXCORIATOR

skis on the ends of its limbs, diamonds winking from its bare skull, oh, it makes you shiver to see it, although a robot cannot feel the cold, of course . . . moving its skeleton limbs with such strange grace, this way, that way, dancing across the ice.

Behind it, a great heavily armed sleigh, being drawn by gigantic wolf-like robots, pounding relentlessly across the ice. In the sleigh a grim figure, deep in snowbear furs, with only the nose peeking out, hidden behind a protective shield.

The wolf-robots and the sleigh were dragging behind them along the fire-ice a yowling, screeching bundle of something, screaming so loud that it pierced the ears almost as acutely as the freeze of the wind.

Neither the robot nor the devil that was riding in the sleigh seemed to heed the noise. But at one point, the caterwauling attracted a shoal of snowsharks, their curving fins cutting through the ice behind the bundle, and the shrieking increased in terror.

The robot in front did not even halt, just sent up a periscope from its back, and two great laser jets of fire catapulted out, hitting two of the snowshark fins.

Vorcxix
(the Vile)

Pow pow!

The snowsharks gave piercing dying shrieks, and the rest of the following snowshark pod stopped in its tracks, and turned back to hunt for easier prey.

The robot and its strange entourage carried on, still ignoring the appalling shrieking coming from the bundle of rags they were dragging behind them. Until the noise accelerated to such an extent that the robot slid to a great curving halt, sending a spray of snow up into the air, and the bundle behind the sleigh screamed, 'It's here, it's here!'

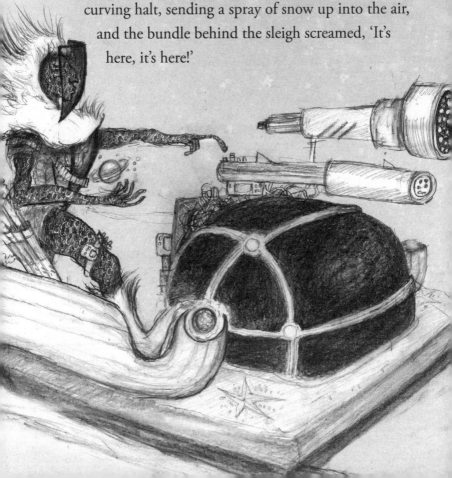

The robot knelt so that the be-furred sleigh-Rider could leap from the great sleigh, on to the robot's back and down to the ice. With one spurred boot the Rider gave the bundle of something a swift, sharp kick, which released the charm that held it, and out spilled from the invisible Spell-Net a spitting, cursing, infuriated Witch, green as emerald and lean as a broom.

'I told you it's here, Curse you! Release me like you promised!' whined the Witch. 'Give me my diamonds and release me!'

The Rider took out a glowing orb from his pocket. 'Tell me the Prophecy again,' said the Rider.

The Witch's spittle rained around the Rider's head in a sparkle of insults, so fruity that they would have set fire to one who was not so Spell-Protected as the Rider was. The Rider moved his finger, and the Witch screamed, as if shot. Shut up.

With a smile, the Rider handed the Witch something from his pocket. It was a child's shoe, tattered, torn. Still smeared green with the juice of jungle vines, for the child-owner had lost that shoe deep in the Forest of the Abhorrorghast, far, far away, in the distant world of Excelsiar.

The Witch sniffed at the shoe like she was a dog, smelling a thing to track it.

'The shoe of the Child-With-The-Atlas-Gift . . .' she crooned.

And then she blew on the shoe, hard, and the Witch Breath took tiny particles of the shoe, far too small for the eye to see, mixed them with the falling snow all around, and blew them into the Rider's orb.

With one finger the Witch tapped the Prophecy into the globe.

The Witch's vision sprang up in the centre of the orb, and the Witch squinted at the moving figures, sprinkles of light, traces of the future, there a moment, then fading like shadows.

'Very pretty, when the vision is made out of sssnow,' said the sleigh-Rider, whose name was Vorcxix. He peered over the Witch's shoulder admiringly. Even pure evil can appreciate beautiful things.

For Vorcxix was one of the Dangerous People I was just telling you about. And he wasn't just any old Bad Person. He was a two-faced member of the High Council of the Universal Government, a Were-dread Enraptor known as 'Vorcxix the Vile', with fingernails sharper than Air Sticks, and more sheer wickedness and devilry in him

15

than a sackful of were-cats.

He and I were deadly enemies, and last time I met him he was making trouble on the planet of Excelsiar behind the Universal Government's back – but we were keeping each other's secrets for our own purposes – *for now* . . .

'So . . . my Plan . . . my Future . . . is it ssstill intact?' smiled Vorcxix, with the hiss of a malevolent snake.

The Witch gave a shiver and a groan, as if she was thoroughly regretting looking into Vorcxix's Future. 'It looks even better than before,' she said sadly. 'For you anyway.'

Vorcxix gave a greedy smile.

'But you need to get rid of the Child-With-The-Atlas-Gift, for as long as his Alternative Atlas is not under your control, you cannot win,' said the Witch.

The Witch peered into the vision inside the orb more closely. 'You need to eliminate the whole O'Hero-Smith family, or your Plan will fail . . . except the baby – the one with the Gift of Magic-That-Works-On-Plastic. Her Gift will be useful to you.'

Vorcxix smiled again, enjoying the prospect. 'The entire nessssst of vipers, good, very good. I know where they are, on that wretched Planet Earth, but someone has closed all the Which Ways that would take me there, and I cannot get in.'

'The vision says the children will come through the

Which Way HERE,' said the Witch, pointing down at the ice beneath them.

Vorcxix stamped his foot on the unyielding surface, and it let out a protesting shriek. 'But there's NO Which Way here, Witch . . . See! Sssssolid ice.'

'Not yet there isn't,' whined the Witch. 'But the worlds will turn, like they always do, the Which Way will appear, and the four O'Hero-Smith children will come through here, one of them being the Child-With-The-Atlas-Gift . . .'

'But why would they do something so perfectly nonsssensical? They are safe as long as they stay on Planet Earth!' puzzled Vorcxix. 'I hope you are not tricking me . . .' He twitched his Spelling Finger, the Witch's body convulsed in an aching cramp, and she screamed protestingly.

'I suppose they *are* humans after all,' she pleaded. 'Humans are known to be disobedient and irrational and unreasonable . . .'

It was a difficult moment for the sweating Witch. But to her relief, the Were-dread Enraptor seemed to believe her.

'Let me go,' begged the Witch. 'I've put the vision into your orb, you can keep it now, what more do you want of me?'

'When?' snapped Vorcxix. '*When* will these ssstupid little humans come?'

'I cannot tell *when*,' snivelled the Witch. '*Where* is good enough, is it not, in the endless stars of the dusty universe? Right . . . *here* . . .'

With the other talon, the Witch drew a bright 'X' in the snow-covered ice. 'And that's the last time I offer a Fortune to a creature like *you*, Vorcxix!'

Vorcxix gave a slow smile, and oh, that smile was unpleasant to see and more like a bite.

He looked in the orb, which had now captured the Witch's vision. Sniffed.

'It sssssseems such an odd coincidence that they should come somewhere where I have so much work going on already . . . Could *they* be seeking *me* out?'

What work is Vorcxix talking about? I thought, with foreboding in my bones. *What is he doing on this frozen forgotten nightmare of a planet? Up to no good, I bet, by the whiskers of Sagittarius, up to no good . . .*

Vorcxix aimed another kick at the rag-wrapped Witch. 'Niccce doing business with you!' He took back the child's shoe, counted out one, two, three, four diamonds into the Witch's greedy palm. One for each child, and an extra ruby for the one with the Atlas Gift.

The Witch bit the diamonds to check they were real, gave a greedy groan of relief – he had not tricked her.

The fire-in-the-ice below and around them was too deeply embedded to keep Vorcxix warm, so the robot was building a fire of his own. Vorcxix lit that fire with his Spelling Finger, and it was not like any fire you see on Planet Earth, for this was a Spell-Fire made out of the falling snow, rainbow colours, bright with a sun-like heat. Vorcxix moved his hands towards it to warm them.

'You will not harm the children, will you?' begged the Witch, with a sudden attack of scruples, now she had her payment.

Vorcxix's smile was, if anything, even more unpleasant

than before. 'What a question from a being like yourself, who is happy to sell these children's futures, for a couple of stinking jewels!' he jeered. The Witch shook her head unhappily, like her conscience was a bubble of water that had got into her ears and she was trying to shake it out.

'My companion is a robot assassin,' Vorcxix went on. 'Isn't it obvious what we are here for, Witch? It's certainly not to enjoy the view? Now be off with you . . . what we mean to do *now* is none of your business.'

'But the Which Way we came through may have frosted up in this weather!' protested the Witch.

'That's *your* problem, isn't it?' snarled Vorcxix. 'I kept *my* promise . . . GO!'

Both Witch and Vorcxix knew that the Witch had greater and more immediate problems than a frozen Which Way. Alone, with no robot protection, on a planet that contained some of the highest concentrations of venomous and dangerous creatures in the whole of the universe, not to mention the artificial intelligence that had made this grim place their home.*

She didn't stand much of a chance out there.

With a scurry of talons on ice, the Witch took off the way she had come, still screeching, in blurry wingbeats.

---

* It was known by the robots who lived there as Brqjk1urblk22! But across the universe more commonly as 'Blink 22', for that is an easier name to pronounce for many humanoid tongues.

Silvery limbs glinting, the robot stuck his skis in the ground and made a start on building a shelter. They would wait for the children to come through the Which Way, like killer whales at a seal breathing hole. The shelter was not for the robot, of course. Robots do not need shelters. The shelter was for his master.

The robot sat down, training his considerable arsenal of weaponry on the 'X' in the ice.

Vorcxix stood up, furs billowing about him, watching the Witch fly away, faster and faster.

The Witch was in a hurry.

Maybe she knew what was going to happen now. But she couldn't change her fate.

Vorcxix was in no hurry.

There was nowhere for a Witch to hide in an empty sky.

Vorcxix waited until the Witch might have thought she was safe.

Pulled out his finger, made good aim.

The Witch didn't make a sound as she dropped from the air.

Landed on the ice.

Green blood spread out in a pool around her body.

Vorcxix grunted.

Sat back down by the rainbow fire.

Put the child's shoe carefully down beside him.

Waiting.

It's fine, thought I.
Vorcxix is waiting in the wrong place.
Looking into the future is such a
complicated process. The snow got in the Witch's eyes,
and muddled the vision. Why would the O'Hero-Smith
children travel *here*? Imagine an entire planet of ice creatures
as dreadful and poisonous as those that live in Australia, but
adapted for the cold conditions.

No one would choose to go here voluntarily. And how
unlikely for the children to go, for the second time, to
where Vorcxix was already conducting business of his own.

Let me give you just a sprinkling of an idea of how
unimaginably vast the universe is.

Mind-blowingly, brain-cell-numbingly large. There are
more stars in a single galaxy than the infinite grains of sand
on an Atlantic beach. Out of all the worlds, were they really
going to choose *this one* to turn up in?

This was the first of the coincidences that would begin
to concern me about what was going on here, and it gave
me a lot to think about.

In the meantime, I had to follow what was going on
with that troublesome O'Hero-Smith family.

So let me take you to a much more hospitable spot

than this strange planet far, far away, to somewhere you aren't likely to freeze to death within seconds or be eaten by gigantic snowsharks. The next chapter takes place in a much more pleasant place, and it is called: Planet Earth.

You better sit tight on that Planet Earth of yours, O'Hero-Smith children.

You better keep your promises not to step through the Which Ways.

On Earth you are safe.

On Earth no one can reach you, as long as you do not open the Which Way doors.

The O'Hero-Smith children, the whole O'Hero family, would be JUST FINE as long as they kept their promise not to use K2's Alternative Atlas . . .

Surely they would not do something so absurd, so unreasonable, so DANGEROUS as to break that promise?

I have a bad feeling about this, as we go to find out.

Hold tight to the hairs on the back of my neck, as I travel millions and millions of space miles to dear old Planet Earth.

Hold your breath.
       We're going in ...

Planet Earth

Chapter 2 There is No Magic on Planet Earth

There is no Magic on Planet Earth.

Or there oughtn't to be.

But apparently nobody had told that to a small creature running for its life through a particularly ordinary part of the perfectly ordinary Planet Earth countryside on a joyously peaceful warm summer's afternoon in early July.

The rest of that countryside was minding its own business. Birds were twittering from tree to tree doing their whole July thing.

Rabbits were hopping about, dashing across the pretty little winding lanes and into their burrows in the hedgerows.

Across the fields there stumbled a round little hairy thing, unsteady on its feet, running as fast as it could make its short legs move, out of its mind with fear.

It was as out-of-place as it could possibly be, and definitely a creature of Magic, because it was odd colours all-at-once, but mostly purple, a funny mixture of owl-like and impossibly fluffy, like an exploding kitten, clumsy and falling over, and limping because it was dragging behind itself in the mud one leg, encumbered by a luminous manacle.

Across the fields it scrambled, letting out the odd squeak, like the *hiss-squeal* of a kettle. Down the hill, through the hedgerows . . .

The barking of dogs, the clink of keys, getting closer, closer.

Four gigantic Alsatians, leaping through the field behind.

Five large humans, swearing, calling, begging for the unknown creature to come back or it would regret it.

The creature let out a low moan and dived into the rows of wheat to hide.

Above in the sky, came the whine of a drone.

ZOOOOOOOOOOM!

At the sound of the drone the little scrambling creature gave a particularly high squeak of alarm, which had the unfortunate effect of allowing the drones to pinpoint it more exactly, and they skimmed lower over the wheat, shooting tranquilliser darts into the crops.

A pause, and then the creature shot out of the cover of the wheat, on, on, poor little thing, balancing on the crumbling dry mud of the edge of the field, falling over, picking itself up again. It wasn't clear where it was going, and it might have been safer in the wheat. But the dogs would catch up wherever it went.

Behind the dogs, the humans on foot were gaining.

The drone spun around.

The little creature was running out of strength.

Panting, whispering soft encouragements and endearments to itself in agitated 'peeping' noises, it staggered on a bit more, but this time it could not dodge the zooming drone.

PEOW! PEOW! PEOW!

Shots rang out, raining around the little creature, and one dart caught it on its shoulder.

The creature gave a terrible scream of alarm.

'They've got it! Over here!' cried a joyful human voice, the excitable barking of the dogs going wild now, straining on their leashes as the humans closed in, plunging through the wheat towards the creature that was now staggering in drunken circles on the edge of the field, quivering and in pain.

One of the humans, a woman restraining her snapping, yelping dog with one gloved hand, grabbed the creature by its leg.

'GOT IT!' she cried.

The other humans arrived, their snarling dogs frantic with excitement.

'We got it, Mr Spink!' said the woman again.

Mr Spink stepped forward. He was the largest of the humans, immaculately but rather inappropriately dressed for the countryside, in a dark suit and tie.

Mr Spink was rather inappropriately dressed for the countryside.

His eyes lit up with greed and excitement.

Oho. He poked the Magic Creature with one finger.

'Lucky for *you*, Ms Right,' snarled Mr Spink. 'If we hadn't caught it, I would have held you entirely responsible for its escape.

'And as for you,' said Mr Spink to the Magic Creature, very loudly and clearly to be sure that it understood what he was saying. '*You're* going to regret putting us to all this trouble.'

The poor little creature was now a very dark purple,

and passing out from the sleeping drug in the dart, but when it saw Mr Spink, and the look on his face, and heard these words, there was an expression in its slowly closing eyes of absolute despair.

One of the other humans moved forward with a small cage in his hand to put the creature into.

Chapter 3 Various Impossible Things Happen Very Quickly Indeed

And then, various impossible things happened very quickly indeed.

The man with the small cage in his hand tripped and fell flat on his face, inexplicably putting his own head into the cage along the way.

Startling one of the other humans, who momentarily lost his grip on the lead holding his snarling, barking, leaping dog.

Who bounded forward, dragging his human behind him, opened his mouth to bite the little Magic Creature, but instead clamped his jaws on the gloved hand of Mr Spink, who was holding him.

Mr Spink let out a small yell, stepped backward, put his foot on the drone behind him, crushing it to pieces, and dropped the Magic Creature, who bounced, once, twice, and was knocked unconscious for a second as it hit the ground for a third time.

Seconds later, the little creature shook itself awake again, rolled into a ball and then bounced down, down the field, which was on a slope, like an extra-fluffy hedgehog in a race.

'After it!!!' screamed Mr Spink.

All four of the dogs' leads had become entangled, so the little Magical-Creature-in-a-ball had a good head start.

The dogs raced after the tumbling creature . . .

. . . but by the time they caught up with it, it had already rolled under the hedge at the bottom of the field, and out the other side into the dust and dirt of the lane behind, where it spun in three neat circles before coming to a stop, spreadeagled like a star, floppy as a slightly plump and squashy glove that somebody had just trodden on.

The dogs were too big to get under the hedge, but they wasted a couple of minutes sniffing wildly at the leaves, barking ferociously and trying to get through.

'Go round to the gate!' yelled Mr Spink, pelting down that field as fast as he could.

The dogs worked out they couldn't get through the hedge and ran around to the gate at the edge of the field.

It would take them only a few extra minutes to reach the gate, vault it and get out into the lane to pick up the little creature, still dead to the world.

But at that second . . .

. . . round the corner . . .

. . . came four children on bicycles. Two girls, two boys.

This doesn't seem like a good moment for introductions, what with all that's going on and everything, and the urgency of the moment, but these children are, in fact, the heroes of this story, so I'll tell you all about them in the next chapter, when I've got a bit more time.

The children were arguing, which is how I know it was *them*. The O'Hero-Smith children, I mean.

I've met these little humans before and they are always arguing.

They seemed to be searching for something. They were looking high in the hedgerows, and down in the ditches, as the older girl called, 'Where are yo-oou?'

The older boy said crossly, 'Why have you been keeping a cat in secret, Izzabird? No reasonable person would do that! When did you say it went missing?'

'This morning,' said the older girl.

'It will be so frightened,' worried the younger girl.

And this was the moment that the older boy leading them came to a screeching halt in front of the Magic Creature, unconscious on the ground.

'There it is!' cried the older girl, pulling up eagerly beside him.

The four children leapt off their bikes. The older boy took one look at the creature lying spreadeagled in front of them and said exasperatedly, 'This is not a cat, Izzabird.'

'Maybe it's not completely a cat,' admitted the older girl.

'It's not even *remotely* a cat!' exploded the older boy. 'Those colours are definitely Magic and we are going to be in so much trouble . . .'

'Is it all right?' the younger girl said anxiously.

The younger boy was gently examining the creature. 'It's still breathing,' he said.

From the other side of the hedge came the sound of frenzied barking. The older girl tried to peer through the hedge. 'Oh my goodness . . . I think there's some dogs after it!

Maybe they think it's a fox or something?'

The barking was getting even more savage.

The children didn't hesitate.

The older boy scooped up the creature and put it carefully into the younger girl's arms, because she was wonderful with animals.

The barking was getting closer, closer. The wheel of the younger girl's bicycle had mysteriously fallen off, so the younger girl got on the back of the younger boy's bike, and the children turned their bikes around, pedalling desperately in the other direction.

So when the four humans and Mr Spink and the four Alsatians vaulted the gate into the lane, they saw . . . no Magic Creature.

And no children, thank the stars.

They had disappeared round the corner in the nick of time. There was only a child's bicycle in the lane, just a small damp patch where the little fluffy thing had lain.

'Where's it gone?' shrieked Mr Spink, as the madly barking Alsatians dragged the humans towards it.

Mr Spink
stabbed the small
damp patch three times
with his tranquilliser apparatus
just in case the thing had turned
invisible, but no, there was nothing
there, he just blunted the needle slightly.

The dogs were going out of control, sniffing around the patch and then whining, crying, trying to drag the humans towards the corner.

Mr Spink's eyes narrowed.

'Something's taken it,' whispered Mr Spink. 'LET THE DOGS OFF!' he yelled.

ROARRR...!

The humans let the dogs off their leads and four leaping, growling Alsatians bounded after the bicycle tracks, followed by Mr Spink and his team.

Round the corner, the children could hear shouts and running boots on the lane.

The children were already exhausted. Hot in the face, knees scratched, desperate. Four bounding Alsatians now appeared around the corner, baring their teeth.

The lead dog quickly caught up with the younger children's bicycle, weighed down as it was by the two people riding it.

'Mabel!' cried the older boy, looking over his shoulder in horror.

As the dogs closed in, the one in front gave a great le-e-eap forward, mouth open . . .

. . . and the larger boy reached for something hanging from his belt, hidden underneath his T-shirt. With one hand he unhitched a small garden spray bottle, and turned round and sprayed the younger children's bicycle.

The bicycle gave a last wild wobble, the tyres screeched on the road . . .

And the bicycle launched up, up into the air.

The older boy sprayed the bicycles belonging to himself and the older girl as well, and they followed the younger children. Low over the hedge, up, up, up.

The dogs halted, barking in confusion, leaping up after them. But dogs do not have wings, and once they realised that they could not follow, they landed down on to the ground again.

And when Mr Spink and

the other humans arrived at where the dogs were barking, they gazed with open mouths at the four children disappearing low over the next field, dissolving into the heat haze of the summer afternoon, still pedalling, such an unexpected sight that it was as if they were a mirage in a desert.

Low over the field, pedalling steadily over the ears of the corn as if it were a road on solid ground, the younger children's bicycle wobbling from side to side, so they were in imminent danger of falling off. Into the trees beyond. And out of sight.

The humans gazed after them, astonished. For children on flying bicycles are not supposed to happen on Planet Earth.

'Impossible,' breathed Mr Spink.

'Impossible,' agreed Ms Right, shaking her head in awe. This *job*. You got to see some incredible things in this job.

Mr Spink had his tranquilliser apparatus in his hand. In a moment of annoyance, he pressed it into the arm of the human next to him, who fell to the ground, quivering.

That seemed to make Mr Spink feel better. He wiped his sweaty hands on a handkerchief he pulled out of his top pocket.

Mr Spink took off his sunglasses and looked around him. The perfectly gorgeous Planet Earth countryside all about him seemed to offend him in some way, as if he had an allergy to joyful little blue-tits and frothy meadow parsley.

'Where are we?' said Mr Spink. 'Remind me. What a dump.'

One of the humans checked on his phone.

'It seems to be called . . . Which Way Corner, Soggy-Bottom-Marsh-Place.'

'Interesting,' said Mr Spink, who worked for the government on Planet Earth. On second thoughts, maybe this mistake could turn out to be leading him to a very big capture indeed. And a promotion that Mr Spink felt he richly deserved. 'Ve-ry interesting.'

'OK. Send the drones after them! I want this whole area put under covert observation while we find out exactly what is going on round here,' said Mr Spink.

Who were these children, where did they live, why were they on flying bicycles and what did they have to do with this Magical Creature? And shouldn't they be brought in for interrogation and investigation and testing and rigorous scientific experimentation, I mean, silly me, examination? In the national interest, of course.

Mr Spink was going to make sure that happened.

Because there is no Magic on Planet Earth.

Or there oughtn't to be.

Chapter 4 Introducing the O'Hero-Smiths

The four children flew low over the next field.

You have probably guessed already that these are the very O'Hero-Smith children that Vorcxix and I were looking for.

The flying bicycles were a bit of a clue.

It seems like a good moment now to introduce you properly, and you can decide which one of these heroes is going to be your favourite.

Izzabird and K2 O'Hero were twelve-year-old twins from a Magical family that was trying to keep their Magic secret in a world that did not think that Magic existed.

And Theo and Mabel Smith were thirteen and nine years old, and from a supposedly *non*-Magical family that had recently discovered that they might not be *quite* as un-Magical as they had previously thought.

When Theo and Mabel's father, Daniel, married Izzabird and K2's mother, Freya, the Smiths had moved to Soggy-Bottom-Marsh-Place, and the two families had become one family, and the children had not been happy about it.

The one thing they could agree they were all happy about was their baby sister Annipeck, whom everyone adored.

When I first met these children, they were all sad and

rather angry. Theo and Mabel were missing their mother, who had died a few years earlier. K2 and Izzabird were missing their father, a great Explorer Hero who had an unfortunate habit of going missing and emptying out the family bank account.

I could smell that they were somewhat less unhappy than the last time I met them, so they had made some hopeful progress.

But they were having some problems keeping their promise not to argue so much.

Particularly Izzabird and Theo.

Izzabird and Theo argued ALL the time because they both wanted to be in charge.

Izzabird was a disobedient, slightly-out-of-control kid with an uncountable number of cheery freckles scattered all over her optimistic little face, and she was pedalling her bicycle with such excitement that she was in danger of going over the handlebars any minute.
She was the kind of person who MEANT well, but who was always getting into trouble because she *acted* first – and *thought* later.

Izzabird acted first – and thought later.

K2 and Mabel

'What are you *doing*, K2?' yelled
Izzabird. 'You have to KEEP PEDALLING
or you're going to crash!'

K2 and Mabel's bicycle was wiggling wildly from left to
right and he was hanging on to the handlebars for dear life.

Unlikely as it may seem, *K2* was the one with the
startlingly amazing 'Atlas Gift' that I was telling
you about earlier.

K2 did all the worrying for both twins. He

was somewhat shy, and unconfident and ordinary-looking, and he had generally got into the habit of doing whatever his twin sister said, in a slightly dreamy, absent-minded way, because Izzabird was such a forceful character it was a lot easier just to do what he was told – but in this case he was having a bit of difficulty. His pedal hadn't quite fallen off yet, but it seemed to be attached by only one screw.

'I'm *trying*!' said K2, as the bicycle plunged downwards.

'UP! Point the handlebars UP!!' shouted Theo from over his shoulder. 'Oh my goodness, we're being attacked by *drones*! *DUCK!*'

Theo was in front, leading the flying-bicycle-party, much to Izzabird's irritation. Theo was the kind of kid who often ended up leading things, whether it's a flying-bicycle expedition, or a sports team, or a chess club. He was highly intelligent and popular, and top in everything, from academics to sports, and he even managed to make riding a flying bicycle look cool, which is tricky because you have to keep pedalling or you drop right out of the sky.

But there he was, not a hair out of place, looking like he was going for a fast-but-relaxed afternoon cycle on the ground, rather than twenty feet up in the air, being bombarded by drones shooting tranquilliser darts, and Izzabird found this profoundly annoying.

Theo swooped down, spraying the drones with the

Flying Poshun in his spray bottle, and they shot upward like rockets, out of control, and out of action, way into the clouds above.

Theo gave a whoop of satisfaction as he turned his head upward to watch them go.

'Nice work, Theo, but stop giving K2 orders!' ordered Izzabird. 'You're so bossy! K2, you need to pedal quicker! Those drones could come back . . .'

'I . . . can't . . . do . . . it . . .' panted K2.

'I think one of his pedals has broken!' said Mabel.

Mabel was kind and quiet and small and shy, and maybe those are Hero qualities, too? The story will no doubt tell us. There's nothing like an adventure to find out whether you are a Hero or not. Like K2, Mabel was a lot less happy than the other two to be in this alarming situation.

Theo even made riding a flying bicycle look cool

Mabel was right, and it's very difficult to pedal a bicycle with only one pedal.

As K2 and Mabel's bicycle plunged downwards, a small whirring robot with helicopter wings flew out of his knapsack.

The robot was called Puck, and he was lopsided, and eager, and always getting things wrong.

Mr Spink would have been as interested in this robot as he was in the flying bicycles, because children on Planet Earth do not normally have robot companions.

Pets, yes.

Mobile phones, often.

Well-intentioned but accident-prone little droids? Not so much.

'I's can help!' squealed Puck. 'I's can SO help!' He thrust out one of his robot arms, and screwdrivers, spanners, oil squirters and slightly less useful things like drills and spoons sprouted out of his arm holes, like an animated and enthusiastic Swiss Army knife.

He zoomed after the plunging bicycle and tried to fiddle with the pedal, but all he succeeded in doing was getting a lot of oil over K2's socks and accidentally sticking one of his arms in between the spokes of the back wheel, causing the bicycle to rear violently forward like a bucking horse, propelling K2 headfirst over the handlebars, and making

Puck the well intentioned little robot

'I's can help!'

Mabel cling desperately to the frame of the bike so she
didn't fall off.

'Whoops,' said Puck.

Down K2 and Mabel plunged, still holding on to the
handlebars of the now upside-down bike, and they would
have had a very nasty crash indeed if it hadn't been for Theo
swooping down to break their fall by grabbing the back wheel
so that K2 could make a slightly more controlled landing.

The other children landed nearby, and ran to where K2
and Mabel were staggering to their feet.

'Is it all right?' said Izzabird anxiously.

'And are *you* all right, Mabel, K2, Puck?' said Theo.

'I izz SO OK!' squeaked Puck, wriggling out from
underneath K2's crashed bicycle, and flying, slightly
wobblily, to the four children, crowded round K2 and
Mabel. 'I izz *werpefickly* fine!'

'Oh, Puck . . .' said K2 sadly, trying to bend one of his helicopter wings back to a straight position. 'Aunt Violet had only just mended you . . .'

Mabel checked the Magical Creature hadn't been hurt by the fall. The creature was small and round and fluffy, like a squashed baby yeti, and at the moment it was all colours of the rainbow, with one extra for luck. This was a Magical colour that no one had ever seen before, which I will call 'yurple'. 'It's so SWEET!' gasped Mabel, tenderly stroking the floppy paw in the broken security manacle around the Magical Creature's ankle. 'Did you see those people in suits? They must have imprisoned it, poor thing . . .'

Theo had one of those faces that didn't change expression much, so you couldn't always tell when he was upset. Now a cold knot of fear and anger was hardening in his stomach. Mabel could have been captured by those people. Or hurt by that dog.

'You know perfectly well we're not supposed to let anything Magic go out of the house, Izzabird,' snapped Theo. 'Why can't you follow the rules?'

'HA!' retorted Izzabird. 'What about the Flying Poshun YOU just used? You're not so very obedient yourself, Theo Smith!'

'I was defending Mabel,' said Theo loftily, even crosser because he knew Izza was right. He couldn't resist trying out

49

all the wonderful Magical spells and potions he'd so recently discovered all around him in the O'Hero-Smith household, and then he felt guilty about it. But at least he had used it to get them *out* of trouble, rather than *into* it.

Like Izzabird, Theo's independent spirit and sense of adventure often mysteriously led him into trouble without him exactly intending it.

'The question is, who were those people, and why were they chasing this creature?' said K2.

The children looked at one another with stiff, scared faces.

That broken security bracelet was very sinister. Nobody was supposed to know about the existence of Magic and the strange things that went on at the House at the Crossing of the Ways, where the children lived.

'Aunt Trudie and Violet will know what to do,' decided Mabel.

They had run out of Flying Gas, so K2 put the knapsack with the Magical Creature in it on his back and Theo gave him a lift on his bike, while the slightly-broken Puck dragged K2's very-broken bike and, hearts pounding, they all pedalled as hard and fast as they could to the House at the Crossing of the Ways, with the distant sound of barking dogs in their ears.

Chapter 5 The House at the Crossing of the Ways

The house seemed to know they were coming.

The nearer they got, the more Theo had the weird sense that it wasn't only his own legs that were moving the pedals, but that there were ghostly fingers stretching out from the house and helping the pedals go round faster, and he himself was just trying to keep up. The back garden door opened for them of its own accord, as if by an invisible wind, and when they bundled through, gasping, panting in the afternoon heat, in an untidy, frightened crowd, the door slammed behind them and when Theo pushed the bolts back with sweaty, trembling fingers, there was the click of an extra-locking of Magic.

For the house *knew*.

It was an old, old house, and it sensed when it was in danger of attack.

The house had been built on an ancient Crossing of the Ways, a crossroads where people had been walking since way before the Bronze Ages, and, less known locally, where beings from across the universe had been travelling through since the beginning of recorded time, through the Which Ways or short cuts that are crossing points between the worlds, and save so much time and expense on space travel.

Above the door it called itself 'The House of the
O'Heros', with a picture of two hands pointing in different
directions and the O'Hero motto underneath: 'An O'Hero
Knows No Limits! The Sky Is Just the Beginning. No Rivers
Can Stop Us, No Mountains Can Stand in Our Way!'

And on the gate it had now added: 'The House of the
O'Hero-Smiths', to mark the fact that the O'Hero and the
Smith families had merged, and this most coincidentally and
fortunately means 'Heros-in-the-making', because a 'Smith'
is another name for a craftsperson, or a maker of things.

New kinds of Heroes were being created in this house. Heroes with new powers . . .

The children were greeted at the back gate by Clueless, the little black-and-white family dog, jumping up and down and barking excitedly. They abandoned their bicycles and ran full pelt up the garden towards the house.

By the time they got to the end of the lawn, the house alarms were blaring all over the peaceful countryside, as if this was some major incident in an urban area rather than the peaceful backwater of Soggy-Bottom-Marsh-Place.

Aunt Trudie met them at the front door, in what can only be described as a total tizzy.

She had her hands over her ears because a number of alarms in the house were going off. Not the usual intruder alarm, but alarms that the kids had never heard go off before. The doors were slamming, the sinks were letting out great foghorn burps, and all the telephones were ringing, even the ones that weren't connected to any wires.

'Oh, thank the stars, you're back!' said Aunt Trudie. 'We have a major problem! We seem to have some unwanted government attention!'

'We've got a bit of a problem ourselves, Aunt Trudie . . .' said K2, Izzabird tugging on his jumper to try and get him to 'Shhh'.

'Not now, not now!' squealed Aunt Trudie in a most

Aunt Trudie-like panicky fashion. 'My plants are escaping!'

Aunt Trudie

'My plants are escaping!'

And she ran out into the garden towards her greenhouses. Most plants, of course, don't move about too much. But Aunt Trudie had a really rather fascinating plant collection from across the universe, some of which had tendrils that they used as legs.

These plants had now escaped from the greenhouses and were running across the lawn, chased by an out-of-control lawnmower crossed with a rocket launcher from Aunt Violet's workshop.

The children ran into the hall.

Freya, K2 and Izzabird's rather
scatty, determined little mother,
had one of her migraines, and she was
looking particularly fierce, her face taut with fear.

'Someone must be investigating us, which is why those
alarms are going off,' she explained, hurrying past them all to
try and turn off the alarms. 'Oh dear, oh dear, oh dear . . .
we should never have taught you about Magic . . . much
better for you not to know . . .'

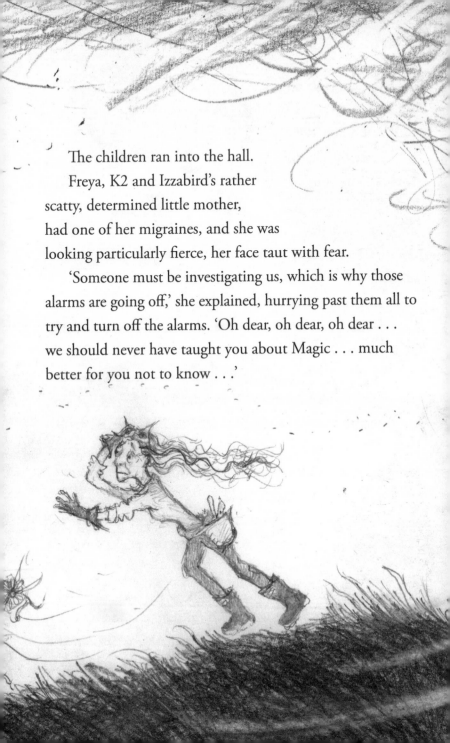

Theo and Mabel's father Daniel →

'You haven't been teaching us MUCH,' said Izzabird crossly.

'You're the eldest, Theo. I hope you haven't been leading the others into any trouble?' said Daniel, Mabel and Theo's father, peering suspiciously at his son through his glasses.

Daniel was the headmaster of Soggy-Bottom-Marsh-Place School, and he should have been having a quiet break because this was the summer holidays – but he often found looking after five hundred students rather easier and more peaceful than looking after his own family.

An entirely un-Magical person himself, Daniel was still getting used to marrying into a Magical family, and he'd *never* got into trouble when he was a child. Why did Theo always seem to be at the centre of any chaos that was going on, either at school or at home? It was hardly sensible Smith behaviour.

'I'm only *just* older than K2 and Izzabird, I can't control them, and why don't you trust me?' protested

Why are you always telling ME OFF?'

Theo, with a strong sense of injury. 'Why are you always telling *me* off?'

'If any of you pesky children have been doing any Spelling outside the house at all, that is the last Magic any of us ever teach you!' growled Aunt Violet, a heavily muscled, tattooed old lady with a mean look in her eye. She sent the four children an absolutely ferocious look from under her brows, as she elbowed them out of the way on her way to the kitchen, from which the most appalling racket was emerging.

Mabel opened her mouth to explain, but Theo gave her a look to say, 'keep quiet'.

Aunt
Violet
↙

You pesky children
better not have been
doing any Magic...

Freya and Annipeck

It didn't seem the best moment to come clean about the Magic Creature.

Freya and Aunt Violet and Aunt Trudie clearly knew about those people running after it anyway. Theo supposed they were the unwanted attention the aunts were going on about and why the weird alarms were going off. There was no point getting Izzabird into any more trouble.

'Oh, no, we haven't been using any Magic, have we?' said Theo. 'Haven't even *seen* anything suspiciously Magical whatsoever.'

Izzabird gave him a grateful look.

'OK, nobody *panic*!' said Freya, holding her head, as the alarms still blared on, regardless of how often she punched the buttons on the controls by the front door. 'It may be a false alarm . . . But just in case someone hears these sirens and the police get involved, we need to make everything look NORMAL . . . Daniel, sort out Aunt Trudie's workshop, and I'll deal with Aunt Violet's, she's going to be busy in the kitchen . . . Could you children take Annipeck upstairs and tidy anything away that looks a little . . . *unusual*?' Freya handed Annipeck to Theo. Annipeck was looking delighted at the chaotic situation, peering around with great interest. 'And Annipeck! Make your toothbrushes play dead!'

A family of three plastic toothbrushes were perched on Annipeck's shoulders, and they were unusually animated for toothbrushes on Planet Earth.

In fact, they looked surprisingly as if they were *alive*.

Annipeck blinked once, twice, and the toothbrushes tucked themselves away in her hand, stiff and proper like nice normal toothbrushes. Her Lego still looked pretty lively, though. Not to mention the second-hand toy telephone that was bumping repeatedly into Theo's ankle, nudging him upstairs.

Creak! One of the paintings in the hall mysteriously unhooked itself and would have crashed to the floor, smashing the glass, if Freya hadn't pushed a sideboard underneath it in the nick of time. She was surprisingly strong for such a small person.

'*What in the name of Earth and all the planets and stars*

and the whiskers of Sagittarius is going on???' said Freya, in distress, running out of the door.

From the kitchen came the sound of banging and clanging. On their way upstairs they peered through the open kitchen door to see Aunt Violet wrestling with some of her own inventions, which appeared to have gone entirely out of control. Her Automatic-Dog-Feeding-Machine was randomly shooting dog biscuits across the room. Her Eazo-Relaxo-Breakfast-Maker was buttering Daniel's important headteacher's papers and then toasting them. Her Ultra-Fast-Baked-Bean-Tin-Opener was scurrying through the kitchen opening up packets of cereal, the top of the bread bin and Aunt Trudie's handbag.

The knob on the staircase fell off when K2 was running upstairs. And there was the distant sound of bath water running from the family bathroom.

They all dived into Theo's room, which was quite quiet compared to the rest of the house, apart from loud banging coming from the chest of drawers. When Theo walked over and opened the top drawer, a large plastic hairdryer shot out and flew around the room like an agitated aerial seahorse.

K2 shut the bedroom door.

Freya was right.

What on Earth was going on??

Chapter 6 What on Earth Was Going On??

Y ou will now know, even if this is your first introduction to the O'Hero-Smith household, that this is not an *entirely* ordinary family.

But this was a chaotic situation, even for the O'Hero-Smiths.

'What on Earth is going on, Izzabird?' said Theo, grimly crossing his arms as the sound of chaos drifted up from downstairs. Theo was a very neat, tidy person, and he found situations like this particularly annoying.

Izzabird opened her eyes wide. She put her fist up in the air, and immediately went into Izzabird's Automatic Defence Mode.

'I'm innocent! I was framed!' she yelled. 'Whatever it is, I wasn't there! Why does everyone always blame ME for everything?'

'Because it's generally your fault!' said Theo. 'You're getting us all into trouble and you're completely out of control!'

I'm innocent!
I was framed!

because it's generally your FAULT!

None of the other children contradicted Theo. Even the hairdryer and Annipeck's toothbrushes nodded solemnly, while Annipeck gave an approving gurgle.

'That's *so* not fair!' protested Izzabird. 'Why do you let Theo bully you into agreeing with him, K2? He isn't the boss of US!'

One of the many extremely irritating things about the Smith children, in Izzabird's opinion, was that since they had appeared on the scene K2 had shown troubling tendencies towards thinking for himself, rather than doing whatever Izzabird told him to do.

Mabel showed everyone the Magical Creature. She gave it to Izza.

'Oooo!' squealed Annipeck excitedly. Clueless gave a bark of delight, and Puck buzzed forward to get a good look.

'You have to admit, Izza, whatever is going on seems to be something to do with *this* creature,' said K2, showing it to Annipeck, and stroking it tenderly.

'Is it all right?' said Mabel anxiously.

'I think so,' said K2. 'It's just a little unconscious . . .'

'The question is,' said Theo, 'what IS it, and where did you get it from, Izza?'

'You all promised you'd help me catch it, no questions asked!' fumed Izzabird.

'Yes, well, that was when you said it was your missing cat! And before I saw it being chased by a whole load of super-scary armed people, and before the house alarms and everything went completely flipping wild,' snapped Theo, as the loud sounds of complete flipping wildness carried on from downstairs.

'Izzabird, we have to tell the grown-ups, and if they stop teaching us Magic because of it I am going to be *so irritated.* Can't you stay out of trouble for *one minute?*'

'HA! I thought you'd decided you didn't like Magic, Theo Smith, that it was too messy for you?' said Izzabird. 'And here you are wanting to be taught it. Not to mention using it yourself on the bikes.'

'Life was a whole lot easier before we joined your weird family,' said Theo.

Theo was torn between wanting the old quiet, happy, safe life for him and Mabel and Daniel, the life they'd had when his mother was alive, and secretly liking the excitement of this new Magic household they'd accidentally ended up in when Daniel married Freya. The confusing-ness of this made him grumpy.

'The point is,' snapped Theo, 'you can learn about Magic and still be disciplined about it. I was wrong before, we have to take this creature to Aunt Trudie, I think it isn't well, and what even is it? WHERE . . . DID . . . YOU . . . GET . . . IT?'

Izza sighed and gave the creature back to Mabel.

She might as well tell them the truth. She was feeling the weight of keeping the whole beastly thing a secret anyway. Even *she* was beginning to think she might have gone a bit too far this time.

'It hatched out of an egg about ten days ago,' said Izzabird. 'I've been keeping it in my room. It's very sweet but a bit accident prone . . .'

She led them all out of Theo's room, into the corridor, and then into her bedroom. Even K2 hadn't been in there for a while, Izza hadn't let him . . . and now he knew why.

'Mess,' said Annipeck, staring around with wide eyes.

Izzabird's room was never the tidiest, but now it looked like a small bomb had gone off in it. The curtains were half torn down, there were shredded clothes all over the floor, half-eaten remains of her schoolbooks, even the chair had a big bite taken out of one leg.

Izzabird closed the bedroom door and locked it. '*This* is where I found the egg,' she said. She reached under her bed and dragged out a large flat object, rather like an oversized surfboard. She pointed to the underside. 'The egg was clinging to the bottom of it,' she said. 'At first I thought it was part of the board's decoration, but then it started growing, bigger and bigger, until it cracked and this little creature hopped out . . .'

All four of the other children recognised the oversized surfboard immediately. It looked a bit like a cross between a hoverboard and a snowboard, with a hole in it, and was stamped with an intricate decoration of stars that looked like real diamonds, and strange symbols that were not to be found on this Planet Earth.

In short it was something that was most definitely Out of this World.

Theo's jaw dropped, along with his ever-so-cool and disapproving attitude.

Why does everyone always blame ME for everything?

'Izzabird,' he said with something suspiciously like slightly reluctant but nonetheless awed admiration, 'did you steal this Flymaster from *Horizabel the Grimm*???'

'"Steal" is a strong word,' said Izzabird shiftily. 'I prefer the word "borrow". I just sort of slightly hid it behind some coats when she was leaving. I've been practising flying on it ever since.' She took something from out of her pocket. It was a beautiful orb, stamped with stars that matched the board's decoration and fitted into the hole at the tail-end. This was how to make it start. 'Every night after bed, I sneak out of the window on it. I've got really good.'

'I BET you have,' said Theo jealously, stroking the beautiful shining sides of the Starwalker. He forgot he was supposed to be sensible, forgot he wasn't supposed to be letting himself enjoy Magic too much, lost in appreciation of this wondrous object and the intoxicating thought that they had it all to themselves, and they could do whatever they liked with it.

'Can *I* have a go?'

'What on Earth are you talking about?' said K2 in complete horror. 'Have you completely lost the plot? You are going to be in SO MUCH TROUBLE. Not just from Mum and Daniel and the aunts either . . .'

'Yes, but look at it, K2, it's totally stunning!' said Theo eagerly. 'How fast does it go, Izzabird?'

'I don't care how fast that thing goes,' snapped K2 crossly. 'Do you think you can steal something like this from a completely amoral intergalactic bounty hunter and she won't come and try and get it back? No wonder things are going wrong . . .'

Puck, who was a bit of an expert on things-going-wrong, entirely agreed with K2. 'Oh yes, I thunks you should really gives that back . . .'

Izzabird ignored them. 'My thinking is, this egg must have come from some planet Horizabel visited. I found a book in Aunt Trudie's library called *Creatures of Excelsiar,* but I couldn't see anything that looked like this one. So it must be from somewhere else . . .'

'It's waking up!' said Mabel excitedly.

The little creature was indeed waking up.

It gave a small yawn, its multicoloured fur lit up like someone had turned on a fluorescent lightbulb deep within it, and it opened its huge, heavily lashed eyes. One pupil was square.

K2 stared fixedly at the Magical Creature.

He had the odd feeling that he had seen it before, in scary

dreams that he had been having recently about the Alternative Atlas, but the details in the dream were a bit blurry, so he couldn't remember anything else about it, apart from . . .

'I think it's called "Bug". . .' said K2.

'How do you know that?' said Izzabird suspiciously.

'Oh, I'm just guessing that would be a good name for it,' said K2 hurriedly, because if Izzabird knew he was having dreams about the Alternative Atlas, she would definitely make him draw it and he didn't want to draw pages of the Alternative Atlas again. He'd promised his mother and the aunts he wouldn't do that any more.

'But a bug is an insect, and this is clearly a mammal!' objected Izzabird.

'Well, *I* think it's a wonderful name,' said Mabel. 'Hello there, Bug!'

Bug seemed to agree.

'Peep!' said Bug happily, turning from all-colours-at once to a warm gold. '*Peep!*'

It looked Mabel deeply in the eyes.

'You see!' said Mabel. 'It likes the name Bug!'

And it likes ME! thought Mabel joyfully as Magical Creature and small human girl locked gazes.

Bug's mouth opened in a wide smile and its tongue licked Mabel on the cheek. Its furry firework of a tail swished forward, intending to tickle Mabel under the arm, but missed, flicking itself in the face instead, like a feather duster, and making itself sneeze. 'Peep peep peep . . . *ATISHYOO!*'

'Oh . . .' sighed Mabel, wiping its streaming eyes and nose for it with the end of her sleeve. 'Bug is *adorable . . .*'

Bug's slightly crossed eyes then wandered around looking at things completely independently of each other, and the left eye landed on Clueless, who was watching with interest, tail wagging. 'Pee-i-ee-i-ep . . .' said Bug uncertainly, fading from gold to pale yellow. It seemed unsure about dogs, not surprisingly as it had just been chased by a snarling pack of them. Smoke drifted out of its ears. And then, as its right eye caught sight of Puck, hovering above, the little Magical Creature and the smoke turned swiftly from yellow to brown, to violet, to darkest indigo, and it gave a sharp '*PEEEP!!!!*' of alarm like an old-fashioned train whistle.

Bug *definitely* didn't like robots.

One of Puck's helicopter blades fell off.

The little robot listed to the left, and Theo only just prevented him from crashing to the ground.

'Watch out!' Izzabird warned Mabel, who was still holding the squirming Magical Creature. 'It's turning purple and smoke is coming out of its ears! It doesn't seem to mean to cause chaos but when it's purple, somehow it does . . .'

'What do you mean?' asked Mabel. '*Oh!*' Bug gave

a wriggle and dropped out of Mabel's hands, landing on Izzabird's skateboard, which then tipped up, bonking Annipeck on the nose . . .

Theo gave a wailing Annipeck a comforting hug and Izzabird picked up Bug, patting it soothingly.

'I know how to handle it, and you don't yet, Mabel,' said Izzabird.

'Don't worry, Bug,' said Mabel, as Theo put the screw back in Puck's helicopter blade so he could fly again, 'Clueless and Puck here are our FRIENDS . . .'

Bug appeared to trust Mabel, and as K2 and Mabel helped Izza stroke it reassuringly, the smoke dissipated, and its fur turned from pale violet to a soft gold, and it began to purr.

'Bug seems to have a Good Luck Mode and a Bad Luck Mode. It's fine when it's all rainbow colours, and really happy when it's the colour yellow,' explained Izzabird. 'But if it gets anxious it turns purple and that's when the trouble starts. It doesn't like being left on its own, so whenever I get back from school I find it's turned this deep purple colour and completely wrecked the bedroom. And when I tried to wash it this morning, it totally freaked out and jumped out of the window. I'm so relieved it hasn't hurt itself.'

Bug now decided that it was perfectly safe, and scrambled from Izza's arms into Mabel's, crawled inside her shirt and fell asleep, purring and snuffling contentedly.

'I think maybe it sends out some sort of negative forcefield when it's unhappy?' suggested Izza. 'Like Aunt Violet when she's in a bad mood.'

'OK,' said K2 bravely. 'I . . . I am putting my foot down here. We need to go to the grown-ups, tell them everything, and they can help us give the Starwalker back to Horizabel and take Bug back to Wherever-It's-From . . . and then the alarms will stop and those scary people with dogs will leave us alone.'

'I agree with K2,' said Mabel.

'Yes, but this has got too big now,' said Theo, frowning thoughtfully. 'We can't say she's stolen Horizabel's Flymaster! They'll never let us do Magic ever again . . .'

'Maybe that would be a good idea!' howled K2, waving his arms around. 'Maybe we're out of our depth!'

'It's fine,' said Izzabird soothingly. 'Isn't it, Theo? K2, you worry way too much. Horizabel doesn't even know we've got her Starwalker. She probably just thinks she left it somewhere by accident. Anyway, she can't get into Planet Earth because my mother and the aunts have closed all the Which Ways . . .'

Ring Ring! Ring Ring!

All four children and Annipeck stiffened in astonishment as Annipeck's second-hand Fisher-Price telephone started ringing.

Annipeck's telephone was a toy.

So this should not, technically, be happening.

However, Annipeck was a rather unusual baby, who had this exceptionally rare Gift of Magic-That-Works-On-Plastic and Annipeck had recently been using her plastic toy phone to successfully *call* her siblings on their mobiles.

Annipeck liked to feel that she was as grown up as everyone else.

She had phoned K2 so often that he had now put her toy phone number in his Contacts. (Her number was 26647325 – which spells 'ANNIPECK' on your regular telephone keypad.)

'Are *you* making that happen, Annipeck?' said K2.

Annipeck shook her head solemnly, staring at the telephone with big eyes.

Ring Ring!
Ring Ring!
Ring Ring!

Who on Earth could have Annipeck's number other than themselves?

Theo picked up the phone, listened for a moment and then passed it to Izzabird. 'It's for you.'

Izzabird took the receiver from Theo, and got a short sharp electric shock.

Serve her right.

To do her justice, she stayed holding the phone. She put the receiver to her ear.

'Hello,' said a chatty, pleasantly musical voice from the other end of the line. 'This is Horizabel Delft speaking. Do I have the pleasure of talking to the Absolute Excrescence of a little human being, Izzabird O'Hero-Smith, who has stolen my precious Silver Starwalker?'

UH-OH..

Chapter 7 A Phone Call with Horizabel the Grimm

Now, as I told you earlier, 'Horizabel Delft', also known as 'Horizabel the Grimm' and I, the Story Maker, are one and the same person.

So Izzabird was having the honour of being rung by the Story Maker herself.

I have to admit that Izzabird was impressively unshaken under the circumstances.

'Hello, Horizabel,' she said politely, the impertinent little burglar. Politeness is always disarming. 'Yes, I *have* got your Starwalker. Were you looking for it?'

The cheek!

Izzabird held out the receiver so they could all hear Horizabel's answer.

'Little human beings,' said the voice of Horizabel, speaking very slowly and clearly, with a hint of a stiletto razorblade to her voice. 'Stealing a bounty hunter's Starwalker is an outrageous crime that puts you in Big Trouble, and now you need to do as you're told. I'm standing behind the Which Way quite close to you, but you have to let me in, so that you can give me back my Starwalker, and then you will escape punishment. Perhaps. Go into Annipeck's room, and you will hear me knocking.'

They all filed into Annipeck's room.

There was a *KNOCK! KNOCK! KNOCK!* from the small bedside cabinet by Annipeck's new big-girl bed.

Knock! Knock! Knock!

Now.

I have told you something about this at the beginning of this story, but I'm going to repeat myself because it's a little complicated.

So, clean out your ears, sharpen your wits and listen carefully. There are, of course, plenty of worlds on which there is life in the universe, but they are gazillions and gazillions of miles away, so most human beings haven't found out about them yet.

But there is another way to move between the worlds, a much quicker way than space travel, and that is through the portal of a Which Way. These are in places where the line between the worlds is so thin that you can actually break through it.

Long, long ago, a distant Ancestor of K2 and Izzabird had a Gift called the Atlas Gift, which was the power of drawing an Alternative Atlas that showed exactly where these Which Ways or crossing points between the worlds were. The crossing places shift slightly and slowly, all the time, because the worlds are constantly moving around their stars. A true Alternative Atlas absorbs these leisurely changes and updates accordingly.

Only *twenty-four* legal, computerised Alternative

Horizabel's LEGAL
Alternative Atlas
↘

Atlases were ever made, on
the instructions of K2 and Izzabird's
Ancestor, thousands and thousands of years ago. Twelve of the
legal Atlases are owned by the twelve members of the High
Council of the Universal Government, (UG for short) . . .
and the other twelve are owned by twelve of the finest bounty
hunters that the skies can provide. Right now, the youngest
and the cleverest being . . . *me*, your Story Maker, Horizabel
the Grimm. The UG declared any other Atlases illegal.

Just after the legal Atlases were made, the original Atlas-
Maker disappeared, in highly suspicious circumstances,
along with his original homemade Atlas. High and low the
Universal Government searched, across the many misty
miles of the dusty distant galaxies, but he and his family
seemed to have vanished into thin air.

What Horizabel had recently discovered was that K2 and
Izzabird's Ancestor with the Atlas Gift had settled right here,
on Planet Earth, and he deliberately built this house on a
Crossing of the Which Ways, where many worlds collide. K2
and Izzabird's family had been secretly using this Alternative
Atlas to travel between the worlds for many centuries. They
made illegal copies of the Atlas over the years, used them
themselves, gave them to Magical Creatures to help them
emigrate, lent copies for pirates to use.

Down the centuries it has been the job of the Twelve

UNIVERSAL GOVERNMENT
ALTERNATIVE ATLAS

BLINK 22

OFFICIAL ATLAS-CARRIER:
HORIZABEL ᵗʰᵉ GRIMM

BOUNTY
HUNTER

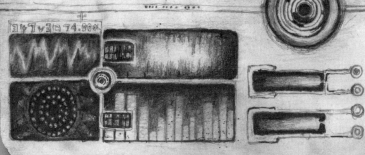

Bounty Hunters to track down any illegal Atlases and destroy them. And last time they saw Horizabel she had been clever enough to remove the original Ancestor's Atlas from the O'Hero-Smith house, along with every single copy that had been made.

Now . . . nobody else had been born in the O'Hero family who had the Atlas Gift for thousands and thousands of years.

But . . .

Unlikely as it may seem, because to the outward eye he looks a bit . . . *hopeless* . . . the first person ever known to have the Atlas Gift since the original Ancestor himself . . .

Was K2.

Horizabel should have got rid of K2 at the end of their last adventure, because that Gift is too dangerous and too powerful for this unlikely hero. But in a rare moment of compassion, Horizabel had made them promise that K2 should never draw another Atlas . . . that they would never travel between the worlds again . . . and so would leave them be.

As the sound of the knocks on the door of Annipeck's bedroom cabinet ring out, you have to imagine me, Horizabel Delft, Bounty Hunter Extraordinaire, also known as 'the Grimm', beautiful as ever and accompanied by my little droid Blinkers, with my robot hand and my tree-branch hand and my wild hair, knocking on the Which Way door in the wind and rain of another world.

Because the aunts had closed all the Which Ways that led into Planet Earth, like you might close a front door. People could only get OUT, they could not get IN. And the House at the Crossing of the Ways had a protection built into it, that even *I* could not overthrow, so in order for me to enter from the other side, the door has to be opened to me.

You have to knock, and the knock must be answered, and then you can step in.

So although my great Story Maker powers allow me to eavesdrop on what is going on, in many places at once, I can't actually *effect* anything unless they let me in.

It's a little frustrating.

Knock! Knock! Knock! from the bedside cabinet door.

'Don't answer . . .' whispered Mabel, eyes round with alarm.

'Open the door of the cabinet and let me in,' said I, the great bounty hunter and Story Maker Horizabel. 'Give me back the Silver Starwalker and the Magical Creature, and I will forgive you for your insolence in stealing my belongings, word of a Grimm bounty hunter.'

Hmmmm.

The little human beings were most mysteriously not answering Horizabel's knock. They seemed to be scared of her for some reason, I have no idea why, she had been perfectly charming to them so far, in fact she had put herself out for them in a way that she had never done for anyone else.

'Why was the egg attached to the bottom of your Starwalker?' asked Izzabird. 'Did you take it from another world?'

'Of course I didn't!' snapped the voice of Horizabel. 'It must have hitched a lift . . . and WHY, is the question? Generally if eggs are hitchhiking in this way, it's an indication that there is something wrong in the place they are coming from. But none of this is any of *your* business . . . I am going to sort all of this out myself . . .'

'Why can't *we* do it?' asked Izzabird, affronted.

'This kind of creature needs delicate handling,' said Horizabel. 'I will take it back to its own world. I have seen what chaos it has created in your world already, and the longer it is there, the worse it will get.'

'So it *is* the creature causing all this trouble,' said Izzabird, eyes alight with interest.

'Besides,' Horizabel went on, 'it will start to die if it stays too long with you. And it is far too dangerous for you to take it yourselves . . .'

'You sound like my mother,' said Izzabird crossly.

'Yes, well, sometimes you should listen to your mother, and not great Grimm bounty hunters from out of this world,' said Horizabel, and the knocking from behind the bedside cabinet door got even more urgent.

'That's a bit contrary,' Izzabird pointed out. 'Should we listen to you or not?' She paused and looked to the others. 'What should we do?'

This showed she had at least learnt something from the last adventure. Six months ago she wouldn't have hesitated for a second. She'd have acted first and thought about things later. Now at least she was pausing a moment, every now and then, and consulting the others.

'If we give Horizabel the Starwalker and the Magical Creature, then *she* can sort it all out,' said K2.

'The aunts said we're not supposed to open any doors of the Which Ways, so that includes doors to Horizabel,' said Theo, who thought Horizabel was marvellous, but even he didn't really trust her. 'And she was the one who told us to grow a little gumption and think for ourselves . . .'

'It might be safer to let her deal with it, but she IS very tricky,' shivered Mabel.

'You can't possibly deal with this yourselves,' said the voice of Horizabel sneeringly. 'This is way too complicated and dangerous for such little human beings with such a basic grasp of Magic . . .'

Well, *this* annoyed all five of them, even K2 and baby Annipeck.

Hadn't they done pretty well last time, on the planet of Excelsiar?

Weren't they O'Hero-Smiths, and weren't O'Hero-Smiths pretty terrific?

Why did nobody trust them? Horizabel was only repeating what Aunt Violet and Aunt Trudie kept on saying, how they didn't know what they were doing, how they needed to learn the Rules of Magic before they did anything interesting.

It was profoundly annoying.

And then something happened that made the hairs prick up on the back of everyone's necks.

In the background behind Horizabel, the children could hear some *thing* or *thing*s whispering something, and it was a nasty, creepy, creaky noise, and it sounded like: *'Bring us the Child-With-The-Atlas-Gift . . . Take out the Child-With-The-Atlas-Gift . . .'*

'Silence!' hissed Horizabel to whoever was making that noise.

But it was too late. It was enough to remind them how at the end of the last adventure, Horizabel had nearly got rid of K2 because of his gift. She *was* a bounty hunter, after all.

'Bad Grimm,' said Annipeck, unexpectedly joining in the conversation from down on the floor, solemnly shaking her head.

A short, thoughtful silence.

'I will open the door and give you the Starwalker, Horizabel, if you make me a promise, Word of a Grimm,'

Horizabel
and her robot,
Blinkers

said Izzabird, 'that you will stop trying to hunt down my father.' Izzabird exchanged a significant look with K2.

Horizabel was still trying to get hold of Izzabird and K2's father Everest O'Hero, who had slipped through her tree-branch fingers on many an occasion since they last met. Everest was the Most Wanted Person in the universe.

'Oh, for the stars' sake,' said Horizabel irritably. 'Why do you think I'd be in the black hole of a world that I'm in at the moment if I wasn't chasing Everest? He's around here somewhere, and not only does he have a bounty on his head, but we think he may have stolen something extremely important!'

'My father is not a thief, and I'll only give you the Starwalker if you stop hunting him,' said Izzabird stubbornly. 'And that's my final offer.'

'Are you trying to bargain with a great Grimm bounty hunter? I don't think you realise who I AM, Izzabird O'Hero-Smith,' said Horizabel, and this time her voice could have frozen the ear tips, so cold was it.

'Those are my conditions,' said Izzabird.

Conditions!

A little pesky human being with no discernible Gift showing itself yet, to offer *conditions* to a being like myself!

'Bargain not taken,' said the voice of Horizabel. 'In which case, you can sort things out for yourselves.'

The phone went dead.

Now, to do Horizabel justice, she hadn't had a lot of experience with human beings so she didn't know yet that the one thing you should never do, particularly with ones like Izzabird and Theo, is to tell them NOT to do something because then they immediately want to do it, however brainless and nonsensical.

I have absolutely no idea why this is, you would have thought that this level of contrariness put human beings at a massive evolutionary disadvantage. But there you go. There it is. It's one of the many reasons that it's an absolute miracle there any human beings left in the universe at all.

Izzabird put the receiver down and gave the phone back to Annipeck.

Theo looked at her and K2, and said gently, 'She's never going to stop hunting Everest, you know . . .'

'I know,' sighed Izzabird. 'But it was worth a try . . . What do we do now?'

They all looked at one another.

Downstairs, the noise of clattering and banging and alarms had finally stopped.

Freya shouted up the stairs.

'Emergency over for the moment!' Freya sounded agitated but relieved. 'Could you all tidy up upstairs before supper?'

Chapter 8
Starcrossers

It took a while for the O'Hero-Smith children to clear up Izzabird's room, and even longer for the adults to clear up the dog biscuits and clean the butter off the Soggy-Bottom-Marsh-Place School Very Important Headteacher Papers and the general chaos of falling-down paintings and cracked china downstairs.

But Bug had taken a real shine both to Mabel, who was wonderful with animals, and also, more surprisingly, to Puck, now Mabel had told Bug that Puck was a *friendly* robot. Which was helpful, because once Bug had woken up again, it started following the robot around making high-pitched peeping noises. That meant they didn't have to leave Bug on its own when they went down to supper. It remained a warm golden yellow colour, for the rest of the evening, and the house returned to normal.

'The house hasn't overreacted like that for years,' said Aunt Trudie as the children sat down. 'Something strange is going on.'

Aunt Violet was thrilled. 'That alarm means the SIA is nosing around again,' she

growled. 'I had a look through Everest's telescopes from the battlements, and I'm sure it's them. I sent out one of my Egg-Whisker-Spy-Drones and it's already returned saying it's found what looks like an SIA laboratory not far from here . . . Something must have drawn them close to the house. It'll be just like the old days . . .'

'What's the SIA?' asked Mabel, eyes round.

Puck and Bug making friends

'The Supernatural Intelligence Agency,' explained Aunt Violet. 'There are secret Anti-Magic governmental organisations all over Planet Earth, investigating paranormal activity, crop circles, UFOs, that sort of thing. Oh, we used to have such fun teasing the SIA when I was a girl!'

'But they haven't paid us any attention in ages,' worried Freya. 'Why now?'

The children exchanged guilty glances . . .

'It's fine,' said Aunt Trudie. Izzabird got her optimism from Aunt Trudie. 'It's all back to normal now. They must have given up.'

Aunt Violet leant back in her chair, cracking her knuckles. 'I bet they haven't,' she grinned, 'but the SIA is nothing to worry about, compared to what happened back in the old days.' She turned to the children. 'I'm talking centuries ago now, starting in the Iron Ages, when people began to get rid of Magic here on Planet Earth. And when this house was built in the sixteenth century it became the centre of an entire Magical refugee operation.' Aunt Violet waved a proud fork at the crumbling old kitchen. 'Oh, the Wizards, the unicorns, the dragons, the nuckalavees, the Magical Creatures that have passed through this house to settle in kinder reaches of the universe!'

'Really?' said Izzabird, very impressed. 'Why didn't you tell us about this before?'

This was *WAY* more interesting than the Magical History that Aunt Violet had been teaching them recently, which had turned out to be just as annoying as *school*. Aunt Violet insisted that they had to have a go at understanding the history of all the known worlds in all the known universe, starting with the Central Galaxy, which was the home of the High Council of UG, where the stars were crowded so close together that you didn't have to travel by Which Way.

And History wasn't as bad as Spellcraft and Wart-Cunning, which were like chemistry, physics and biology all mixed together, but with more complicated ingredients and equations. And the potential for louder explosions. Which Izzabird and Theo might have enjoyed, except Aunt Trudie wouldn't let them actually try anything at all until they had grasped the theory.

'Yes, back in the sixteenth century, the countryside was full of Witch-Finders and Magic-Hunters,' explained Aunt Violet, 'and that's when an incredible intergalactic Starcrosser called Madam Swish made this house the centre of an underground Magical emigration operation.'

'How noble!' exclaimed Mabel.

'Of course she was a Starcrosser. *I* want to be a Starcrosser . . .' said Izzabird longingly. 'Starcrossers are so cool.'

The Starcrossers are the Universal Police Force and the children had been learning about them in their Magic lessons.

In order to qualify to be a Starcrosser you have to be a brilliant Flymaster, an accomplished Spellcaster, an Advanced Laser-Sword-Worker, a great big show-off . . .

. . . *and you have to have a really cool Gift.*

Izzabird's natural optimism meant that even though she showed absolutely no signs of Magical Giftedness whatsoever, she was nonetheless entirely confident that eventually said Gift was going to manifest itself, and when it did it was going to be considerably better than anyone else's.

Daniel pushed his glasses more resolutely on to his nose. 'Being a Starcrosser sounds a little . . . dangerous, Izzabird.'

'Of course it's dangerous!' said Theo scornfully to his father. 'That's the whole point!'

Starcrossers

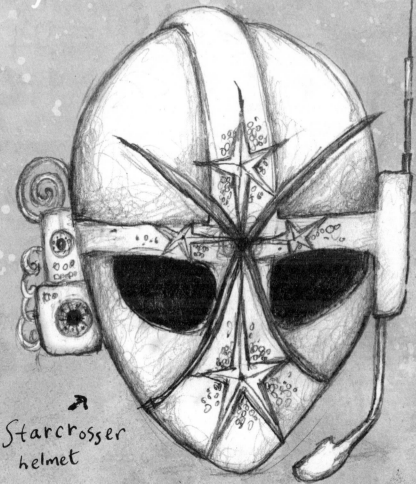

Starcrosser
helmet

Sword of magic ↘

The Sky is not the Limit

'Anyway,' K2 tried to bring the conversation back to the point. 'You were telling us about the Magical refugee operation . . . well, there's something that we—'

'What K2 is trying to say,' Izzabird interrupted, giving K2 a quick warning look, 'is if these "SIA" people have captured some Magical Creature in that laboratory of theirs, shouldn't we be taking it back through the Which Ways to safety like this Madam Swish person?'

Aunt Trudie and Aunt Violet quickly looked at one another, and looked away.

Daniel tried to sound as commanding as possible. 'We've closed all the Which Ways. We promised Horizabel, so that K2 doesn't get into trouble, remember?'

'Besides, there's absolutely no need for anybody to be a Starcrosser OR run a Magical Escape Service,' said Freya, very firmly indeed. 'There isn't enough Magic left here on Planet Earth to make that necessary. What we need to do now is stop the Supernatural Intelligence Agency from hunting down US.'

'Attack is the best method of defence,' growled Aunt Violet. 'We should get out the old Amnesia Blasters and Powders of Forgetfulness, fly over to that SIA laboratory and shut it down before they start telling everyone else, and every secret governmental organisation from across the world starts moving in on Soggy-Bottom-Marsh-Place.'

'Can *we* come too?' asked Izzabird eagerly. 'We can help – we have before!'

'Absolutely not,' said Freya.

'Too dangerous,' said Daniel.

'You all promised that you'd let us practise some Magic!' cried Izzabird, facing up to her mother furiously. 'You promised you'd help me find my Gift! When are you going to start keeping those promises? And now you're stopping us doing anything interesting all over again! Why don't you trust us?'

Freya put her hand on her throbbing forehead. Her Seeing-Into-the-Future Gift was giving her terrible trouble and she seemed to have an entire *team* of headaches ganging up on her. 'It's not the right moment, Izzabird. I told you, we can't do any Spelling AT ALL right now. It might draw the attention of the Supernatural Intelligence Agency even further.'

'Oh, for the stars' sake!' exploded Izzabird, slamming down her spoon and storming out of the kitchen. 'If my father was here, *he* would let us join in! He's a REAL HERO.'

There was a time when Theo would have been very happy to be from a perfectly ordinary non-Magical family. But now he was just as disappointed as Izzabird.

'For once,' said Theo, standing up and stalking out after her, 'Izzabird is right.'

Daniel drooped sadly. He was already wondering how he

could ever live up to being a Hero like Everest.

'Theo didn't really mean that, Dad,' pleaded Mabel to her father, giving him a big hug before following them, 'he's just a bit . . . *confused.*'

Trembling with annoyance at his father and the other adults' lack of trust in him, Theo went to his neat, tidy room to get his Plan Book.

He opened his desk drawer. And there, next to his Plan Book and a precious photo of Theo's mother, was a letter that Daniel had given him a few weeks earlier.

It was addressed to Theo and Mabel in their mother's handwriting.

To Theo and Mabel, it said.
To be opened on your 13th birthdays.

Just seeing the handwriting made him ache with longing for his mother.

To Theo and Mabel
To be opened on
your 13th birthdays

Theo hadn't opened the letter yet, even though he had now turned thirteen. He didn't know why. It made him feel so guilty. Guilty that he hadn't opened it. Guilty that he didn't *want* to open it. Guilty that he was excited about this next adventure even though his mother would probably agree with his father about not using Magic. Guilty that he was enjoying being in the House of the O'Hero-Smiths, because it felt like being happy was leaving her behind.

He stood staring at the letter for a moment.

But why aren't you here? he thought longingly. And then

he felt such a mixture of cross and sad and guilty that it was overwhelming.

So he put the letter back in the drawer, carefully, where it would be safe, next to the photograph, and the phone that his mother had given him a long time ago, the one that Aunt Violet had mended when Izzabird broke it.

I'll look at it . . . some time . . . he promised himself.

He joined the others, who were all in Izzabird's bedroom (except for Annipeck, who was very cross about having to go to bed straight after supper).

'We're going to start up a Magical Escape Service,' said Izzabird, as a bright buttercup-yellow Bug bowled around the room, giggling and playing Hide-and-Seek with Puck, Clueless barking excitedly, 'just like that wonderful Starcrosser back in olden times, Madam Swish.' Izzabird was sitting on her bed with her own Plan Book open, furiously scribbling. 'We're going to save Bug and show our parents just how much we don't need their boring training because we are already brilliant all by ourselves! Then they'll HAVE to start trusting us!'

Theo started writing down ideas as fast as she was.

'OK,' said Theo, in a business-like fashion. 'We need to find out what kind of Magical Creature Bug actually is, and then we can narrow down the worlds where it's likely to be from . . . Izzabird, you're the best at sneaking around this place. I assume you have a secret key to Aunt Trudie's Library of Magic?'

'Of course I do.' Izzabird grinned, producing a key from a little box on her bedside table with the air of a magician. 'This is the master key to *every* door in the house. And once we know where we need to go, we're going to need thinking-caps, food, that Steri-gas sanitising spray . . .'

K2 was staring at both of them with his mouth wide open.

The only thing worse than Izzabird and Theo arguing was when they got together to plan some sort of military operation of disobedience. In which case they were unstoppable, like petrol meeting fire.

'Are you actually thinking of *doing* this?' he said.

'You mean "we",' said Izzabird. '"*We're*" going to be doing this. You're going to be drawing the Atlas, of course, K2.'

'But I promised I wouldn't use my Gift any more!' said K2, panicking. 'Mabel, help me persuade them! Remember, Mabel's supposed to be the Leader!'

On their last adventure they had all agreed that Mabel should be the Leader because Theo wouldn't hear of Izzabird being Leader, and Izzabird wouldn't accept Theo being the Leader.

'OK, Mabel,' said Izzabird. 'What do you want to do?'

They all turned to Mabel.

Shy, gentle little Mabel was often on K2's side about things.

But Mabel's eyes were shining as she watched Bug playing with Clueless and Puck on the floor, giggling as the dog covered it with licks.

'Horizabel said it needed to go back to its world, it would get sick if it stayed here,' said Mabel. 'Look how frightened it was when we found it. And the poor thing has a sore ankle from where the bracelet was around it.'

Annipeck had broken open the plastic handcuff for them using her Magic-That-Works-On-Plastic but the Magical Creature was still limping.

'It's fine, we're just going to find out where Bug belongs, then pop through one teeny-weeny Which Way to take him there,' said Izzabird briskly. 'And then we'll pop right back again.'

'But Mum says not to! And we'll be on our own! It's mind-bogglingly risky!' protested K2.

Theo examined his own Plans. On one page he had written 'RISK ASSESSMENT' in large capitals. 'I think we can really cut down on the risks if we're well prepared,' said Theo, frowning thoughtfully. 'I don't want to put Mabel in any danger, of course. But we've travelled on our own before, K2, and last time we had to rescue your tricky father from that prison.'

'Our father is NOT tricky!' objected Izzabird.

'This time it's going to be far easier,' continued Theo,

ignoring Izzabird. 'No robot assassins, no terrifying Beasts, no treetop prisons. Just a question of dropping this Magical Creature home, really. It could be as simple as dropping Annipeck off at nursery school.'

'What could *possibly* go wrong?' said Izzabird, opening wide her eyes.

So it was three to one in favour of embarking on this big rescue mission without telling the adults, and K2 had to give up trying to sway the others.

They all went off to bed.

K2 helped Izzabird tuck the Magical Creature under the end of Mabel's duvet where it curled around Puck and Clueless, all golden and fuzzy and purring.

'You see?' said Izzabird triumphantly to K2. 'All we have to do is keep it feeling safe, and it's going to be perfectly fine. It's just as I said. What could possibly go wrong?'

K2 left Mabel's room, eyes raised to the heavens.

I have to admit, I agreed with K2.

There were quite a number of things that could possibly go wrong.

Chapter 9 Just Two of the Things that Could Possibly Go Wrong

My own mind is absolutely boggling with the amount of things that could possibly go wrong.

If the O'Hero-Smith children do carry out their plan to go travelling through any Which Ways . . . and let's hope that they don't . . .

Hang on tight to the hairs on the back of my neck as I take you in one great Story Maker's leap, truly mind-bendingly, stomach-churningly, heart-meltingly far away across the great calm ocean of space, back to the forbidden fire-frozen planet of Blink 22.

WE'RE GOING IN.

To where that long drip of evil, Vorcxix, was opening up the Witch's vision in the middle of his orb once more. Three times, Vorcxix tapped on the orb, warmed it in his long reptilian fingers, blew on it, and then spun it round and round so fast, that the globe smoked and spat as it spun on the end of his finger.

The Prophecy leapt up brightly in the centre of the sphere, and Vorcxix's eyes gleamed with glee to welcome it. *'They are coming,'* whispered the voice of the dead Witch out of the orb. (The fact the Witch was dead made her vision only the stronger.) *'Be ready, they are coming.'*

'*When are they coming, you dead old HAG?*' spat Vorcxix. 'I can't wait here forever! I have thingsssss to do! I can't keep sitting around here with my eyeballs freezing up, I want to know exactly WHEN!'

Vorcxix gave the orb a vicious poke with his Spelling Stick, and though the Witch was dead it seemed to shake her up a bit, for the Dead-Witch-Inside-the-Orb shrieked in dreadful pain just as if she were still alive.

'They'll be here within the week,' groaned the voice of the Dead-Witch-Inside-the-Orb. 'It's hard for me to work out more than that because of the time difference.'

Blink 22 was situated a little too close to a black hole, so time ran slower there.

'And . . .' Vorcxix prompted.

'. . . And when they come they'll leave the Which Way open,' said the Witch.

Vorcxix smiled, showing very sharp serpent teeth. 'Ssso I can go back through the other way . . .' He finished the Witch's sentence for her, hissing with delight at the thought of it.

Vorcxix grunted, satisfied. He whacked the orb again and again, the Witch screaming over and over, until the light died inside. Vorcxix bent, picked up the orb, put it in his pocket.

THE EXCORIATOR stepped forward. 'I have been summoned for a meeting at the Universal Government on the Planet of the Evergods,' said he.

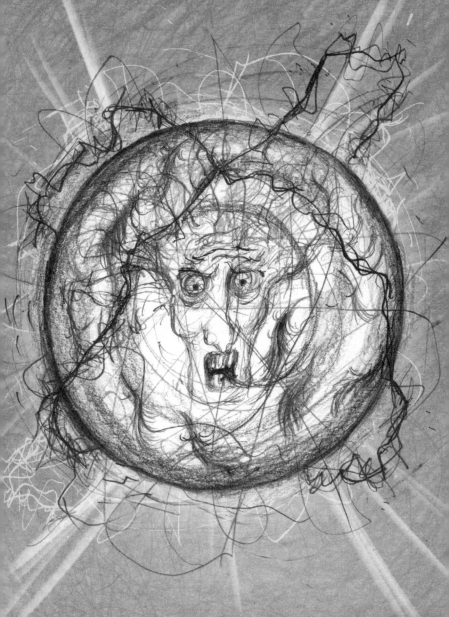

Such a summons could not be ignored.

'Go, then,' said Vorcxix. 'But return here as quickly as you can.'

The great grim head of THE EXCORIATOR nodded. Wings appeared from THE EXCORIATOR's back and the robot leapt into the sky.

Vorcxix snapped his fingers. A robot far larger than THE EXCORIATOR, who had been standing in the background, now stepped forward.

Its name was Blunderbore, and it was enormous, green as emerald, with muscly synthetic limbs shining and gleaming, the smooth glass planes of its face impassive as a piece of stone. It had an extraordinarily huge skull, way out of proportion to the rest of its body, to hold the gigantic size of its memory databank.

'In the meantime YOU are in charge,' spat Vorcxix to Blunderbore. 'When they come through the Which Way, bring the human beings straight to me. I want to deal with them personally. And *I* will head the expedition back to the O'Heros' nest myself . . .'

'As you wish,' said Blunderbore, who was a Pure-of-Heart robot. Pure-of-Heart robots have no heart and no emotions, they are built entirely for obedience purposes.

The robot drew out his most fearsome weapons, sat down once more, staring steadily at the still-solid fiery ice where the

Witch had drawn an 'X' with her talon when she was alive.

Vorcxix turned.

Behind him, there were six other robots standing on the great desert of fire-ice, or hovering above it.

One, a Scorpio-cyborg, built like a giant scorpion, equipped with the tracks of a tank, gleaming a silver so brilliantly bright that it made the eyes sore to look at it.

Two, a Workerbot, the soldier of the robot world, more humanoid in construction, in full combat gear, loaded down with lasers, and screens, and heat-sensors, and other military equipment.

Three, a Hellsfire-heliraptor, hovering above with wings that made no noise, rockets at the ready.

Four, an absolutely massive Giganti-automaton, the fire-ice creaking complainingly beneath it as it stood fifty feet tall, with crane attachments, head dizzyingly high, fists as large as houses, dripping with chains, Glacier-Blasters at the ready.

Five, a Stealth-derk, made out of some strange ectoplasm-meets-liquid-metal material, and as transparent as a ghost.

Six, a Murgadroid, red as blood, with eyes on the ends of its fingers.

A robot with a bad heart can be much, much worse than a robot with no heart at all. Someone way back in history designed an extremely bad heart for the Murgadroid.

A treacherous, twisting, computerised nightmare of a heart, all poisoned batteries, and nasty memories, and horrible wishes, and twisted manipulators, with strychnine in its tubes and cyanide affectors.

When you turn up somewhere and there are Murgadroids about, you know there's bound to be some really bad stuff going on.

My heart sank to see them. What was Vorcxix doing with such a collection of some of the most dangerous military robots from across the universe and gathering them together on the fire-ice? 'On your kneess!' cried Vorcxix. The terrifying robots dropped down into the kneeling position of submission, or bowed their heads if they had wheels or tracks instead of limbs. Vorcxix was taking no chances. The important thing with artificial intelligence was to show it who was boss.

'Hear me well, O brainless ones,' spat Vorcxix. 'Listen hard, O heartless, soulless, clockwork things. You obey my creature, BLUNDERBORE here, as if he were me. One aluminium *toe* out of line, one single stray mechanical *thought* of your own, and I will annihilate you into scratchings of rust, you hear me, maggots?'

Vorcxix spat a long gob of spit right in the centre of the Witch's 'X'. He snorted with satisfaction.

And vaulted into the sleigh, screaming the wolf-robot into action, and settling down in his snowbear furs as the sleigh rocketed across the ice.

Leaving behind the kneeling robots. Waiting.

With Blunderbore in the centre, sitting by the ever-burning fire-that-robots-did-not-need.

As slowly, slowly, the ice around the Witch's 'X' began to melt.

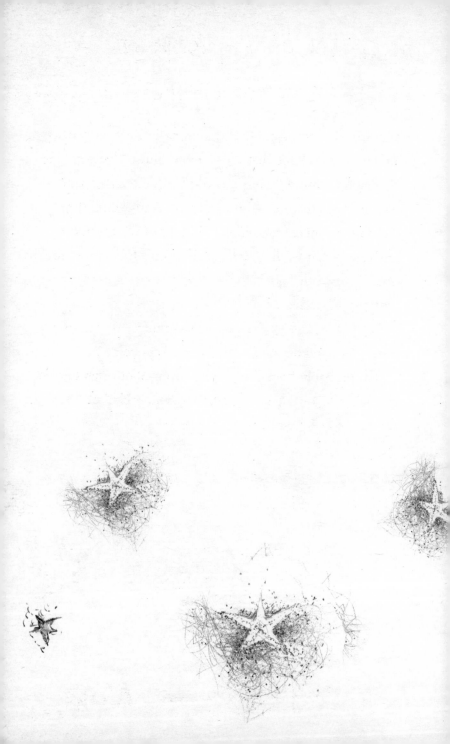

But let us hope that the Witch's Prophecy is incorrect,

and Vorcxix and his robots are waiting in the wrong place. And also let us hope that the O'Hero-Smith children change their minds about proving everyone wrong and rescuing the creature all on their own. And even if they did do that, there are so many millions of worlds in the universe. What would be the chances of the O'Hero-Smiths turning up in this one? It doesn't seem like somewhere a fluffy ball-like creature would belong.

It's terribly difficult to predict the future, as you can see from Freya and her headaches, as I've said before.

I'm probably even going to be wrong about that knock that will ring out on sleeping baby Annipeck's door . . .

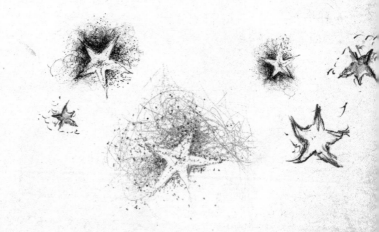

. . . any moment NOW . . .

Chapter 10 The Knock on Annipeck's Door

Much, much later, when the stars were shining brightly in the soft clear summer's night sky, when the wood-pigeons were calling peacefully to each other from the branches of the trees in the garden, when all of the moon flowers in Aunt Trudie's greenhouses were turning their faces up to the full harvest moon, when little baby Annipeck was sleeping all alone in her room, snuggling tight to her Lego and her toothbrushes . . .

She was woken by a knocking on the door of her bedroom cabinet.

KNOCK!

KNOCK!

KNOCK!

Annipeck opened sleepy eyes.

But the knocking would not stop.

Annipeck's toothbrushes *strongly* advised against responding to that knock.

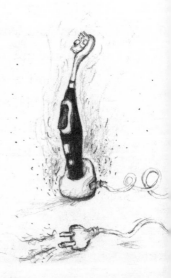

Or at least that she should call for assistance from the rest of the family first.

Even the Lego, a bit bolder than the toothbrushes, were heavily in agreement about getting help.

But Annipeck was a brave and curious child, and she liked doing things on her own if she could.

So she brushed aside the toothbrushes and the Lego, they were always worrying unnecessarily about stuff, climbed out of her new big-girl bed (Annipeck was very proud that she had graduated out of her cot), toddled over to the bedroom cabinet, and whispered, more loudly this time, 'Bad Grimm! Go away!'

But the voice that replied to Annipeck through the bedroom cabinet door was not the voice of Horizabel the Grimm.

'It is I, Everest O'Hero!' said the voice, very muffled, very faint, very harassed. 'Quick, open the door! I'm being *chased*!'

Well, there's a surprise!

We haven't seen *him* in a while.

Everest O'Hero, remember, was K2 and Izzabird's frequently absent father.

Annipeck had met Everest once before, and this did sound like Everest's voice, but, very sensibly, Annipeck knelt down and peered through the keyhole to make sure. He looked a lot smaller than she remembered but maybe that was because she was looking through the keyhole. It was definitely him, and it did sound like he was in trouble.

K2 and Izzabird would want Annipeck to help their father.

So Annipeck opened the door.

Everest shot through it, dishevelled and clearly terrified, and slammed it shut behind himself. 'Thank you!' he gasped. 'By the heavens, that was a close one . . . Horizabel really is going to catch up with me one of these fine days . . . I don't know how she works out where I am each time!'

Annipeck took a while to reply.

She gazed at Everest with her mouth open in a mixture of astonishment and delight, before eventually saying:

beep beep

'Efferist teeny-weeny!'

'You is *tiny* . . .'

Annipeck was right.

Everest was, indeed, much smaller than when she'd seen him last.

Much, MUCH smaller.

In fact he was miniature, not even as tall as her largest toothbrush.

He hadn't been that small last time, Annipeck was sure of it.

This was *memorably* titchy.

'Is you – Efferist?' she asked, now a little more uncertain that she had the right person.

Ragged and torn and minute as he was, Everest drew himself up to his full height, puffed out his proud chest. Gathered himself together.

'Yes, it is I, Everest O'Hero,' said Everest with as much dignity as was possible under the circumstances. 'Also known as World-Walker, the Uncatchable One, who once tracked the stars beyond the Outer Limits, the Darer of the Lost Black Holes, the Great Discoverer of so many of the Hidden Planets, it is indeed, I.' (Everest didn't normally list his accomplishments like this but he was feeling the need to buoy himself up a bit right now.) 'And I may be – *ahem* – a trifle on the diminutive side at the moment, but I still have the old Everest fighting spirit.'

'Yes, it is I,
Everest O'Hero...
also known as
World-Walker...'

beep
beep

Everest demonstrated a few of his more complicated karate moves.

But Annipeck seemed unable to move on from the microscopic aspect of Everest's present appearance.

'You is *teeny-weeny*!' said Annipeck in an awed voice.

'Yes, yes, let's not dwell on that, shall we?' said Everest tetchily, for he was a bit touchy on this subject. 'I am, I admit, perhaps a little less consequential than normal . . . I had an unfortunate confrontation with a Witch over a card game and she put a Curse on me. I'm so sorry, I do apologise, I know we've met before, but I can't remember your name?'

'I is Annipeck,' said Annipeck proudly. 'Annipeck O'Hero-Smiff.'

'Well, never play poker with Witches, is my advice to you, Annipeck, never play poker with Witches,' said Everest with a solemn and sad shake of his head. 'That's a lesson for life, right there.'

Annipeck nodded her head gravely back, even though she hadn't a clue what he was talking about, because Everest seemed to expect some sort of response.

'The Curse the Witch laid on me after our rather lively disagreement was one of those beastly shrinking ones,' continued Everest. 'Which is why you find me somewhat . . . diminished. But at least the Curse shrank all of my clothes and belongings as well, otherwise I'd have been in quite the predicament.'

Everest pointed to his teeny-weeny gas mask, his teeny-weeny boiler suit, his teeny-weeny backpack, and ever a lover of small things, Annipeck was enchanted. Best of all, *ta dah!*, a teeny-weeny Alternative Atlas that K2 had drawn and given to him on the last adventure. 'So I can

So I can still travel!

still travel!' said Everest, looking on the bright side. 'Plus it's a lot easier for me to hide from Horizabel like this,' said Everest, putting the teeny-weeny Atlas back in his teeny-weeny backpack, 'so although I wouldn't call this the ideal situation, there's a lot to be thankful for. And, of course – another bit of life advice for you here, Annipeck . . .' Everest held up a bitty but pompous finger, '*Size is not important.* Size is not important, Annipeck. I've always said that, and I want you to remember that.'

'Efferist *teeny-weeny*!' agreed Annipeck, still fascinated.

'Well, I wouldn't say *teeny-weeny*!' protested Everest. 'That's going a bit far, isn't it! Just slightly on the more modest side than normal – not that that is important,' he added hurriedly. 'You can be small, but you can be mighty. Anyway, let's move on, shall we? So,' said Everest, briskly, rubbing his minute little hands together, 'thank you for opening the door to me, Annipeck, and I'm now going to get on with my mission . . .'

The introductions seemed to be over so Annipeck got up and pointed at the door. 'Mummy?' she asked, 'Annipeck call Mummy?'

'Oh! *No!*' said Everest, horrified. 'No . . . absolutely no need to bother Freya . . . this is more of a flying visit . . . there's a few things I need to get my hands on, something Aunt Violet has been keeping safe for me, hopefully, and one of Aunt Trudie's antidotes to rectify this . . . um . . . *undersizing* scenario that I have going on at the moment . . . and then I'll be on my way . . .'

'Iz-bird?' suggested Annipeck. 'K2? Annipeck call K2?'

'No,' said Everest sadly. 'No, not this time, Annipeck.' Everest heaved a big sigh.

He sat down.

Annipeck sat down too.

'Let me explain,' said Everest confidentially. 'Just between you and me, Annipeck, I haven't, perhaps, been the best father in the world. No, really, that's kind of you to look sceptical, but I mean it. I've been away a lot. I may have accidentally emptied the family bank account a few times to fund some of my more ambitious expeditions. I meant so well, I had so many dreams . . .' Everest raised his eyes to the heavens, tutted, shook his head ruefully. 'However, life, and the stars, kept getting in the way. But last time I saw my children I made such a great farewell speech, so moving, so final . . .' Everest threw wide his tiny arms and repeated a bit of that speech: *'Know this, flawed as I am, I will be in your hearts forever. And I will be watching you from a faraway star . . .'*

Everest was overcome at the memory of these wonderful words, blew his nose on his teeny-weeny handkerchief. 'It was a great speech, and I really, really meant it. So how can I pop back up again so soon? Particularly looking like *this*? I've made so many mistakes, but at least they still look up to me! Their father, the great Hero. At least they have *that*. I can't bear for them to see me looking so . . . inconsiderable. There, that's it, Annipeck. You've got the truth out of me. I cannot bear for my children to see me looking so SMALL.'

Everest sighed again. 'And I would much rather Aunt Trudie or Aunt Violet or Freya didn't see me like this either, not to mention that husband of Freya's, even if he doesn't have any moustache to speak of, and it makes things slightly awkward . . . But an O'Hero never gives up!' he said, brightening.

'I'm going to make amends, and finish my mission, and hopefully get a little taller, and then perhaps I can face them again. Do you understand, Annipeck? Do you?'

Annipeck hadn't the faintest idea what he was talking about.

She was only two and a bit.

But she caught the sadness in his voice and sighed sympathetically, holding tight to her Lego.

There was a long, thoughtful, melancholy silence.

And then Annipeck got up.

'Annipeck go to bed now,' she said firmly.

'Oh! Right! Yes, of course!' said Everest.

So Annipeck took her toothbrushes and her Lego back to bed, and Everest set off on his mission, squirming on his stomach like a commando under the crack at the bottom of the door and sprinting off down the corridor, stopping for a moment and sliding in underneath the door of K2 and Izzabird's room. He whispered them a few bedtime stories and kissed them goodnight. And then he heaved a heavy sigh and turned back into the corridor again, getting out his teeny-weeny ropes and crampons and climbing harnesses, and headed for the stairs.

When you are less than the size of half a pencil, the journey to Aunt Trudie's and Aunt Violet's workshops becomes quite the expedition.

Luckily Everest was extremely fit and had considerable experience of battle conditions.

Luckily Everest had considerable experience of battle conditions...

beep beep

Chapter 11 Everyone Was Keeping Secrets from Everyone Else

or the next couple of days, everyone was concerned with their own business.

There was a lot going on.

Freya and the aunts were planning an invasion of Mr Spink's laboratory, following Aunt Violet's opinion that attack was the best method of defence.

They were keeping their preparations secret from the children, because no one could face another confrontation with Izzabird; entirely unaware of the fact that the O'Hero-Smith children were not paying any attention whatsoever to what the adults were doing, because they were secretly planning a much more exciting and point-proving mission of their own.

So it was only Annipeck who noticed a thoroughly overexcited Aunt Violet unsubtly winking at Aunt Trudie as Trudie hid their flying Hoovers behind the coat-stand by the door ready to go. And Freya whispering to Aunt Violet, 'Do you think we're going to need more Amnesia Blasters?' And Aunt Violet suddenly slapping her forehead during breakfast muttering, 'Uh! I forgot to recharge the Spelling Sticks!' and rushing out of the kitchen chomping on half her toast and Marmite.

In Mr Spink's S.I.A. laboratory, some poor captured Magical Creatures had lost hope...

Meanwhile, Izzabird went on secret raids to Aunt Trudie's library to try to identify what kind of Magical Creature Bug might be.

And Theo drew up Risk Assessments, which got more and more elaborate, and he collected together thinking-caps and he found some travelling wetsuit thingies from Aunt Violet's wardrobe that were a bit like the one that Horizabel wore. He had to cut these down a bit, to fit the four of them, but he was determined that this was going to be a more efficient and professional travelling operation than last time.

K2 and Mabel concentrated on keeping Bug happy – feeding it Bounty bars mixed with spinach, which it loved, playing with it and singing it happy songs. Nobody tried to wash it.

But even so, it was fortunate that the grown-ups were so distracted, for Bug's good luck and bad luck modes were often activated.

When Bug was feeling joyful, extraordinarily lucky things happened.

Aunt Trudie found those shapeshifting pills that she had mislaid for absolutely ages. The exact location of Mr Spink's laboratory swam magically into Freya's mind when she was having a quiet 'Seeing into the Future' moment in her empty workshop. Aunt Violet made a massive breakthrough in her invention of an Automatic-Window-Cleaning-Machine that would clean every window in the house in less than ten minutes.

But when Bug was sad, or frightened, extremely unlucky things happened.

One time Bug was playing Hide-and-Seek in Izzabird's bedroom with Puck during supper, and Izzabird had forgotten to lock the door, so it got out and rolled downstairs, pursued by a frantically panicking Puck. Bug toddled gleefully into the sitting room . . . where it mistook the television for a dangerous robot, about to attack.

It went violently purple, its tail shooting sparks of alarm, the television exploded, the curtains fell down, and the lightbulbs in all the lamps turned electric blue.

Puck only
just had time to
swoop down, pick
up the bright purple
Bug, and fly away with it back upstairs again before the
family stampeded into the room to find out what all the
noise was about.

On that occasion, not only did all the lamps in the
whole house stay a deep periwinkle blue, but so too
did the windows, the mirrors, the bathwater, and, most
mysteriously, the end of Aunt Violet's nose.

'Strange things are going on,' said Aunt Violet, moodily,
scrubbing away at the sapphire tip of her handsome snout,
as her rubber duck floated around her in the sapphire blue
bathwater. 'We must have upset the poltergeists again . . .
Bother.'

Aunt Violet had her own reasons for suspecting why
she and Aunt Trudie might have accidentally upset the
poltergeists.

It took Freya and Aunt Trudie and Aunt Violet two days to turn everything the right colour again.

But Mabel noticed that the purple incidents and the contented rainbow moments and the joyful yellow times were getting fewer and fewer, and Bug was turning a sort of pale blue as time went on, and it was playing less energetically, and 'peeping' and giggling more faintly.

Hopefully they'll all change their minds about telling the grown-ups, thought a very troubled K2.

And every night, Theo set his alarm for 2 a.m. and the four children crept outside the house and practised flying on the Silver Starwalker. Even K2 and Mabel enjoyed this. It was a much smoother ride than the Flymaster Homemade-Os, or Aunt Violet's Hoovers.

Luckily it was the summer holidays so they could sleep in.

And amid all of this was Annipeck, the only one noticing the odd behaviour and highly suspicious that the family was planning to go somewhere without her, so she was toddling around saying hopefully, 'Annipeck come too?'

And Aunt Trudie or Izzabird or Freya or Theo would turn to Annipeck with big innocent eyes and say, 'Where, Annipeck, where? We're not going ANYWHERE . . .' before looking surreptitiously out of the corners of their eyes in the hope that no one else had noticed.

In short, everyone was keeping secrets from everyone else.

These human beings! They promised to be more open with each other!

Daniel found it quite peaceful. He had the kitchen table to himself to do his entire lesson plans for the autumn term undisturbed by Theo and Izzabird arguing or Aunt Violet turning up the telly too loud, as everyone tiptoed around whispering to each other and collecting things and wondering whether they were packing enough *firepower.*

And they were all too busy to notice, under everyone's noses, the little figure of Everest, who every now and then swung from the light hangings like a teeny-weeny Tarzan or sprinted athletically across the floor like some sort of highly trained SAS *mouse,* off on his *own* mission, which seemed to consist of searching the entire house for something small and terrifically important.

Clueless the dog and Annipeck did try to point Everest out to the others, when he abseiled down the kitchen table leg, for instance, and ran behind the sink. Clueless had never seen or smelt a human being this minuscule before, so the poor dog barked wildly whenever she spotted him, and Annipeck clapped her hands delightedly, or bashed her spoon on the table crying, 'Go, Efferist, go!'

It was a shame that everyone was so busy that they assumed she was talking nonsense.

But people often don't pay quite enough attention to what babies are trying to say.

It's important to slow down sometimes.

Everest, for instance, was getting increasingly frantic.

That first night, Everest had searched and searched for a certain mysterious object that he had put in Aunt Violet's pocket for safekeeping during the last adventure, when he thought Horizabel was going to carry him off to the Prison of the Evergods.

And now he was coming back to the House of the O'Hero-Smiths to retrieve it.

But he couldn't work out where Aunt Violet might have put it, so he looked everywhere: Aunt Violet's workshop, her bedroom, the loose tile behind the bath.

However, things take so much longer when you are extremely small.

Eventually Everest got so tired of looking that he had to give up and go to bed in the Fisher-Price garage in the playroom. And even though Everest was used to roughing it, having slept many a night of his life rolled up in his sleeping bag on the cold hard ground, there was something particularly gloomy about sleeping in a toy garage, it felt rather demeaning.

He took up the hunt again the next morning, thoroughly searching Aunt Violet's garden shed and the secret hiding place called a 'priest-hole'*.

No luck. He resorted to less likely options. The haunted dresser in the hall. Under Aunt Violet's pillow. The disused lavatory under the back stairs, which rather surprisingly he found already occupied by a couple of tiny

beep beep

---

* Madam Swish used to hide Magical Creatures in this 'priest-hole' in the old days behind the chimney in the kitchen, and Aunt Trudie's greenhouses.

mer-bears*, swimming round and round. Eventually, to his enormous relief, at about lunchtime three days later he found what he was looking for during a perilous expedition down into the cellar.

There it was, hidden behind a crate of Aunt Violet's homemade nettle wine, enclosed in the most fizzingly powerful Spell of Protection that Aunt Violet could possibly cast, so strong that there was a glow all around it of luminous yellow light.

No wonder Aunt Violet had concealed it, for there was something truly terrifying about this little object. It looked a lot like a large old-fashioned wind-up alarm clock, beautifully encrusted and engraved with constellations of diamonds and Magical symbols, and its clock face was very unusual, for the numbers descended inward in what was called a 'Time' or 'Infinity Spiral'. But there was something that turned the stomach about it, an aura of danger that came off it, and despite the power of the Spell of Protection, it had still turned all of Aunt Violet's neighbouring wine to vinegar.

Everest was too little to pick it up for the moment, so he left it where it was and turned his attention to part two of his mission, which was to find a potion in Aunt Trudie's workshop that would undo the Shrinking Curse.

He made the perilous ascent up to Aunt Trudie's Spelling

---

* These are like seahorses, but in fact they are bears.

Cubbard, and found the Antidote to the Shrinking Curse somewhere in among all the other bottles, at the back of the second shelf from the top.

Once he made it to the apex of the bottle, it took quite a lot of heaving, arms around the cap, to unscrew it. He dropped a pen cap attached to a thread down into the liquid, hauled some up and poured it into his own water bottles, so that he could carry it away with him.

He was so small he couldn't take a normal dosage, only very tiny drops. He had to be patient, because growing too rapidly was extremely bad for you, if not fatal.

So there was nothing to do but hide around here for a couple of days, dosing himself up until he got big enough to lift this important but appalling object and take it away with him through the Which Ways.

That evening, he took refuge in the second-hand dolls' house in Annipeck's room. It was a bit of a comedown for an ageing Hero, but it was better than the toy garage.

At least the mattresses on the dolls' house beds had been stitched and stuffed with cotton wool by Aunt Trudie herself, so they were actually pretty comfortable.

By the afternoon of the same day, Bug was now the palest blue it had ever been, and they were all extremely worried about it. Its light had got dimmer, its peeps were softer, and it had stopped playing with Puck entirely. K2 looked at it anxiously, as Mabel gently stroked it, all curled up in the nest that she had made for it under her duvet.

'We don't know what it needs! We have to find out where it lives!' said an anguished Mabel.

'Well, I've been meaning to tell you,' confessed K2, 'I *did* have this dream about Bug and maps did come into my head . . .'

'Brilliant!' gasped Izzabird, so thrilled she didn't even tell K2 off for not telling her immediately. 'So DRAW THE MAP!'

'But the map was so scary I hoped you might change your minds about telling the grown-ups,' admitted K2 with a shiver. 'We could still tell them?'

'*NO!*' said Theo and Izzabird, both at the same time.

'I think it's *dying*, K2!' said Mabel, her eyes filling with tears.

'Perzaps you should just TRY drawings that map,' suggested tender-hearted little Puck.

'OK,' said K2 determinedly. 'We have to at least *try* and get it home. I can't promise this will work, though, it was only a dream . . .'

Izzabird fetched K2 one of his old Geography exercise books to draw in, Theo gave him a complete set of pencils organised by colour, and Mabel put the Magical Creature gently down beside K2's right hand to give him inspiration.

Bug was so weak that it just lay down and went to sleep there.

'You can do this, K2,' whispered Mabel. 'You're brilliant . . .'

'I have to admit,' said Izzabird, 'you are wonderful at this, K2, step back, everyone!'

And they all stepped back, watching expectantly, as K2 took a deep breath and began.

He hadn't used the Atlas Gift in a while, but oh, the glorious mixture of relief and terror and excitement and joy when he started the drawing!

He held the pencil lightly in his hand, so he could guide it but let it go free.

And as the familiar, almost trance-like state came over K2, the pencil seemed to take on a life of its own.

To start off with, bizarrely, K2 drew the beginnings of maps of many other worlds, so quickly that it was hard to make them out very clearly . . .

. . . Diamonticon, a world made entirely out of diamonds, where Pure-of-Heart robots lived wild, free lives, in perfect harmony with each other . . . Posideon, a world covered entirely in oceans, where creatures like the mer-bears Everest found earlier lived alongside sea-dinosaurs and great coral underwater cities inhabited by selkies occupied miles of the sea-beds . . . Trio-Life, three worlds grouped so close together that the inhabitants had long ago built space bridges from one to the other . . .

He turned the pages in frustration, starting a new idea, a new map each time, then quickly seeming to decide that these weren't the right ones either.

Until finally, on a crisp, new page, white like a blanket of snow that no foot has ever trodden in before, he wrote in large shaking capitals:

BRQJK1URBLK22

'What does that spell?' whispered a fascinated Theo, leaning in to look.

'Shhhh . . .' said Izzabird, as K2 wrote in brackets the words:

Blink 22.

UH OH. UH OH, UH OH, UH OH, thought I, listening, helpless.

Things were taking an extremely bad turn for the worse.

Chapter 12 The Map that K2 Drew

As K2 mapped out the outlines of the extraordinary fire-ice deserts, the great undersea Drowned Forests in the pin-sharp freezing oceans, the incredible dropping gorges of Blink 22, the world came to life beneath his fingers.

And when he began to add more detail, he started drawing the incredible creatures that lived there too.

There were starfish that walked, and killer whales that talked, and the odd snowcat and snowbear padding their way through the endless snows, their thick Magical fur giving them some protection against an astonishing number of other, more venomous creatures.

And as he drew, such was the power of K2's Atlas Gift, you could begin to *hear* the ferocious spitting of the snowsnakes with fifty times the venom of the most venomous snake on all the planets, *smell* the sulphurous stench of the explosive insects born deep in the fire-ice. (K2 was writing down exactly how dangerous they were in brackets by their pictures.) You could *see* the glow of the crabs that lit up in the night with pincers so large they could take off your hand with one snip, and the reptiles with frighteningly large claws and jaws that made Tyrannosaurus Rex look like a pussy cat, so close that Izzabird, looking over K2's shoulder, felt she could almost reach out and *touch* them.

Always as K2 drew, he was flipping the page over, this way and that, to draw the House of the O'Hero-Smiths on the other side of the paper, and an 'X' to mark the crossing points between the worlds.

Because a piece of paper has two sides, doesn't it?

On one side you draw your so-called imaginary world. On the other, you draw somewhere you know well, your house, your garden, the cupboard under the stairs. And then on both sides of the piece of paper, you draw the crossing points between the worlds. And that is how to draw an Alternative Atlas – every place you have ever imagined is true somewhere . . .

It was when K2 started drawing the twisting crystal pinnacles balancing strange mountain-top oases that Bug's tail twitched and the little Magical Creature stirred in Mabel's arms.

It wasn't quite clear whether these pinnacles were made out of rock or ice. But they were supporting vast tabletops of rock that seemed to be slightly protected from the terrors below.

There were huge packs of snowbears and snowcats here,

K2 O'Hero
Geography
Form 70

THE
ALTERNATIVE
ATLAS
(Mark 2)

For the O'Hero-Smith Starcrossers

where there were only a few elsewhere. Unicorns and unideer and frost wolves and Hurlyhobs and . . .

. . . and K2 took up two coloured pencils at once, one in his left and one in his right hand, and started drawing a creature that looked incredibly like Bug.

The other three children held their breath in wonder.

There it was, coming to life, a little eccentrically as K2 couldn't draw with his right hand quite as well as he did with his left, a rather comical creature with soft ears and colourful fur, and big eyes and feet so huge in proportion to the rest of its body that it looked like it might trip over itself any minute.

As K2 wrote beside the drawing the name of the little creature, Mabel said it aloud: 'UTCHIMABUG. Oh my goodness! It IS called Bug, after all!'

Bug's pale blue eyelids fluttered and it opened sleepy, weary eyes. It staggered to its feet, wobbling unsteadily it was so weak, and stomped right across the map, breaking K2's trance, and smudging what he had drawn already.

It blinked down at the picture of itself. 'Peep!' it said, and if a peep could sound astonished, that peep certainly did. It looked around at the rest of the map and whistled 'Peep!' very loudly, stamping its feet on the part of the map where the snowbears and snowcats seemed to live, its fur prickling into soft rainbow life.

When it looked up at them all with an unbearable longing in its eyes, they didn't need Puck to translate the next 'Peep!' for them.

'Home!' the Utchimabug was saying.

Home.

This was the Utchimabug's *home*.

Just looking at K2's drawing seemed to make the Utchimabug happier and stronger and a little more golden, and its tail waggled away furiously, smudging the drawing a bit more as it waggled and stamped and peeped.

Home! Home! Home!

Well, after that there was no question. Even K2, coming out of the trance he had got himself into, like a swimmer coming up from the depths, was convinced of their mission.

Gently Mabel lifted Bug off the page, and kissed it. 'Don't worry, Bug, we're going to get you home.'

Theo picked up the exercise book and flipped the Blink 22 page back and forth.

'You see,' he said excitedly. 'I knew we could reduce the risk if we planned things properly. There are various Which Ways to Blink 22 from this house. It'll be much safer if we take the *right one*. There's one, for instance, through the back of the boiler room in the upstairs bathroom that comes out slap bang in the middle of the most dangerous bit, with the worst amount of scary-looking creatures . . .'

Mabel made a face.

'Not that one, then . . .'

'But there's also a Which Way direct to those mountain tops where Bug seems to come from. Look here,' said Theo pointing to the old tower where Everest's workshop used to be.

'It's like I said,' he went on. 'We can pop straight through this Which Way and back again, it wouldn't be any more dangerous than dropping Annipeck off at nursery school.'

It was an enticing thought.

'But Dad's workshop is the one place I don't have a key for,' admitted Izzabird. 'Even the master key doesn't work for that one.'

'That's OK,' said Theo, eyes shining. 'We can get up there from the *outside*, on the Silver Starwalker. We'll be like Madam Swish, and the Starcrossers of ancient times . . . I'm going to call this Operation Blink 22 and Back Again . . .'

'And we need to go TONIGHT!' said Mabel urgently. 'Before the Which Way shifts, and before Bug *DIES*!'

So over the next couple of hours K2 drew more maps and Theo made more Risk Assessments in his Plan Book, under the heading Operation Blink 22 and Back Again. Meanwhile, Izzabird found books on Blink 22 in Aunt Trudie's library that gave them more information about the atmosphere on this planet and the kinds of Magical Creatures they might meet there, and even a book about Utchimabugs.

'The purple and yellow episodes Bug has really are called Bad Luck and Good Luck Modes!' said Izzabird, reading up about Utchimabugs with great interest.

Izzabird took an Air Stick, to get them through the Which Way, and Spelling Sticks, just in case they needed to defend themselves (*not that the aunts have taught us how to use them properly yet, but how hard could it be?* thought Izzabird).

She found an Omni-babel-o-phone[*] lying around Aunt Violet's workshop that she thought might be useful, so she took that too. Theo packed the Enchanted Hairdryer, which was excellent at tracking things, in case Bug or any of the rest of them got lost in the alternative world they were heading to.

Bug was so pale it was almost white now, and it slept all afternoon.

By supper time, the three grown-ups and the four O'Hero-Smith children had all their plans finalised and their equipment hidden under their beds, ready to leave that night.

---

[*] A handy translation device you put in your ear and it enables you to speak and understand any language. Elf, Werewolf, Tree, for example.

BUG in GOOD LUCK MODE

When slightly happy the Utchimabug will be yellow or orange, and good things will happen around it.

yellow or orange in colour

rainbow colours
very fluffy

Rainbow colours and fluffy tail indicate very good luck indeed. Can even make the weather turn sunny.

BUG in BAD LUCK MODE
Know the signs...

Violet or lavender in colour and
lifted paw means bad luck might
be about to start.

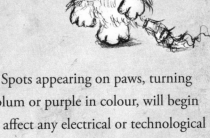

Spots appearing on paws, turning
plum or purple in colour, will begin
to affect any electrical or technological
equipment. An odd number of spots
means greater bad luck.

Deepest indigo, lots of spots and patches on
paws, smoke coming out of ears, BEWARE!!
An Utchimabug in full Bad Luck
Mode can make equipment
explode, boats sink or
change the weather
for the
worse.

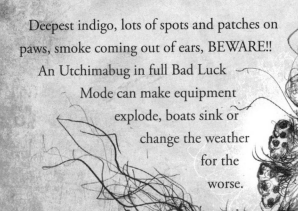

At Annipeck's bedtime, K2 and Mabel sat on her bed, reading her a bedtime story, and when they finished, Annipeck said hopefully, 'Annipeck COME TOO? Efferist come too?' She pointed to the dolls' house. 'Where to, Annipeck?' K2's eyes widened. 'Nobody's going anywhere. And it's too late to play with the dolls' house now, we'll play with you tomorrow.'

'You IS going Anywhere!' insisted Annipeck, as if 'Anywhere' was an actual place. 'You need Annipeck. Annipeck is a VERY BIG GIRL.' She frowned. 'Annipeck GO ANYWHERE.'

Freya came in to turn out the light, very harassed. 'K2 is right, nobody's going Anywhere . . .' said Freya.

Annipeck might be old beyond her years, but she was also still a baby.

She started to cry, big rolling tears. 'Annipeck go Anywhere! Annipeck COME TOO!' she wailed. 'Toofbrushes want to COME TOO!'

The toothbrushes did *not* want to come too.

'Safety first', was the toothbrush family motto.

They made their feelings known by tucking themselves up in bed extremely firmly. The baby toothbrush had already fallen asleep on Annipeck's pillow some time ago, curled up like a little plastic jellybean. The larger toothbrushes, realising Annipeck wasn't getting the message, jumped back up and pulled gently on Annipeck's pyjamas to get her to lie down.

'We're all staying here, Annipeck,' Freya insisted, a little frantically. You could always tell when Freya was lying because her ears turned bright red. 'Particularly Daniel, you're not going anywhere, are you Daniel?'

'Absolutely not,' said Daniel, coming in behind Freya. 'Although,' he said longingly, 'I wish we could afford a holiday. And it's way past your bedtime, Annipeck . . .'

Annipeck knew perfectly well they weren't telling the truth, because of course *everyone*, apart from Daniel, had Plans that night, that nobody was telling anyone else, in case they should worry.

Very grumpily she allowed them all to put her to bed.

And after Daniel turned out Annipeck's light, she crept out of bed, toddled over to the dolls' house and opened up the front.

Everest was settling down in the kitchen to a nutritious meal of one baked bean, a pea, and a crumb of mashed potato, served on a cheeringly handsome-looking miniature fake silver plate. And he was drinking the Anti-Shrinking Antidote out of a cheeringly classy little fake crystal glass (these things matter when you're down on your luck). The Antidote was working disappointingly slowly, so Everest was only a tiny bit bigger each day.

Annipeck played with the dolls in the other rooms while Everest told her stories of his wonderful exploits over the years. How he had stolen the great Spelling Stick, the Dreadblade, from the ghastly robot Ironshanks. How he had discovered the Lost Black Holes. How he had once sailed in the crew of the pirate spaceship *The Terror*, captained by the most terrifying pirate of them all, Chief Aero-Ruthless the Skyripper.

'That old rascal Cyril Sidewinder and I were part of the crew of that spaceship . . .' said Everest, waving his teeny fork around.

Annipeck, quietly chatting away to herself as she dressed up one of the dolls in a Superwoman outfit, stopped at the mention of Cyril Sidewinder's name. 'Grandpa?' she asked eagerly.

'Um . . . no . . . not your Grandpa, Annipeck. *Cyril Sidewinder*, highly unreliable fellow, half Lurkim – never trust a Lurkim. The chap who stole you last time and took you to Excelsiar.* I'm so sorry about that, by the way, it was possibly a little my fault. Cyril and I – er – well, we sort of *borrowed* some treasure Chief Aero-Ruthless had hidden in his hold, part of which was this scary Infinity Clock that everyone seems to be so keen to get hold of, as well as myself. I mean, how were *we* to know how important that clock was going to be to everybody?'

Everest held up a stern, pompous finger.

---

* You can read about this in *Which Way to Anywhere*.

'Never volunteer for a pirate crew, is my advice to you, Annipeck, never volunteer for a pirate crew,' said Everest, with a solemn and sad shake of his head. 'That's a lesson for life, right there.'

Everest was feeling a little sorry for himself and regretting some of his life choices, the life he had lost, how far he had fallen to end up in the dolls' house, talking to a baby.

'These are desperate times, Annipeck,' continued Everest, 'so I am going to use that Infinity Clock to Turn Back Time, and put things back the way they were. It's a dreadfully dangerous business, of course, Turning Back Time, but unless I Turn Back Time, how else am I to have a second chance at being a better father to K2 and Izza, and a second chance with Freya? She can't spend the rest of her life with a man with no moustache. I'm saving her from herself, really.'

'Which reminds me,' said Everest. 'When you and Cyril were in Excelsiar, did you by any chance find a box with a key in it?'

Annipeck was a good-natured child so she politely stopped the far more important thing that she was doing for a second to try and answer Everest's question.

She looked at him, puzzled.

'Did Cyril dig up a box?' tried Everest again. 'Large treasure chest thingy with a key inside it?' He mimed unlocking something with a key. 'Buried somewhere in the scariest place I could possibly think of because I was trying to stop it getting into the hands of anyone trying anything so careless as to Turn Back Time, and never imagined that said careless person would be me, and I would one day be going back *myself* to find it! Did you and Cyril come across that box when you were in Excelsiar?'

Annipeck stared thoughtfully into the distance.

And then she waved her arms around excitedly as she remembered her recent adventure.

'Ersersiar! Tickle tickle ickle *STAR*! Box! KEY! Grandpa! Key! *Yes*, Efferist! Yes!'

Annipeck nodded her head enthusiastically before turning back to the more vital task of tucking the smaller dolls into their bunk beds.

'That's a relief,' said Everest. 'I just need to track down Cyril and get the key off him, then. I wasn't fancying going back to Excelsiar again. Although . . .' A thought occurred to him and he sighed. 'Cyril is now in the Prison of the Evergods so if I'm going to get back that key, I have to head there next and you could say that the Prison of the Evergods is a considerably worse spot to visit than the planet of Excelsiar.'

Everest shook his head gloomily before perking up again. 'But my family is worth it, Annipeck, the kids are worth it, Freya is worth it. Love is *always* worth it.'

'Now, I know what you're thinking, Annipeck,' Everest went on, mouth full of baked bean and a carving of pea, 'I should just tell Puck I'm here, and then he can carry the Infinity Clock for me, and I can get on with my mission. But I've had that little robot since I was a child, and he looks up to me, almost as much as my own children do, and I can't let him see me like this. And where I am headed is too dangerous for a small droid like him . . .'

Annipeck nodded as if she understood while tucking up the Mummy doll in bed, saying, 'Night, night, darling' in a sing-song voice. Then she turned and stared at Everest, deep in thought, in a way he found unnerving.

And ve-ry gently she made a move to try and put one of the Playmobil Viking helmets on Everest's head.

'You stop that right there, Annipeck!' Everest said, mightily offended. 'I am still a Great Hero, not one of your toys . . . That reminds me, it's way past your bedtime. Into bed, Annipeck, into bed, and I'll sing you a lullaby . . .'

Annipeck had the considerable size advantage, but teeny as Everest was in his present incarnation, he was nonetheless an adult, and he had the voice of authority, so she obediently shut the dolls' house door and hopped into bed.

Everest still had a wonderful singing voice, smaller though it might be right now, so the night ended with Annipeck falling asleep as he sang her beautiful, haunting songs drifting faintly out of the windows of the dolls' house. Everest was in a melancholy mood, so the songs were filled with longing.

Footsteps in the dark night sky
I left my love and I don't know why
Longing for her as the time goes by
Can't get back to my love.
Wished for a world and the wish came true
Wish I had wished to go back to you
It's too far now in these worn old shoes.
I got them Sad Old, Bad Old, Wishing Blues . . .

Which way Witch, and Wish Way Where?
Could go Anywhere, just don't care
Returned for my love but she's not there
Can't get back to my love.

'There's a hole in my heart,' sighed Everest, once he'd got to the end of his song, 'where my children used to be . . .'

Annipeck was about to go to sleep, and sat up in bed and

There's a hole in my heart where my children used to be

demanded something a little more cheerful. 'Wuz upug a Galixy song, Efferist!'

'All right, then, Annipeck,' Everest called back, 'but this is the last one . . .'

'Once upon a Galaxy,' sang Everest,
'When dreams will all come true . . . !
You'll come home to a family
And we'll be home to you . . .'

Annipeck was nearly asleep now, all snuggled round her toothbrushes and her Lego, but she joined in, singing woozily.

'Wuz upug a Galixy
Wer derms ar all come ter-ooo . . . !
You'll car home to a famery,
Ar war be home to yooo . . .'

The last bit turned into a yawn and a snuffle. Annipeck was asleep, so she didn't hear Everest carrying on the song without her.

'I love a starcrossed journey
flying fast and flying slow
But home is where my dreams are, however far I go . . .'

Chapter 13 Which Way There and Back Again

Theo had set his alarm for 1.30 a.m. but he was woken a good hour or so before that, by some banging about downstairs in the hall.

He crept out and peered over the bannisters.

Aunt Trudie and Aunt Violet and Freya, heavily armed with all sorts of Spelling Sticks and Magical equipment, were making their way to the big, heavy old front door, which Daniel was holding open for them.

'Ssshhh . . .' whispered Aunt Trudie, because Aunt Violet was making quite a racket, dragging her ancient old Hoover behind herself.

Theo could just about hear his dad say something like: 'Do be careful . . . I wish I could come with you . . . this person sounds extremely dangerous . . .'

And then Freya replying: 'Don't worry, Daniel, we've done this sort of thing so many times before. Besides, we have to do this. I've looked into the Future, and if we don't, the whole family is in jeopardy. And someone has to stay here to look after the children . . .'

She leant forward, kissing him on the cheek.

The three women climbed aboard their Hoovers, Aunt Violet revving hers a few times, before they took off into the night. Daniel watched them go, and then turned and closed the door.

'Ha! Look after the children, indeed!' Theo jumped as Izzabird appeared, whispering at his elbow. 'We went on a whole adventure in Excelsiar without *them*, when will she stop treating us like babies?' she fumed. 'All they say about not doing Magic unless it's absolutely necessary. They're doing all the fun stuff on their own! Well, we'll show them – they'll *have* to believe in us after this!'

They scrambled out of the way to hide in the shadows as Daniel climbed the stairs, passing them so closely in the corridor they could have reached out and touched him. He paused a moment to pop his head round Annipeck's door, to check she was still sleeping, and then turned the corner to go back to his own room.

Theo and Izzabird waited enough time for Daniel to go back to sleep, and then tiptoed back to wake up Mabel and K2.

'Have we got everything?' said Izzabird, thoroughly overexcited. 'Travelling suits? Spelling Sticks? Thinking-caps for thought powers? Pencils and papers for finger powers? Eye glasses for looking powers? And some things that we love for luck and protection?'

Izzabird took her scallop shell, K2 had his drawing pad, Mabel her favourite book and Theo his skateboard. They put Bug and Puck in Mabel's arms, because Bug was happiest with Mabel, and Puck was its friend. Bug was clinging very sweetly to Mabel with its other arm wrapped around the little robot, weak as a kitten. Mabel and Puck hugged it and stroked it, trying to keep it calm.

'You mustn't worry, Bug,' whispered Mabel. 'We're going to SAVE you . . .'

'You promise, we're not going for *long*?' said K2. 'Just enough time to take Bug back to its planet and then we come straight home again . . .'

'Oh no, not long,' said Izzabird reassuringly. 'But I've left a note, just in case . . . Operation Blink 22 and Back Again, *here . . . we . . . go . . .!'*

Chapter 14 Unexpected Consequences of Going Through a Which Way While Accompanied by an Utchimabug

What happened next was really very unlucky indeed.

(Or lucky, depending on your viewpoint.)

I am not sure whether it was the fault of the Utchimabug, or the Silver Starwalker.

But I have to admit the Silver Starwalker played a considerable part in it.

Either way, the minute Izzabird put the orb into the back of the Silver Starwalker to make it start, and as soon as it lifted off the ground, things started going wrong.

The Silver Starwalker hummed into life, purring like a cat.

It shot smoothly upwards, blowing back Theo's hair.

Theo tried not to look down as they lifted higher than the garden wall, and then up higher still, level with the upstairs windows. He would never get used to this bit . . .

He could feel his stomach lurching uncomfortably.

But to everyone's alarm, the Starwalker lunged wildly to the right, turning away from the house.

'Izzabird! You're steering it in the wrong direction!' said Theo.

'It's not me!' panted Izzabird, frantically moving switches on the Automatic Fly System. 'I'm *trying* to steer it but it's going the other way!'

'I thunks there's a problem . . .' said Puck, as Mabel tried to hang on to the Starwalker with one hand and soothe Bug with the other. 'Bug has gone vile-let . . . no . . . Bug has gone burple . . . no . . . MAYDAY! MAYDAY! Bug has gone . . . INDIGO!'

Bad things happened when Bug went indigo.

'OK . . . Abort mission!' exclaimed Theo. 'Land the thing again, Izzabird, we can't risk it if Bug is in Bad Luck Mode . . .'

However, the Silver Starwalker was not listening to instructions.

It shot low down over the vegetable garden, so low that it sliced off the top of the sweet peas . . . then up into the air again . . . then it got thoroughly confused and darted into Aunt Violet's maze, twisting through it with such violence that K2 nearly threw up. It reached the centre . . . screeched vertically upwards . . . and then sped towards the large tree at the bottom of the garden with the old abandoned treehouse in it.

It began to circle the tree.

And K2 realised the door of the treehouse was very faintly . . . humming. And there was a shimmering piece of air that formed a darkening of the atmosphere at that one precise spot. Both of which were markers of a Which Way.

None of this made sense.

K2 was *sure* there wasn't a Which Way in the treehouse. He'd never drawn one, and he'd been drawing plenty of maps recently. Maybe it had just opened up?

'Pass me the Air Stick!' yelled Izzabird.

She had dropped down on to her stomach, and was lying right at the front of the Starwalker.

K2 handed her Aunt Violet's Air Stick, and as the Starwalker made one last circle around the tree, Izzabird reached out and made a great wild slash in the shape of an 'X',

and Theo caught his breath as the air itself fell apart
in the great Starcross of a portal between worlds. Izzabird
held the Air Stick steady, like a great lance. The Starwalker
paused a second in the air, moved back and forth a little,
like a horse preparing to make a final charge.

And then LAUNCHED itself, full speed, at the door of
the treehouse, Izzabird on her knees, Air Stick first, as if she
were a knight with her steed in a jousting competition.

Theo closed his eyes in anticipation.

BREARRRRRRWIRROOOOWWKKKKKKK!

There was the most extraordinary exploding noise as the

Air Stick seemed to *rrrip* through the air itself. The door of the treehouse *smooshed* into smithereens, and bits of door went flying in all directions.

And the Silver Starwalker shot like a great speeding bullet into another world.

Chapter 15 Never Play Games with Horizabel the Grimm

Before I continue with the story . . .

Please Note.

You should NEVER play games with Horizabel the Grimm.

Story Makers are tricksy, tricksy people, with more twists in our tales than the most wind-y of tornadoes.

And stealing Horizabel's Silver Starwalker was the *height* of foolishness.

For oh, that Silver Starwalker!

It's a wild one, it is.

It is no *ordinary* Flymaster.

The Silver Starwalker is a particularly rare and unusual hoverboard (you mustn't call it that, though. Flymaster is the correct term). It is made out of a patchwork of curious and rare metals that could once be found deep in ocean mines on the lost planet of Ixcellion, which was swallowed by a black hole, oh centuries ago, my loves, so precious few of those metals are left wandering around the universe . . .

The Silver Starwalker has a mind of its own and can only be ridden by experienced Riders, by those with the truly Great Minds and clever fingers and strong will of a Story Maker like myself.

And even then it must be flattered and coaxed and reasoned and cajoled into flying the course you want it to.

And you must know its name, of course.

If you don't know its name you haven't a *hope* of controlling it.

So inexperienced ignorant little humans with no idea of the years of practise, the centuries of knowledge, the patient skills, haven't a chance in Andromeda of staying on board if Horizabel didn't want them to.

The minute Horizabel realised they weren't going to open the Which Ways to her, she switched on a button on her left ankle, to activate the Homing System of the Starwalker.

When the Starwalker was on Planet Earth, it would be very obedient and do everything the little human beings wanted, so they would think, poor uneducated little dustlings, that they had it under their control.

But if ever they were so foolish as to open up one of those Which Ways and do some travelling . . .

. . . the Starwalker would wake into life, and take the little human beings to wherever Horizabel was in the universe.

It was for the little human beings' own good, after all.

Terrible dangers might await them if they landed up somewhere unexpected, like Blink 22, Horizabel *had* been telling the truth about that.

So Horizabel was doing them a favour and teaching them a lesson at the same time.

My favourite kind of story.
And Horizabel was not
particularly worried that they would try
and go travelling *without* the Silver Starwalker,
because of the human beings' extreme youth.

A wiser, older human being, if faced with the
choice of going into an adventure on the back
of one of Aunt Violet's reliable old Hoovers or on
Horizabel's unpredictable Silver Starwalker, would
always choose the Hoover.

But little human beings are not born wise.

Look in your *own* heart, if you happen to be a little
human being reading or listening to this story.

Hoover or Starwalker?

Be honest.

Which would YOU choose?

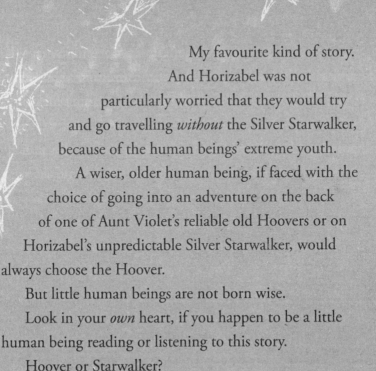

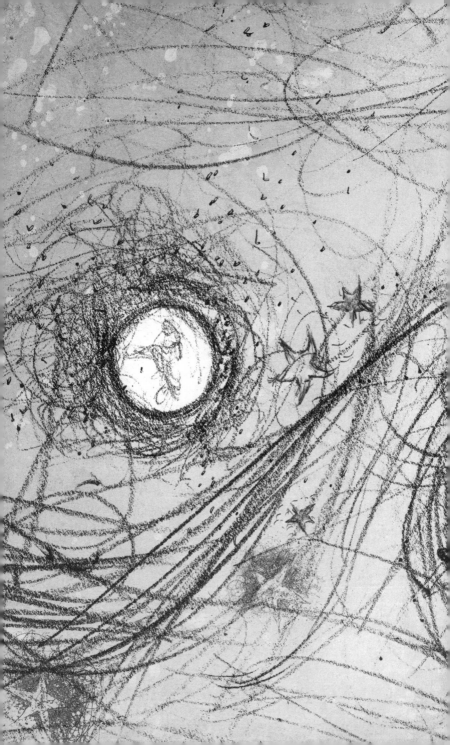

part Two

Chapter 16 Things Go Terribly Wrong

Travelling through the portal this time was not at all like the last few times K2 had travelled through a Which Way.

Before, they had had to force their way through what felt like very thick air.

This time, the combination of the Starwalker and Aunt Violet's Air Stick seemed to have set off some sort of explosion, and as bits of two worlds erupted all around them, an airbag effect momentarily detonated around the Starwalker to protect them.

The Starwalker was travelling so fast that it was difficult to see where they were going, and the children only had brief glimpses of each world they were travelling through before the wildly careering hoverboard tore through another Which Way and on into another world, and then another, and another. Theo and Izzabird kept the Air Stick pointed straight in front of them throughout, only just having time to draw the 'X's in the air so they could get through the Which Ways.

I can tell you where they went, though, of course, for I was tracking their journey with increasing alarm.

Cimmerian, a dark world, where it is always night-time, and the Sound Warriors, and the Giant Bats, and all other creatures who live there, have to use their advanced senses of smell and taste and echo-location to move around the murky shades.

Mercurian, the world with quicker seasons, where it is spring, summer, autumn, winter, in a single day.

Colossic Titanica, the truly gigantic world, far larger than Jupiter, where the great giants and ogres and leviathans headed after they were so persecuted on Planet Earth. Now they move lazily through the grasses, taller than skyscrapers, or riding on the backs of tame dragons or brontosaurus.

And so many others, the Silver Starwalker getting faster, and faster, and faster . . .

The final Which Way they burst through was where it all went terribly wrong.

Clever and tricksy as Horizabel is, there were some unfortunate circumstances that even as ingenious a Story Maker as Horizabel had omitted to take into account. She had slightly forgotten that said little human beings would be accompanied by an annoying Utchimabug, blinking on and off, yellow and purple, like a furry traffic light.

To do Horizabel justice, she was *awfully* busy.

There were battles between galaxies she had to sort out.

There were dreadful robot outcasts she had to outwit.

There were some really scary people that she owed money to from a card game on Who-llevion that she was trying to avoid.

In short, the whole O'Hero-Smith story was just *one* of *many* stories that Horizabel was trying to keep on top of. She was zigzagging across the universe like some sort of cool but ever-so-out-of-control little spider, dispensing justice here, causing trouble there, and it was no wonder that she got her web-lines crossed sometimes.

Even a Grimm makes the odd tiny mistake, there *was* only ONE of her, after all.

But the fact that she had forgotten about the Utchimabug, well . . .

That set the path of the Starwalker and the path of the story off in a wildly unpredictable direction and out of Horizabel's control.

It could not have been worse timing.

As you will see.

For as bad luck and ill-chance and crossed-stars would have it, a little while earlier, Horizabel had received a summons from the Leader of the Universal Government calling for an Extraordinary Meeting of the Twelve Bounty Hunters.

So she had to drop everything and head straight for the

Planet of the Evergods.

And most unfortunately, in her rush, she forgot to turn off that sensor on the Starwalker's homing device.

Which meant that the O'Hero-Smith children and the Starwalker were now heading straight for Horizabel, who was currently standing . . .

Right . . .

In the Heart . . .

Of Universal Government.

Or UG for short.

And unfortunately that means . . .

YOU have to go there too.

the capital of U.G.
planet of the
Evergods

Please Note:
For security reasons,
I am unable to show
you any visuals of
what happens in the
Blue Room.
Thank you for
your understanding.
H. D.

Chapter 17 In the Heart of Universal Government

There is a centre to things.

It may look as if the stars are randomly splattered across an indifferent sky like a child who does not know how to paint, but there is, in fact, a centre to things.

I am not saying, of course, that there is an actual *physical* centre, for that would be to suggest that the universe has an edge or an ending.

No, by 'centre' I mean, the centre for the social life of the universe.

The centre is where, by apparent accident, there are a considerable number of inhabitable stars placed sufficiently close together so that hopping about by spacecraft was possible for intelligent life several million years ago.

One of the oldest grandest stars of all is where the Universal Government has its headquarters, and by that, again, I do not mean that the star is *physically* older than any of the other stars because they are all mind-bogglingly, gobsmackingly, ridiculously old.

But this is a star where life began in the seas, in the soups, in the strange chemical mists, particularly early, and therefore sophisticated thinking life-forms were building civilisations on it before other planets, so being born first gave them an edge.

The star is very very rich, which makes it very very desirable, and vulnerable to attack.

So it hides itself from such attacks using a refined system of invisibility, and spaceships regularly pass by it without knowing it is there. In itself that is a towering design achievement. A star cowl, like my own invisibility cloak, is one thing. Something that hides an entire planet is quite another. Furthermore, ever since the existence of the first Ancestor O'Hero and the first Alternative Atlas, every Which Way to that planet is alarmed and controlled, so that if some foolish being were to try to enter without being invited or without permission, they would be instantly liquidated.

All those who live there, even the smallest, most put-upon cog wheel of a robot, the titchiest sprite, clinging desperately to the bottom of the social ladder, prides itself on being a citizen of the Planet of the Evergods.

This is where everything begins – or thinks it does.

The Planet of the Evergods is flawed, of course, although it is not recommended to suggest such a thing in public.

It is flawed even by the nature of its make-up, for half of it exists in daylight and the other in darkness, yet that flaw is part of what has given it its great power.

The capital is set right on the dividing line, a great

gorgeous astonishing construction, built always to impress, a grand harmony of astronomically high historical buildings and even taller and higher new skyscrapers, always trying to out-do each other. Imagine Imperial Rome constructed in an Age of Technology. And a complication of citizens, Magic and robotic and everything in between. And how to describe the stately Seven Gated Heart of Government, which is the only place in the capital that straddles the Light Side of the Evergods and the Dark?

For on the Light Side of the Evergods no stars are seen. On the Dark Side it is always a brilliant night sky. The Light Side turns in on its own internal politics, enjoys the incredible riches that it feels are its birthright. The Dark Side faces out, to the rest of the universe.

Right in the centre of the Heart of Government, there is a Blue Room.

You are not allowed to go there, or even know about this room's existence, and I am not allowed to tell you about it.

But I am not someone who always obeys the Rules, and it appears that *you* are not either.

So follow me here at your peril. I have warned you.

This is the Room Where Everything Happens.

The only beings allowed in the Room were the Twelve Members of the High Council of Universal Government, and the Twelve Bounty Hunters.

And about half an hour earlier, when the O'Hero-Smith children were making their last travel arrangements before climbing on board the Silver Starwalker, the Twelve Bounty Hunters had been called to an extraordinary meeting in the Blue Room.

They had flown there from all corners of the universe, and were standing still as statues.

They were waiting for the Leader of the UG to appear.

They were waiting for HER.

Everyone in that room was terrified of HER but they would not show it.

I shouldn't really be describing any of the bounty hunters to you, so for my safety and yours I will restrict myself to those who are relevant to this story. Some are Living Beings, both Magical and non-Magical, some are Artificial Intelligence, or robots, in common parlance.

There is me, of course, Horizabel the Grimm, standing on the end, the finest and youngest and best, the most dazzling and brilliant bounty hunter of them all, totally justified in my healthily high opinion of myself, and with elegantly beautiful arms, one robotic, and one shaped curiously like the five-twigged branch of a tree.

(I always talk about myself in the third person when I am in my physical form.)

Beside me hovered my own small companion robot,

Blinkers, who has been with me since I was a baby. She can transform into many sizes, but she was in her most usual mode, small and round and huggable like a flying cushion.

And then there were the others.

Most of them were hiding wings of some sort, either natural or artificial. Some were terrifying-looking. Others were sneakily nondescript. All were heavily armed. There was the skeleton diamond-studded EXCORIATOR, glamorously scary, the one who was secretly working for Vorcxix on the side, but only Vorcxix and Horizabel and you know that.

The bounty hunters were all perfectly still, waiting.

They must be still as a sign of their absolute control.

POWER this great demands a show of restraint, even from Horizabel.

They were waiting for THE LEADER.

Nobody knew HER name. Names are powerful things, so SHE kept HERS a secret. SHE was just known as 'SHE' or 'THE LEADER'.

There was nothing but the bounty hunters in the Blue Room Where Everything Happens, nothing but the ultra-modern mirror blue of the floor meeting the glass of the walls and the ceiling so high up above it might as well be sky. There were windows as tall as trees that looked out on the glory of the Everlasting City in permanent triumphant daylight to the left, and over the cold wastes of the Dark Side of the Evergods in permanent star-studded glorious night on the right.

While they waited, there was a piece of music playing that filled the room so completely that the very glass walls seemed to *hum* with the noise. Horizabel's whole body, as she stood there as still as an icicle, vibrated with the exquisiteness of it.

The music of the stars.

Slowly, gradually, the room began to fill with a hum deeper than the beautiful music. The bounty hunters all stared intently at a piece of air in the centre of the room, and that air seemed to thicken and bulge.

The Blue Room turned even bluer.

Blue electric sparks played along the walls and fizzled around Horizabel's head as the air in the centre of the room began to break a hole in itself.

The music gentled to a whisper.

There was an extraordinary tearing noise, like somebody ripping a cloth. And a gigantic, yelling head thrust itself out of thin air, just as if it were forcing its way through an invisible curtain.

They weren't supposed to look at THE LEADER, but Horizabel could never resist.

There was HER head, at exactly the place where a

Being's head SHOULD be . . . but there was no body below it. The head appeared to be levitating about seven feet up in the air, right in the still blue centre of the beautiful blue room. HER mouth was open in a ghastly bellow of anger and effort, eyes burning like stars on fire, veins bulging out of the furious forehead.

All of this was a performance. THE LEADER wasn't really angry. It was a display of power. The bounty hunters weren't allowed to show emotion so SHE was showing them that SHE could.

SHE stopped yelling.

Nothing more was going to materialise for the moment. SHE'd clearly decided to restrict herself to just the floating head, now emotionless.

Only THE LEADER could do that. Everyone else had to have their limbs clearly visible so that no weapons could be reached for, no wars could begin.

In theory, all members of the High Council were equal.

In practice, as the oldest member, SHE took precedence over all others. Every now and then the members were uneasy about this, because it reminded them of the Sovereign Era, but as SHE had never shown any inclination to rule alone, they had allowed HER unspoken priority to continue. The truth was, fear of HER kept some of the more – how can I put it? – possibly unruly members, such as Vorcxix, in their place. And nobody, apart from Vorcxix perhaps, wanted to return to the dreadful days of war on the High Council.

So only THE LEADER could call a meeting of the bounty hunters without the Members of the High Council present.

SHE spoke.

HER voice, low, calm, terrible.

'Bounty hunters,' SHE began, 'we are living in turbulent times. There are comets ablaze that have not been seen for many a hundred year. Stars with trains of fire and dews of blood, warnings impossible to ignore. Worlds knocked off their axes, sinister forces forming, Things of power like the Infinity Clock going missing, Magical Creatures on the move, fleeing their home planets, destinies unlocking from their set course . . .

'And I have called this Extraordinary Meeting,' continued THE LEADER's calm voice, 'because all of these happenings suggest trouble is building out there. And I have reason to believe that we face a threat to our Alternative Atlases.'

SHE could hardly have opened with more dramatic news. The bounty hunters stiffened in horror.

'Six months ago, we had an anonymous donation of the First Ancestor's Atlas to the Universal Library –' (that was clever old Horizabel, of course, donating said Atlas, and quite the Quest she had doing it without discovery, but that's another story) '– a cause for celebration, indeed . . .' HER cold, hard voice now had an edge of pure steel to it. 'The Atlas we have been searching for, for millennia, the ORIGINAL ATLAS, finally under our control. No more pirates, no more unauthorised copies of the Atlas can ever be made without it. As soon as we have tracked down the outstanding copies out there, a chance for peace at last.

'Except . . . I have reason to believe that now . . . after thousands and thousands of years . . . a child has been born to the O'Hero family . . . *who has the Atlas Gift.*'

The bounty hunters were so surprised that some could no longer hold their tongues.

'Impossible!' snarled one.

'The Atlas Gift is unique!' cried another. 'Why would it suddenly reappear after all this time?'

'If this is so,' continued THE LEADER, ignoring the protests, 'there is a danger that this child will start creating new Atlases, that not only could be used for illegal, irresponsible intergalactic travel, but, my soothsayers tell me, also runs the dreadful risk of making our own Atlases eventually obsolete. Which is why the child must be hunted down as a matter of urgency. Every inch of the galaxies must be searched. No asteroid is too small, no spiral arm too far away . . . we must peer into every galactic nebula, every star cluster, search each shining elliptical galaxy. Which is where all of *you* come in . . .' said SHE, her voice silky with menace. 'The returned First Atlas CAME from somewhere. Whoever found it has not come forward to claim their reward. My suspicion is that it came from the O'Hero hiding place, for the Atlas has survived pretty much intact. And whoever deposited it in the Library must have had extraordinary abilities, in order to elude the Library Guards without detection . . .'

Oh thank you, thought Horizabel, smugly, in the secret recesses of her soul, undetectable even from the searching thoughts of THE LEADER.

'. . . and what THAT means,' continued SHE, 'is that it was probably one of YOU.'

Bother it!

There was another nasty silence, even more tense with suspicion than the first.

'Someone here in this room knows where the O'Hero hiding place is,' continued the relentless voice of SHE. 'Someone in this room knows where the Child-With-The-Atlas-Gift is. Someone in this room is withholding important information from the High Council, and someone in this room . . .

'. . . is a TRAITOR.'

Uproar.

Now, I have to confess Horizabel was not entirely concentrating during this last bit, because down somewhere in the region of her left knee a sensor was very gently vibrating, and this was causing even ice-cool *Horizabel* a little alarm.

Why didn't I turn that beastly sensor OFF as soon as I got the call to the Meeting? she was thinking, concentrating with every fibre of her being on not moving.

Because the sensor was alerting Horizabel to the fact that somewhere a gazillion miles away on Planet Earth those wretched little human beings, the O'Hero-Smith children, had chosen this very poor moment indeed to be disobedient and to travel through one of the Which Ways on the back of her beautiful Silver Starwalker.

And *most* unfortunately she had instructed said Silver Starwalker to bring itself immediately to Horizabel, wherever she was, if they ever did such a foolish thing.

Under normal circumstances this would have been another of her most excellent plans, but right now the idea of them turning up anywhere in the vicinity of the central galaxies was making Horizabel's twig fingers sweat slightly at the edges.

So unless she could turn that sensor to *off*, without anyone noticing, the Silver Starwalker would be programmed to head straight for the Planet of the Evergods and that would be, I have to say, apocalyptically bad timing.

They would never get in, of course.

The Which Ways to the Evergods are rigorously patrolled and guarded.

But every knock on the door of a Which Way that leads to the Evergods is investigated, and the Evergods' crack troops are sent out to hunt down and annihilate the impertinent possible invaders, and their entire home and planet if necessary.

Which would be sad, naturally, because if truth be told Horizabel had an irritatingly soft spot for those little human beings, and it's always such a waste when a whole ecosystem is destroyed – however, unfortunately the UG is completely ruthless regarding matters to do with their own preservation.

But more importantly . . .

People would ask themselves, what on Earth the closest relations to one of the universe's most wanted outlaws were doing flying through the galaxies on the back of Horizabel the Grimm's Flymaster?

And even the bold and tricksome tongue of Horizabel, quicksilver and sometimes merrily oblivious to the truth as it was, would struggle to convince when she denied all prior knowledge of said little human beings, and therefore also her involvement in the recapture of the First Alternative Atlas or knowledge of K2.

Yes, it would all be very awkward.

The High Council would tear her apart.

Or worse, imprison her forever.

She *had* to turn off that sensor.

Hoping to be covered by the extraordinary uproar that had now broken out in the Blue Room, Horizabel moved one finger infinitesimally slowly towards her left knee and the sensor, in the expectation that a lightning movement might jog it down to *off*.

HER eyes instantly swivelled towards Horizabel.

Horizabel froze.

How could SHE have sensed even that tiny weeny movement amidst all this chaos?

All might have gone very badly for Horizabel, if something completely astonishing had not happened the very next second.

CCCRASSSSSSSSHHHHHHHHHHHHH!!!!!

Chapter 18 Unprecedented Chaos in the Blue Room

The unbreakable crystal glass on the Light Side of the Blue Room EXPLODED . . .

As a Which Way opened up, seemingly almost spontaneously, and through it . . .

. . . flew Theo and Mabel and Izzabird and K2 on the back of Horizabel's Silver Starwalker.

Right slap BANG into the Heart of the Universal Government.

Impossible, unbelievable, preposterous as it was . . .

It happened.

And chaos ensued in the Blue Room.

In the fraction of a second where everyone else was ducking and trying to defend themselves, Horizabel had the presence of mind to do two things. One was to press the camouflage button on her left elbow, which automatically disguises the Starwalker, to make it look like the sort of regulation army-issue Flymaster that you can find knocking about most of the stars in the Central Galaxy.

The other was to turn off that sensor by her knee, thus cutting off the Starwalker's homing device.

Now Horizabel just needed to disassociate herself entirely from both the Starwalker and the little human beings.

Which was only going to be possible if the little human beings escaped.

And that was a big 'if'.

The O'Hero-Smith children did at least seem to be wearing some of Aunt Violet's homemade armour, which was covering their faces, but their muffled voices were going to give some of them away as relations of Everest's as soon as anybody put them through a voice recognition system. Mind you, for security reasons, none of the meetings in the Blue Room were supposed to be recorded.

'Where are we?' cried Izzabird.

One of the problems with the armour was that it was quite difficult to see anything through the eye slits. 'Can anybody tell?'

'I's not sure!' moaned Puck. 'But I is pretty *absquolootely* CERTAIN we is not supposed to be here! Turn back!'

Bug had turned thundercloud purple and was peeping wildly in alarm.

'It's *fine*, Bug, don't worry,' lied Izzabird. 'It's all absolutely fine . . .'

'Oh my goodness, the place is stuffed with robots! And other horrible monster-y type things . . .' gasped K2.

'Put us into Stealth Mode, Theo!' ordered Izza.

'I'm *trying*, but it doesn't seem to be working!' said Theo, desperately pushing the button that should make the

201

Starwalker turn invisible. 'Mabel, calm Bug down, I think its Bad Luck Mode is interfering with the Stealth Mode system . . .'

'Calming it down isn't working either!' cried Mabel, tenderly stroking the Utchimabug, who was snuggled deep in a sling around her neck, its fur as dark mauve as a bruise.

'Go back through the last Which Way, Izza!' yelled K2.

'But I can't *see*!' cried Izzabird.

Mabel could feel her stomach melting with terror. Wherever they were, this was BAD, she knew it.

'MAYDAY! MAYDAY! MAYDAY!' shrieked Puck.

The Starwalker careered wildly this way, that way, turned upside down, shooting across the ceiling. They clearly had absolutely no idea what they were doing.

But they *did* have the advantage of total and absolute surprise.

Because nothing like this had ever happened in all of the umpteen millennia of the Universal Government's existence.

The Planet of the Evergods was supposed to be impregnable.

The Blue Room was supposed to be unassailable.

The bounty hunters weren't even supposed to *move* in the Blue Room, let alone *fight*, so for vital seconds most of them were uncertain what they were allowed to do in these unheard-of circumstances.

And the O'Hero-Smith children, entirely unaware of the

full scale of the unutterable sacrilege they were committing as they sailed wildly out-of-control through that room like they were on some ridiculous homemade aerial *skateboard,* had another momentary blessing on their side.

There was a being in that Room other than Horizabel who had a vested interest in the O'Hero-Smiths escaping.

THE EXCORIATOR. Because if the O'Hero-Smiths were captured now, THE EXCORIATOR would have some awkward questions to answer.[*]

So just as the bounty hunters sprang into action, through the rain of bouncing crystal and confused shouting, THE EXCORIATOR and Horizabel locked eyes. They gave small nods to one another, making an unlikely temporary alliance.

One of the Witch bounty hunters pointed their Spelling Stick in attack, finally deciding that Magic must be an option in such extraordinary circumstances, and THE EXCORIATOR bumped into her, making it look like an accident.

Horizabel deliberately dropped one of her Spell Canisters, and the oily contents spilt all over the mirror-floors. Then she sent off a particularly smoky Magical bolt, supposedly trying to target the Starwalker, but actually

---

[*] The O'Hero-Smiths knew from their previous adventure that THE EXCORIATOR was illegally working for Vorcxix – bounty hunters weren't supposed to work for members of the High Council.

hitting various bounty hunters, intending to cause more confusion – and the flaming vapour of the bolt activated the internal sprinkler systems.

'No Magic,' ordered SHE serenely, her soft cold words somehow penetrating the pandemonium and creeping into the ears of all in the room, as the water poured down like a monsoon. 'They must be captured ALIVE.'

Only SHE appeared unruffled by the strange course of events.

The Blue Room was in torrential downpour. Crystal glass was everywhere. The beautiful background music had ceased, to be replaced by the loud grating scream of the fire alarms.

'Where do we go? We can't go back!' yelled Izzabird.

They had already attempted to fly back the way they came but SHE must have closed the Which Way. Goodness knows how they had opened it in the first place.

As they streaked through the air, swerving to avoid the missiles and bolts from the bounty hunters slipping and sliding on the oily floors as they tried to catch them, a gigantic Harlequin Centaur just caught hold of the Starwalker between thumb and forefinger, before it was hit by a stray Magic bolt. Twisting free of the Harlequin Centaur's fingers, which had opened in pain, Izzabird steered the entire Starwalker down and right through the legs of a Devilogre Behemoth, and then on, swivelling and turning, desperately seeking an exit, anywhere to get out of here . . .

On the Light Side the fire alarms had alerted the Evergods' troops, whose helicopter whine could now be heard as they launched off the top of the spinning towers and flew towards the Room Where Everything Happens.

To give the ridiculous little human beings a gentle hint of their only hope now, Horizabel 'accidentally' knocked her finger on the gigantic window on the Dark Side of the room. The blast of energy caused when the Which Way opened had been so great that it had fractured the unbreakable crystal glass of this window too, into an immense crazy paving of cracks, shaking furiously, barely holding itself together. One tiny scrape of Horizabel's robot finger, and the entire thing collapsed.

The wild wind of the Dark Side of the Evergods tore into the Room Where Everything Happens.

It took all the strength and power of the Twelve Bounty Hunters to stay upright.

Initially the O'Hero-Smith children on the Starwalker were plastered against the ceiling like flies against a windscreen.

But Theo pushed the speed of the Silver Starwalker to its utmost extent and Izzabird steadied the orb of power at the back.

'This way!!!' Izzabird shouted. 'Brace yourselves, everyone, and never forget! *AN O'HERO-SMITH KNOWS NO LIMITS! THE SKY IS JUST THE BEGINNING! NO RIVERS CAN STOP US, NO MOUNTAINS CAN STAND IN OUR WAY!!!*'

Most inspiring, of course, but not very subtle, under the circumstances, and may have given away once and for all who they were. The wild wind of the Evergods tore at Horizabel's star cowl, sending it swirling behind her as she closed her eyes in horror.

With a high-pitched squeal, the Silver Starwalker launched into the face of the wind and shot straight out into the Dark Side of the Evergods.

Every single one of the bounty hunters unfurled or shot out their wings to follow. Horizabel was determined to be the first to catch up with them, but. . .

'Nobody move,' said THE LEADER. 'The Guards will catch them.'

REEEOOWWWW!

XERROOORR!

REEEOOOOOOOOOOOORR!

Above the heads of the bounty hunters the advanced flyers of the army of the Evergods set off after the O'Hero-Smiths.

Horizabel spat her hair out of her eyes as she watched them go.

Yup.

I think I can safely say it had all been a bit of a disaster.

The alarms shrieked on, and the water poured down in the Blue Room.

'As I said,' said SHE, calmly, 'there is a traitor in our midst. And until I know who it is . . .

Nobody . . .

Leaves . . .

This . . .

Room.'

It looked like the O'Hero-Smiths were on their own.

Chapter 19 The Dark Side of the Evergods

The O'Hero-Smith children were entirely unaware of the special significance of the Room they had just blundered their way into and out of.

In the Alternative Atlas, the planet is labelled 'Planet with No Name', which doesn't exactly reek of authority.

So from their point of view, they had just lost their way, found themselves under attack somewhere with a whole load of robot and other weird-looking attackers, and cleverly managed to elude them.

What with all the glass flying around, and smoke, and general chaos, the children hadn't spotted Horizabel or THE EXCORIATOR in there, which might have alerted them to the fact they had made some sort of more glaringly ominous error.

Nonetheless, they were deeply relieved to find themselves flying swiftly into a dark expanse of nothingness, too busy to take in the staggeringly beautiful canopy of stars spread out above them, Izzabird steering, Theo trying to get Stealth Mode to work, K2 desperately drawing a new map, trying to find a nearby Which Way that would lead them to Blink 22, Mabel anxiously trying to cheer up poor limp, purple Bug so their luck would change again.

And for one joyous second it seemed like that might be working.

'Found one!' said K2 triumphantly. 'And it's quite close . . .'

'Brilliant!' said Izzabird. 'I knew you would . . .'

Bug's tail tried to quiver upwards . . . and then fell down again.

'Oh dear!' said K2 in horror. 'But it isn't coming out in the Tabletop Territories that are Bug's home, it comes out in one of the really scary bits where the poisonous creatures live!'

But they had no choice.

The guards of the Planet of the Evergods were launching themselves over the walls of the Light Side into the Dark.

Theo finally got the Stealth Mode button to work so at least the guards wouldn't be able to follow.

The children and the Starwalker vanished like breath into mist.

Izzabird reached out with the Air Stick to make the great 'X' of the Starcross.

And Theo steered the Starwalker the wrong way through the Which Way, or the right way through the wrong Way, or the why Way through the Where Way, or . . . well . . . who knows what was going on, but whatever it was . . .

. . . they were flying straight into the trap that had been lying there waiting for them . . .

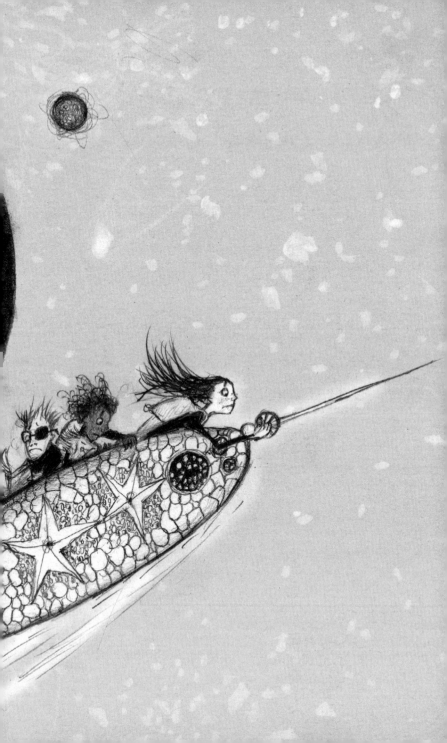

Chapter 20   On No Account Should You EVER Visit the Planet Called Blink 22

A s they burst out of the sea through the Which Way of the Witch's Prophecy, in an explosion of ice and water, the air was pin-sharp bitter, pressing in on them like a thousand pinching needles.

'Is this Blink 22?' panted Mabel anxiously, taking in great gasps of freezing air.

'It seems to be . . .' said K2 consulting the pages of his new Atlas.

'OK,' said Theo, with relief, 'we're back on track . . . I knew we could do this . . .'

Well, at least they were in the right *place*.

Now they could get back to proving that they were capable of Which Way adventuring all on their own.

'Look! The Tabletop Mountains!' shouted K2.

There, far in the distance, where K2 was pointing, were the strange, tall, twisting ice constructions supporting the Tabletop Oases, bright with colour.

Izzabird steered the Silver Starwalker round in that direction. They could fly straight there without even having to set foot on the hostile, venom-ridden terrain, surely.

'PEEP!' cried Bug, stirring in Mabel's arms, opening up

its weak eyes, and shakily pointing towards the mountains.

The fur of the Utchimabug blinked faintly into grey, then a cautious gold in colour, its tail pointing upwards briefly.

And for one second they were all exultantly happy . . .

Until their eyes adjusted properly to the light, and they stopped looking at the distant horizon, and instead looked DOWN, at what was going on below them.

Bug turned unbelievably quickly back to darkest indigo and the Silver Starwalker reared up, trembling in the air in shock. The horrified children gazed over the edge of it.

Seven menacing robots were below them on the ice.

The robots were talking to one another and shooting bolts into the alarmingly exploding Which Way below them, and they had not noticed the children yet because the Starwalker was in Stealth Mode.

'What . . . are . . . *they*?' whispered K2, his stomach curdling with anxiety.

'Oo dear . . . oo dear . . . milisquary robots . . . a Hellsiraptor . . . and a Stelf-derk . . .

and a Murgadroid!' Puck whispered back. 'Worse and worse! What is they doings here? This isquant a Robot Planet, is it? But don'ts worry . . . we is in Stealth Mode . . . they can'ts see us . . .'

The children froze in the air like statues. K2 hardly dared breathe.

Ve-ry cautiously, Theo moved the Starwalker forward so they could softly make their getaway while they were still invisible.

But Bug's Bad Luck Mode was kicking in again, and one of Puck's limbs, a little fork attachment, chose this extremely bad moment to wriggle its way out of its setting . . . and fall off.

Down it fell, way, way down, landing on the gigantic oversized skull of an emerald-green robot shouting orders at the others, with a bright, sharp

Cling!

The emerald-green robot stopped talking, and turned the smooth green glass planes of its face up to look in their direction. It adjusted its eyes in its eye sockets to stare directly at them.

The children froze again.

'And what is *that*??' whispered Izzabird.

'Oo dear oo dear oo dear . . .' moaned Puck. 'Izz a Grand Crystal Robot . . . a Blunderbore . . . one of the Pure-of-Hearts . . . but I's NEVER seen ones with such a big head, is spooky . . .'

'Now, don'ts you look, little Bug,' said Puck soothingly, putting out a soft duster and a teacloth from his arm-holes to cover the pitch-dark-with-horror Utchimabug's eyes. 'Is *nuffink* bad goings on here . . . we is goings to get you home to your family lick quick-ety-split in no time at all . . . Don'ts worry, they can'ts see us . . . we is in Stelf Mode . . .'

'Oh, for goodness' sake,' said Theo, eyes popping out of his head because, presumably thanks to Bug's Bad Luck, Stealth Mode seemed to be wearing off for no apparent reason, however hard Theo flicked the switch on, off, on off, and they were slowly turning visible in front of Blunderbore's eyes. Blunderbore gave a great shout to the others, and the robots, as one, turned their heads, or their protruding eyes, their screens, or whatever passed for the brain-centre of their construction, and whatever they used to see things with, to stare straight up at the Starwalker.

'Just pop through the Which Way and back again in time for tea, you said, Theo . . .' whispered K2 through numb lips. 'Like dropping Annipeck off at nursery school, you said . . .'

Blunderbore adjusted the lenses in its eye-sockets so it could gaze more intently, and whispered in an entirely emotionless voice: 'The Child-With-The-Atlas-Gift . . . the O'Hero-Smith family . . .'

And all around the robots on the fire-ice whispered in reply, in terrifying unison, getting louder and louder, in creaking, terrible, robotic intensity: 'Bring him the Child-With-The-Atlas-Gift . . . Bring-him-the-Child-With-The-Atlas-Gift . . . BRING him THE CHILD-WITH-THE-ATLAS-GIFT!'

'Nuffinks going on here, Bug,' said Puck, tenderly wrapping more and more attachments round the little Creature to try and calm it down. 'Nuffinks at all . . . No danger . . . no worries . . .'

'AFTER THEM!' screamed Blunderbore, spreading its great emerald wings and jet-launching into the air.

'Puck . . . sing something soothing to Bug to change our luck!' yelled Theo, as he and Izzabird fought for control of the Silver Starwalker, streaking through the sky towards the distant Tabletop Mountains.

Puck searched through his memory systems and came up with a song that Everest used to sing in particularly happy and comforting moments.

'Once upon a Galaxy, when dreams will all come tru-u-eee . . .' sang Puck, as they swerved wildly this way, that way, in desperate haste. *'You'll come home to the family, and we'll come ho-o-o-ome to you!'*

The shaking Bug seemed to be trying its hardest to change colour and help, and at this joyful little tune with its happy associations, it did indeed turn just a smidgen towards yellow.

A whine of helicopter blades, and all around them the robots sprang up from their knees and into life, the Workerbot snapping its ski blade attachments on to the ends of its legs, the Scorpio-cyborg adjusting its snow tracks, the Hellsfire-heliraptor, the Stealth-derk and the Murgadroid launching into the air behind Blunderbore. The flying and skiing robots pursued the accelerating Starwalker at unbelievable speeds, the Giganti-automaton covering vast distances with every stride, legs as tall as buildings and

its staggering arsenal of rocket launchers and ice-blasters shaking the ice as it ran.

The Starwalker was fast. Very, very fast. But the Stealth-derk was fast too, and catching up.

ZZINNNNNAORRW!

'Head for the mountains over there!' yelled Theo.

'I love a starcrossed journey, flying fast and flying slow . . .' sang Puck.

Long lines of silken threads shot past the children's heads, coming from the pursuing Stealth-derk.

'But ho-o-ome is where my dreams are, however far I go!' sang Puck.

One of the nets shot out by the Stealth-derk caught on to the edge of the Starwalker, and would have tipped them over if Izzabird hadn't whacked it with her Spelling Stick.

'Pe-e-ep peep peep pe-e-e-i-ep . . .' sang Bug, to the same 'Once Upon a Galaxy' tune. It seemed to understand how important it was that it calmed down, and was valiantly doing its best to help. *'Peep pe-ip peep peep peep . . .'*

K2 looked over his shoulder. The Stealth-derk was horribly close now.

'Do yous wants the good news or the bad news?' asked Puck, who was turned towards the pursuing army of artificial intelligence, watching anxiously as the nets just missed them. 'The good news,' shouted Izzabird from the front. '*Always . . .*'

'Those could have been lasers. They is not shooting for the kill,' said Puck. 'They is trying to catch us . . .'

'And the bad news?' said K2.

'The bad news is . . . they ISS going to catch us . . .' said Puck.

'Slow down!!' yelled Mabel. 'You're going to crash!'

'I'm . . . not . . . completely . . . in . . . charge . . .' said Izzabird through gritted teeth as she tried to control the wildly zigzagging Starwalker.

And now they ALL joined in the defiant singing. '*Once upon a GALAXY, when dreams will all come tr-u-u-u-e . . .*

You'll come ho-o-ome to the fam-i-ly and we'll come ho-o-ome to YOU!'

But to Mabel's horror, Bug remained as darkly purple as the most gloomy of thunderstorms.

'Turn yellow, Bug,' begged Mabel, tickling the little Magical Creature behind its floppy ear.

'Just gives us ones more squitchy minute . . . one little bit of the Good Luck Mode just so we can get away from these robots . . .'

But Luck sometimes does not respond to orders.

The Utchimabug's colour would not change from deepest indigo. 'Peeeep,' it said softly, regretfully, with a sad, sorry wag of its tail, before the tail turned from pointing up to pointing down.

Its ears drooped.

One of the nets launched from the Stealth-derk robot wrapped around the Silver Starwalker.

They were caught.

They were caught.

Chapter 21 Meanwhile, Back on Planet Earth...

I hate to leave the children on Blink 22 in such peril, but back on Planet Earth, Daniel and Annipeck were about to get into a little trouble of their own.

Aunt Trudie and Aunt Violet and Freya were having a highly successful time raiding Mr Spink's research laboratory and gathering up the poor Magic Creatures being kept captive there. It turns out, there were quite a few. Quietly on their Hoovers, they had flown over the warning signs that read *Keep Out*, the barbed wire, the trenches and the towers, overwhelmed the armed guards, interrupting all the radio and mobile phone wavelengths so that nobody could call out to alert for help, surrounding and muffling the entire, miserable place with their Magic.

It was a truly impressive operation, worthy of Horizabel herself, with absolutely no violence, only Spells of enchantment and stunning and amnesia.

Excellent work.

Apart from one small, important point.

Mr Spink was not in the laboratory at the time.

Mr Spink and a small band of his elite team had set out in the opposite direction some time earlier – Aunt Trudie and Aunt Violet and Freya probably even flew over them, all unknowing – and they were even now approaching the undefended House at the Crossing of the Ways. They were still a couple of fields away, but moving ever closer as the moon shone down gently on a perfectly beautiful summer's night in Soggy-Bottom-Marsh-Place.

Somewhere a nightingale was singing, and barn owls were calling to one another. The dahlias and the roses and the more unusual plants from everywhere-in-the-universe in Aunt Trudie's greenhouse were sending out heady perfumes into the still night-time air.

Daniel and Annipeck, snoring peacefully away in their beds, had absolutely no idea of what danger they were about to wake up into.

Ring! Ring! Ring! Ring!

Daniel sat up electrically straight as the mobile phone beside him on the bedside table jerked him abruptly out of sleep. He grabbed the phone.

'Wossat? Werrami? Whoisit?'

'Daniel, don't be alarmed,' whispered the voice of Freya down the line.

It's never a good sign to be woken at four o'clock in the morning by your wife telling you not to be alarmed. A phone call at four o'clock in the morning, with fighting and strange animal noises going on in the background, is generally a big hint that there is some reason for concern.

'Wossat? Werrami? Whoisit?,'

'All going well except their big boss, Mr Spink, isn't here . . .' said Freya.

'Mr Spink?' spluttered Daniel, blinking owlishly at the empty place in the bed beside him where Freya ought to be. 'Who's Mr Spink, my love?'

'No time to explain,' whispered Freya. 'I have this nasty feeling that he's headed in your direction, but I don't have time to do a proper reading – *Aunt Violet! DUCK!' Crack! Zzing!* A confused clamour of Spelling and shouting before Freya continued soothingly, 'It's probably fine and the house will defend you . . . but . . . call me if you see anything suspicious . . . and don't answer any knocking . . . We'll get back as soon as we can . . .'

And she ran off.

'Freya? *Freya?*'

You see, this is the major downside of marrying into a Magical family, however wonderful Freya might be. Sometimes it can be a little *too* exciting.

Daniel got out of bed, padded into the corridor, trying to phone Freya back, but she wasn't replying. He checked Annipeck's room, and that was OK. She was sleeping soundly, thumb in her mouth, damp curls sticking to her forehead, having kicked off all her covers because of the heat. Her toothbrushes were awake, though, looking a little agitated it has to be said, and her telephone opened a sleepy eye.

Daniel shut Annipeck's door and went into Mabel's room and –

Oh my goodness, *Mabel wasn't there*!

Theo was not in his bed either, as Daniel ran from bedroom to bedroom.

Now he was *properly* panicking.

He threw open K2 and Izzabird's bedroom door. No children, but he instantly spotted Izzabird's note, which she had left on her bed.

It said: *We're just going through one of the Which Ways to drop off something important. Back soon. Don't worry. Sorry, but you really should trust us to do things on our own. We'll explain when we get back.*

P.S. If by any chance we don't get back immediately, maybe you could rescue us? We have gone through the Which Way outside in the window of my father's workshop.

Aaaaghh!

K2 must have drawn another Atlas! The Which Ways were supposed to be closed! What were they doing? Maybe he could catch them before they left.

Daniel ran down the stairs, trying to phone Freya at the same time. No answer.

He dashed across the hall and, not really thinking properly, he unlocked all the bolts and dragged open the heavy front door.

Aaaagh again! The gate was wide open and beyond in the front garden the treehouse seemed to be half hanging out of the tree.

Where were the children?

Daniel had only got a few steps out of the house to investigate further, when someone caught him around the shoulders, and he felt a sharp pain jabbing into his right foot.

He looked down in astonishment to see a tranquilliser dart sticking out of his toe. And then he passed out cold.

Not again!

I mean, I know Daniel wasn't Magic or anything, so he might not have been all that helpful anyway, but you'd have thought he could at least stay AWAKE, he spent most of the *last* adventure completely unconscious too.

This was becoming a bit of a habit.

And now things had got rather worse as the sinister figure of Mr Spink and five of his crew crept through the open front door, shutting it quietly behind themselves.

It looked like the only person left defending the House of the O'Hero-Smiths was sleeping baby Annipeck.

And Annipeck had some great Magical powers, but she was, after all, only two and a bit.

Chapter 22 OH DEAR

Things were taking a turn for the worse on Blink 22 as well.

The O'Hero-Smiths were caught.

The great robot net had closed around the four children, Bug and Puck, and the bucking Starwalker, rearing up like a great silver stallion in the air. It wrapped around them, and, as they fell, the net was caught in the talons of the Murgadroid, swooping to catch the Starwalker like a bird of prey, who then dropped it down to the waiting pincers of the Scorpio-cyborg on the snowy ground below.

One of the pincers immediately dropped off.

'Peeep peeeep peeeeeeeep . . .' sighed Bug, which probably meant 'sorry' in the Utchimabug language, although it really wasn't the poor creature's fault, Bad Luck was just in its nature. None of us can help being our true self.

The Utchimabug couldn't prevent the chaos that followed wherever it went, it just happened.

'The Child-With-The-Atlas-Gift!' cried Blunderbore, turning to the other robots. 'We've captured the Child-With-The-Atlas-Gift!'

'The Child-With-The-Atlas-Gift!' roared the others in robotic voices.

'Follow me!' cried Blunderbore, flying off in some unknown but probably ominous direction across the snow.

The Scorpio-cyborg was built like a giant scorpion, equipped with the tracks of a tank, made of a silver so shiny that it was almost white, and its great shovel of a pincer held the children caught in the net triumphantly high, like a warrior returning with a kill from the hunt.

Puck was still busily chirping, 'Mayday! Mayday! We are being abducted by Ice Robots! On no account panic, but I would suggest escape and a full-scale retreat as soon as humanly possible . . .' And, 'Wrong direction! Wrong direction!' stretching out one, two, three, four, five, six little arms and a couple of helpful arrows. 'We should be going THAT way!'

All of which may have been excellent advice but wasn't very helpful, under the circumstances, given that K2 and Izzabird and Mabel and Theo were firmly grasped in the talons of the Scorpio-cyborg and travelling full speed in whatever direction the robots wanted to take them.

The children were trembling with cold and terror as over the great fiery snow plains they flew, deeper and deeper into the frozen desert. On top of his fear, Theo had a horrible feeling, deep in his bones.

There is something wrong with this planet . . . thought Theo. *Something dead about it.*

No birds flew. Not a sound came from the ice below them. There was not a sign of all the lovely wild things, poisonous though they might be, that K2 had drawn on his map in his Atlas. All was dreadfully quiet.

'Bug is still so sick,' Mabel whispered miserably to Theo. 'I thought when we got to its home planet it would get better . . .'

'It's still in peril,' said Theo. 'It won't get better until it gets to its parents, who will know what to feed it, and how to look after it.'

Oh dear, oh dear. *Maybe we've all made a horrible mistake*, thought Theo. Maybe they should have told those adults after all. Because wherever they were being taken right now, it certainly wasn't in the direction of the Tabletop Mountains, where Bug's parents lived.

On they travelled, until they reached a particular point, indistinguishable from the miles and miles of snow all around.

The Scorpio-cyborg stopped, flicked out a great digger attachment from its underbelly, and began to dig at the ice beneath, more like a gigantic mole than a metal arachnid.

Down, down, the cyborg burrowed, soaking the children as it threw the shovelled snow and ice over its back. It continued downwards, the children still trapped in its pincer, all wound up in the net of the Stealth-derk, until finally landing on its tracks in an enormous tunnel, a long way beneath the planet surface. Blunderbore and the Murgadroid thumped down behind them, but the Giganti-automaton and the others remained on the surface. The Scorpio-cyborg shook off the snow and set off down the tunnel at a brisk trot.

I need to give you a sense of where K2 and Izzabird and Theo and Mabel were now. And I'm not going to lie, I'm as surprised about it as you will be – which is unusual for me, and not something I am terribly comfortable with.

Imagine an entire network of tunnels, maybe the size of New York, or Paris, or London, but underground.

Admittedly, after the fierce cold of the world above, it was momentarily glorious for the children to descend into an underground world that was much more temperate. There was an eerie greasy green glow, and a strong smell of burning oil.

They arrived at what appeared to be their destination, a gigantic door covered in strange symbols, where two more Murgadroids were waiting on either side. The Scorpio-cyborg stopped, dumped the children on the floor, and rumbled off back down the tunnel they had come from. Blunderbore ordered the three Murgadroids to cut them loose from their net prison.

'Ooooo dear ooooo dear . . .' said Puck, anxiously

looking around him, and trying to protect Bug and
Mabel by putting his arms lovingly over their eyes.
'*One* Murgadroid is badly enough . . . but THREE? . . .
Murgadroids is bad bad news . . . What is *goings on* down
here? What is squeeze milisquary robots doing in this
Magical planet anyways?'

I was beginning to wonder that myself, and a hollow
feeling of anxiety was starting to gnaw
at me as I watched from far away.

The Murgadroids talked to
one another in nasty,

ear-scraping voices that so tweezered the nerve endings that you had to put your hands over your ears. They spoke in a language that Mabel really wished wasn't translated instantly by the Omni-babel-o-phone, because it did not make pretty listening.

'Do we *have* to keep them alive?' said one Murgadroid, as they cut the final strand of net trapping the O'Hero-Smiths and they scrambled free.

'His Excellency wanted them delivered to him *whole*, such a bore,' sighed another.

'But maybe we can break up *this* one a little,' said the third, cruel eyes on the ends of its fingers gleaming as it picked up Puck, dangled him in the air, reached out a mean, probing hydraulic hand and . . .

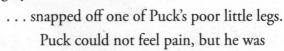

. . . snapped off one of Puck's poor little legs.

Puck could not feel pain, but he was

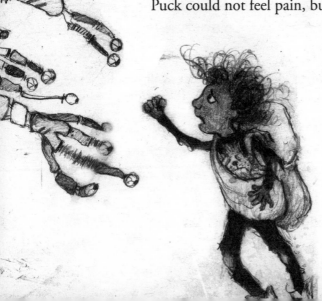

programmed to know that this was bad, and he gave a moan of alarm, withdrawing all of his limbs abruptly back into his body cavity, like the retracting head of a tortoise.

'Is it crying?' cooed the Murgadroid excitedly, shaking Puck so violently that all of his limbs came back out at once, and his head extended madly, wobbling from side to side. 'Look at this pathetic excuse for a cyborg! What a wretched little collection of weak-ly microchips and metal shavings it is!'

'Where are your weapons, you miserable tin can?' jeered another of the horrible cyborgs.

Puck held out his spoon, his corkscrew, his knitting needles, his entire pathetic array of implements, and that sent the Murgadroids into gales of ghastly laughter. 'It's got a spoon on the end of its hand!'

'Oh, by the stars, is that a tin opener?' crowed another, pretending to duck behind his leering cyborg friend. 'Hide me, I'm terrified!'

'Ha! Ha! Ha!'

Puck trembled, looking around at their blank cyborg faces and seeing no mercy.

The first Murgadroid reached out again and snapped off another of Puck's little limbs, offering it to the cyborg to his left. 'There's a fork on the end of this one – how useful! Shall we take off his head next time?'

Not for the first time, the peril of the adventure brought

out a surprising side to gentle, shy Mabel, who loathed bullies.

Trembling just as much as Puck, Mabel balled her hands into fists, and shouted up at the appalling androids at the top of her voice: *'STOP IT!'*

The Murgadroids turned, horribly slo-o-o-owly, to look down at her.

All those eyes, staring straight at Mabel, and then holding up their hands so that the eyes on the end of them stared too.

So many eyes.

'You *LET HIM GO!*' shouted Mabel.

'Yes, *LET HIM GO!*' yelled Izzabird.

'Right NOW!' cried K2.

'Maybe,' purred the nearest Murgadroid, putting its head on one side and reaching out a hand towards Mabel, 'maybe we should break YOU instead . . .'

Theo could feel something strange building up inside him. Anger, definitely, but something other than anger, too. The cold stone that he carried inside himself, deep in his core ever since his mother died, was shaking, rumbling, and inside it was *power,* he could feel it, the red-hot power of explosive lava about to erupt.

He kept that so contained, so locked up. But fear for his sister was going to make him let it go. He forgot his unsureness about Magic, about being part of this new family, forgot his fear of betraying his mother's memory or leaving her behind. He forgot everything.

Theo . . .

LET . . .

IT . . .

GO.

And as he held out a shaking forefinger, pointing at the Murgadroid's arm reaching for Mabel, he felt an odd prickling sensation of pins and needles on the surface of his skin, like spiders were crawling all over his body.

'Don't . . . you . . . *dare* . . . lay a finger on my sister,' said Theo quietly. 'And Puck is one of us. Let . . . him . . . *go*.'

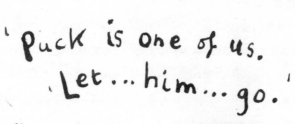

'Puck is one of us.
'Let . . . him . . . go.'

Nothing appeared to emanate from Theo's pointing finger, no visible spell or force, but the hand of the Murgadroid holding Puck crumpled in on itself.

Mabel and K2 and Izzabird watched with round-eyed desperate relief.

The Murgadroids stayed death-like static a second.

They didn't say another word.

Then they carried on disentangling Izzabird and K2 from the remains of the net. One of the Murgadroids even gave Puck his broken-off limbs back.

Shaking, Theo lowered his hand.

'Bug's Bad Luck must have kicked in at just the right time,' he said quickly.

K2 and Izzabird nodded. That must be it.

But Mabel was looking at Theo strangely.

Because Theo could feel a slow tear running down his cheek.

Theo never cried.

'It's nothing,' he said, swiping away the tear quickly, careful to hide his hand in the sleeve of his hoodie as he did so.

But it wasn't *really* nothing.

Theo had noticed something odd that had happened to his pointing finger as he concentrated all his rage into it with his mind's eye. The end of it had turned invisible, and strangely numb. And the invisibility had begun to spread up from the finger, through the back of his hand, up to his wrist – until he realised the Murgadroids weren't going to hurt Mabel after all, and then he switched 'it' off. Whatever 'it' was.

But when he cautiously brought his hand out from his sleeve a moment later and had a secret glance at it, the hand looked and felt perfectly normal. He wiggled his fingers. All there.

And Theo knew, with the same clear certainty with which he'd known that he'd broken his arm, age six, falling from a swing on to the cold ground of a playground in the big city, long before they'd moved to the House at the Crossing of the Ways.

Oh, he'd thought. *I've broken my arm.*

And this was just the same.

Oh, thought Theo. *I have a Magical Gift.*

It wasn't quite clear what that Gift *was,* exactly, and Theo didn't have time to think about what this all meant.

The O'Hero-Smith children had more pressing concerns.

For at that moment, a panel on the wall of the tunnel beside them lit up, and a truly chilling voice spoke out of it, a voice they thought they vaguely recognised, a voice that sent tingles of alarm down Mabel's spine:

'Bring them to *me,*' said the voice.

The Murgadroids jumped in alarm, put their arms around the children and began dragging them off.

The children did not know where they were being taken. But *I* did.

The Murgadroids were taking them to see Vorcxix.

Chapter 23 Oh. My. GOODNESS...

They rounded a corner, and all four children let out a gasp of horror.

OH. MY. GOODNESS.

Watching invisibly from far, far away, I felt a prickle of horror going down the back of my neck too, as I saw what the children were looking at. And it wasn't Vorcxix.

Even Puck's eyes popped out on springs and he passed out for a second, through sheer fear. Perhaps it was lucky that Bug had already gone back to its pale blue weakened state, eyes closed tiredly, so that it didn't see this latest development, because the children's luck couldn't really get any worse.

In front of them was an unimaginably large cavern, and a sight almost impossible for the human brain to take in. Glinting dully in the low light, laser eyes glowing in row, after row, after row, a low electrical hum pulsing through the charged air . . .

Three *million* Murgadroids, three *million* Workerbots, three *million* Hellsfire-heliraptors, three *million* Giganti-automatons, three *million* Stealth-derks, three *million* Scorpio-cyborgs.

A robot army large enough to fill a small country on Planet Earth, all packed together tightly in one space.

A robot army large enough to take over an entire galaxy, in fact . . . Oh dear, oh dear, oh dear. I felt nearly as sick as Theo.

This was what was wrong with this planet.

This was why the creatures of the planet were in hiding, this was why Bug's parents allowed their egg to hitchhike on the bottom of a Flymaster, to get their young one out of the way of danger. Something very terrible indeed was going on.

The individual robot warriors of this secret underground army were kneeling obediently in ranks, neat columns and squares, mile after mile after mile of them, silent and still as statues, in hibernation. You could tell from the rhythmic blinks of the lights on their weapons, steady as heartbeats, reliable as pulses, that these soldiers were not built to sleep forever. The wasp-whisper-hum in the air was a persistent reminder that they could wake at any moment, when they were needed.

K2 was trembling as violently as if he had got pneumonia, as he was carried through the caverns. The hostility that came off the rows of sleeping warrior robots was so dense it was almost visible, a cyanide reek that stretched out tendril fingers and pinched every human nerve end, until K2 nearly passed out in sheer fear, just like Puck.

As well he might, for even in sleep every single one of the robots was whispering, 'Bring him the Child-With-The-Atlas-Gift . . . Bring him the Child-With-The-Atlas-Gift . . . Bring him the Child-With-The-Atlas-Gift!!'

'Don't worry, K2,' whispered Izzabird, 'it's going to be OK . . . We won't let them get you . . .'

'We'll protect you,' said Theo.

'Absolutely,' said Mabel.

On they were dragged, past more caverns, with even more robots, through a great door that closed behind them, and into a room.

And there, sitting on the most magnificent throne of impossibly never-melting fire-ice* was someone who the children instantly recognised from their adventure back on the planet of Excelsiar and quite rightly, a cold drip of fear went down all of their spines when they set eyes on him.**

He was a tall, extremely elegant reptilian Being, covered from head to toe in beautiful shining scales and dressed in the shifting rainbow colours of snowbear furs, making him rather difficult and dazzling to look at. Dark wings curved outwards from his shoulders and spread

---

* There are many impossible things in this universe of ours.
** You can read about this in *Which Way to Anywhere*.

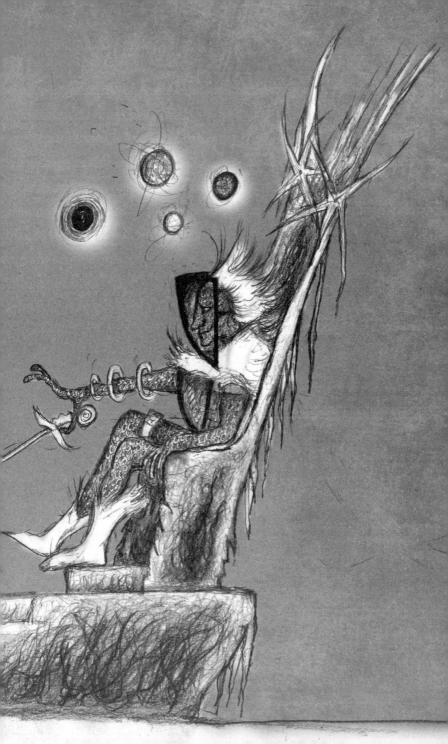

gloriously wide. He blinked his sideways eyes and flicked out a forked tongue.

'*Vorcxix the Vile . . .*' Izzabird whispered.

'Oh dear, oh dear, oh dear, oh dear . . .' whispered Mabel.

'*Your Exxxxcellency* to *you*, you impudent little earth-grubber,' hissed Vorcxix, long snaky fingers tapping on the edge of his throne, but despite the snapping of his words, Vorcxix was smiling a very nasty smile indeed, filled with triumphant glee.

'The Child-With-The-Atlas-Gift . . .' he whispered with relish. 'And accompanied by three of the other O'Hero-Sssmith children, as I live and breathe!'

'I told you,' whined the Orb-With-The-Dead-Witch-In-It, from Vorcxix's hand.

Vorcxix smashed the orb hard with his Spellstick. Its light abruptly went out.

Oo dear. That Vorcxix was *scary*.

He continued smoothly.

'The Witch WAS right, though. You HAVE come to vissit me in my ssslightly out-of-the-way humble holiday home. And the question is . . . *why*? I know why I want YOU, Child. But why in the name of Beelzebub and Betelgeuse, of all the infinite planetsss in all the universe, have you turned up on mine?'

It was a good question.

The children didn't like to say that the reason was to deliver Bug back to its own world, because drawing attention to the Utchimabug might put it in danger somehow – you just never knew with Vorcxix. Especially now he seemed to own an army. So Izzabird said the first thing that came into her head. Which was:

'Horizabel's Flymaster brought us here of its own accord . . .'

Which was sort of true. One of the Murgadroids stepped forward to present Horizabel's beautiful hoverboard. 'They were travelling on *this*, Your Imperial Highness . . .'

Vorcxix licked his lips. 'The Starwalker! So where is that *baggage*, that treacherous Grimm, then?'

'We have no idea,' said Izzabird, staring straight into Vorcxix's curiously yellow eyes. 'I stole the Starwalker from her when she came to our house.'

Luckily for Izzabird, both of these statements were entirely true, for the gaze of a Were-dread Enraptor is uncommonly good at knowing when you are lying.

Vorcxix gave a slow smile. 'Oh, she must have hated that. Excellent.'

He stared into the distance a moment, thinking. Izzabird and Theo exchanged glances as they looked around the room desperately, at the Murgadroids guarding them. Miles underground. There was nothing else in the room apart from Vorcxix's throne, and gigantic screens on all the walls showing them footage of the inconceivably immense sleeping robot army in the caverns all around them. How were they ever going to get out of here alive?

'I can deal with Horizabel later, but this is a very strange coincidence,' said Vorcxix thoughtfully. 'An extraordinarily unlucky one for you . . . but a ssstupendously lucky one for me. You see, the Universal Government wants to get rid of the Child-With-The-Atlas-Gift. Because if new Atlases can be created, our own precious twenty-four Atlases will become obsolete. And what that means is . . . your brother has become extremely important. Anyone who gets their hands on this child here, will be very powerful indeed.'

Which was why, thought all of the O'Hero-Smiths at the same time, *Horizabel was so insistent that they should stay safe on Planet Earth, of course, because K2's gift in the wrong hands could be very* very *dangerous.*

A bit late now, however, to listen to some truly excellent advice.

'The UG has got wind of that business in Excelsiar . . . rumours fly from star to star . . . luckily no one knows that I was involved, but the stories fly on the dust of one's feet, by the time I got back to the Central planet it was the TALK of the galaxy. THE EXCORIATOR has informed me that the Twelve Bounty Hunters are going to be scouring the universe looking for the Child-With-The-Atlas-Gift.'

Vorcxix looked virtuous, and popped a little snack of snowbear liver popcorn in his mouth, and chewed on it ruminatively. 'But *I* have a different plan. My Witch source has advised me to gain control of K2's Atlas; rid the world of K2 and his Magical family . . . and once I do, I have MORE plans. Big plans. Master plans. This galaxy will finally be mine!! Blunderbore!'

Blunderbore stepped forward.

The children looked up at the green robot with the extraordinarily big head. It was an impressive, scary sight. 'Blunderbore' didn't seem an appropriate name for such a beautiful piece of machinery.

'I am going to upload the entire "Atlas" part of your brother's brain into Blunderbore,' said Vorcxix. 'All of his wonderful mapssss, the whole Alternative Atlas that is in his heart and soul and Magic imagination . . . I could have uploaded it into a computer, I suppose, but Blunderbore's legs make it more portable, the weaponry makes it more defendable . . . Yesss, a copy of every winking cell will be transferred from your brother and uploaded into the brain of this magnificent artificial humano-robotic conssssstruction. So you, ssssnivelling humans, will no longer have access to it. I will have control of K2's Atlas. Just like the Witch said I needed.'

That would explain Blunderbore's oversized skull, constructed to hold a vast memory databank.

'What an appalling idea,' said Izzabird, horrified, as poor K2 shrank back.

'And surely a very dangerous one?' said Mabel.

'Well, it *could* be . . . for your brother,' purred Vorcxix. 'He might never be the same again . . . In any case, there is definitely no risk for *me*, and that is the important thing. K2's Atlas will be in my control. And then I can get on with my master plan . . .'

'So building a big robot army, that's part of your master plan?' said Izzabird. 'Does the Universal Government know what you're doing here on this planet?'

'Of course not!' admitted Vorcxix. 'They may have their suspicions and predictions, but they haven't been able to track me or my army to this incredibly clever location.'

It didn't really matter if these children knew his plan now, because Vorcxix was intending to get rid of them anyway.

'THE LEADER is getting old,' grinned Vorcxix. 'And twelve people in charge of a whole Universe is still eleven people too many. I think a High Council of ONE – *me*, in fact, Vorcxix the Magnificent, as the Sssole Ruler of the Universe, would be a much better idea, don't you?'

So THAT was his plan!

'No,' said Izzabird, crossing her arms. 'I think you'd be

the most dreadful ruler of the universe, you amoral, wicked, treacherous lizard.'

'Politeness with Were-dreads, alsqways a good idea, Izzabird!' muttered Puck nervously.

Vorcxix looked irritated for a second. 'That isn't really any of your business, you repellent child,' he snapped. 'My armies are going to take over, planet by planet. If I were you, I would concentrate on getting yourself out of your present predicament, rather than concerning yourself with intergalactic politics.'

Chapter 24 Doing a Deal with a Were-dread Enraptor

Vorcxix looked at K2 expectantly.

K2 said nothing, because he wasn't sure what Vorcxix was waiting for.

'Well, quick, quick, boy, give me your answer!' snapped Vorcxix, after a long pause. 'I need your consent.'

A bit like inviting one into a house built on a Crossing of the Ways, K2 had to *allow* his imagination to be uploaded to the robot's computer.

'And if I don't agree?' asked K2.

'I kill you all even quicker,' smiled Vorcxix. 'You don't have a lot of choice here, really. You should have stayed put on your sad little planet.'

K2's heart was pounding so hard it felt like his ears were ringing with the sound of it, but his head was cool and clear, as a Plan of his own started to formulate in his mind.

He didn't want to agree to Vorcxix uploading his brain, of course.

But the other option was Vorcxix killing them all there and then. Never mind proving themselves to the grown-ups any more, it was up to K2 just to keep them alive right now. And perhaps there was a way . . .

'I agree,' said K2, bowing. 'You're way too clever for us, Your Excellency.'

Vorcxix's eyes narrowed suspiciously, but he smiled even more widely nonetheless, because everyone likes being told they are way too clever, that is always acceptable, even if the person saying it is a little pesk of a human being they suspect may be lying their head off.

'But I agree under two conditions,' said K2. 'I will let you upload my Atlas into your Blunderbore if: one, you promise you won't kill us. Two, you let us go free to leave this world and go back to our own home planet without following us.'

Oh dear, oh dear, oh dear.

K2 had already shown his inexperience here.

You can't make a deal with a Were-dread Enraptor without being much more careful with the wording. It's generally considered a good idea to have both a top intergalactic lawyer and a philosophy professor present, to get the phrasing entirely precise.

Language has such power in the universe, you see. There's a reason for the phrase: 'Magic words'. Words have the power to create, the power to spell, the power to bind, the power to curse, and if you're going to wander about from star to star, you have to be very aware of how you use them.

Just 'I won't kill you' was way too vague to tie down Vorcxix, who was a twistier twister than an eel on a date with a corkscrew.

And K2 should have asked for exact time-frames for setting them free, such as 'two-and-a-half minutes after the upload is complete', and given more accurate definitions of what 'without following them' meant, such as 'neither I, nor any of my minions, or anybody-associated-with-me-here-there-or-anywhere-in-the-universe will either follow, go before, accompany, hover over, or burrow beneath you back to your home planet, neither now or yesterday or for ever after until the next Big Bang and Beyond.' Something like that.

And even *that* might not be enough to hold down Vorcxix, who, as I may have mentioned before, was the slipperiest customer since a boa constrictor slid down an icicle.

Vorcxix smiled a very nasty smile.

His forked tongue flicked out and he licked his lips appreciatively.

This was going to be easy-peasy.

'All right, then, you repellent child,' said Vorcxix. 'If you will allow your Atlass to be uploaded properly, I give you my most sacred word as a Were-dread Enraptor and a member of the High Council of Universal Government that *I* will not kill you. And I will let you go back to your boring Planet Earth without *following* you.'

'It's a deal,' said K2.

Vorcxix traced his forefingers in the air in the shape of an 'X', and the 'X' lingered in the air briefly in bright purple Spellwriting, to signify his acceptance of the deal, as if he were signing some document in olden times.

'Does this mean Vorcxix can't break his word?' Mabel whispered to Puck.

'Absquolootely,' Puck whispered back. 'That's a squit like signing a contract, is Universally legally binding and he can't undo it . . . but Vorcxix is a tricksly, slimesly, swivel-sly one, oh he is, and ever so evilsome . . . you has to watch your back with him . . .'

'K2 . . . Puck isn't sure we can trust him, contract or no contract . . .' whispered Mabel urgently to her step-brother.

'You don't have to do this, K2,' whispered Izzabird.

'We'll think of something *else*, K2 . . .' whispered Theo.

'Too late,' K2 whispered back.

'No point whispering between each other now, you have made your deal, there's no turning back. Step forward, boy!' commanded Vorcxix.

Shaking, K2 stumbled forward, looking up at Blunderbore . . .

. . . and added casually, as if it were an afterthought,

'Can I hold my pet during the uploading process?'

Now this should have made Vorcxix suspicious, but he was so busy congratulating himself on how easily and cleverly he was about to trick these ignorant little life-forms that he forgot to be wary on his own account.

'Stroking it always calms me down,' K2 went on. 'And if I feel relaxed, the whole process will be a lot quicker and easier.'

Mabel gave K2 a quizzical look, but she handed Bug to him nonetheless.

The little creature opened a weary eyelid, took one look at Vorcxix, gave an anxious *PEEP!* and tried to scramble back into Mabel's arms again. K2 gently prevented it from doing so, and tenderly rubbed it behind its ear in exactly the right spot to calm it down. But now it was awake it was already turning violet.

Vorcxix looked at the Utchimabug and gave a shiver of revulsion.

He had a particular aversion to things that were small and cute and fluffy. I'm afraid the first thing he thought when he looked at the Utchimabug was:

'Wouldn't that make a nice pair of mittens?'

And if he had done his homework properly, and paid more attention to the natural history and ecology of the planets he had a nasty habit of meddling with, he would have recognised what this creature was, and what its Magic powers could do.

But not only did Vorcxix have no idea what this creature was, or where it was from, it was becoming increasingly apparent that he didn't even realise it was Magic. And that was interesting, because I had always assumed that Vorcxix, so powerful, so clever with Magic himself, could see the children's auras. For the first time I realised that perhaps that wasn't the case. He knew K2 was Magic, he knew Annipeck was Magic, because he had seen them use their gifts. But he couldn't see what I could see.

He couldn't see the auras of the other children . . .

Very good.

That meant that he would underestimate them.

'All right, all right,' said Vorcxix impatiently, pale green with excitement. 'Just hurry up . . . You can sit on my throne for the process, boy.'

K2 sat down gingerly on Vorcxix's cold prickly throne,

stroking the trembling Utchimabug.

To K2's relief, the little creature was turning a deeper purple.

That meant that something was going to go wrong in some way. But it was still an enormous risk, because it was going to have to go wrong in the *right* way – and who knew if that would be the case.

Blunderbore knelt in front of K2. He put out his great green metallic hand, and closed all his fingers around K2's head. He began.

Chapter 25 The Defence of the House of the O'Hero-Smiths is Now Depending on Annipeck

It's the most *terrible* time to leave the four older O'Hero-Smith children, with the perilous situation K2 is now in.

But we have to, because unfortunately too many miles away across endless dusty space for a person to get their head around, two other members of the O'Hero-Smith family were also about to get into some deadly trouble.

Back on Planet Earth in the House of the O'Hero-Smiths at the Crossing of the Ways in Soggy-Bottom-Marsh-Place, Annipeck had woken up.

She gave a small yell of complaint. 'Mummy!' shouted Annipeck. 'Daddy!'

Nobody came.

Where are they? she thought.

She climbed out of her bed and checked inside the doll's house.

'Efferist?'

But Everest had gone, just as he said he would.

She toddled into her parents' room.

No Mummy. No Daddy.

Hmmmmm, thought Annipeck.

She looked under the duvet and under the bed.

The baby toothbrush helped.

No Mummy. No Daddy.

The toothbrushes, the Lego and the plastic telephone went to look in the other bedrooms. Nobody was there, not Mabel, not Theo, not Izzabird or K2.

The toothbrushes were thoroughly alarmed, but in Annipeck's experience, the toothbrushes spent a lot of the time being concerned, so she tended to ignore that.

Annipeck herself was intrigued, and not as upset by seeming to be alone in the house as most babies would be.

And then she heard a noise coming from downstairs.

Annipeck put her finger to her lips to tell the toothbrushes to be quiet.

She peered over the bannisters.

There were strange people, dressed from head to toe in bright yellow overalls, walking this way and that way, across the hall, going in and out of the downstairs lavatory and through the doors that led to the workshops, which had been rather brutally bashed in.

She could hear the distant sound of Clueless barking in the kitchen.

'Bad people,' Annipeck whispered to the toothbrushes.

Meanwhile, Mr Spink was feeling *terribly* pleased with himself.

He had spent his entire career working for the top-secret Supernatural Investigation Agency (SIA for short), and perhaps once a decade they came across something that was truly worth investigating, such as an odd Magical Creature, or some phenomenon that could only really be satisfactorily explained by the interference of Magical forces, or an interesting UFO, or other compelling possible proofs that life on Earth was not alone in the universe (any discovery, however small, being kept absolutely secret from the general public, of course, so as not to cause alarm).

About five years ago he had discovered a tiny insect that could speak ten different languages and move things with the power of its mind.

It didn't live very long – insects have short lives, and Mr Spink conducted so many experiments on the poor creature, he probably hastened its end.

Mr Spink had never found another one, but that single discovery had made him a hero in the hush-hush and rather unpleasant global community of covert government organisations of which Mr Spink was a member.

So when, after a lifetime of hunting, Mr Spink discovered not just Bug, but *seven* more Magical Creatures in the vicinity of Soggy-Bottom-Marsh-Place, he couldn't believe his luck. But he kept his discovery quiet from his superiors, sensing, with his hunter's instinct, that there were more where these came from, and not wanting any of his colleagues and rivals to share in the glory. And now, here, in this funny old falling-down house, he had hit the absolute mother lode in supernatural detection!

He couldn't contain his excitement. An actual real live KELPIE in the loft! Weird mer-bear-like creatures in a cupboard. A library full of strange books about Magic, a room decked out like a chemistry lab with cauldrons and lists and lists of Spells. Plants he'd never seen before in the greenhouses, a workshop full of the most extraordinary robotic constructions. The whole thing was absolutely mind-bogglingly thrilling.

This would keep Mr Spink and his prison-cum-laboratory in work for the next fifty years. The experiments they could conduct! The undercover reports he was going to write! The medals and the congratulations and the money he would receive for his discoveries and keeping his mouth shut, it was all too good to be true.

If Mr Spink had been the kind of man to break spontaneously into song, he would have done so. As it was, he just strode around rubbing his gloved hands together and barking orders at everyone, while inside his heart was skipping with joy.

Mr Spink was ordering everyone to put on their gas masks in preparation for an evacuation of the creatures in the loft, when he realised there was a little girl toddling down the stairs, holding very carefully on to the bannister.

And following the little girl were three hopping toothbrushes, a whole load of Lego and a small toy telephone, bumping from step to step, as she made her regal progress down the stairs.

When the little girl reached the bottom, she folded her arms. For now, she meant business.

'Bad people,' said the little girl. The Lego formed itself

into a small shield.

Mr Spink was extremely surprised.

But frankly this was a house that was full of extraordinary surprises, so he took this latest one in his stride.

It was just an ordinary-looking little girl, after all, more like a toddler, in fact.

The idea that a toddler might pose any kind of *threat* of course didn't even begin to cross his mind.

Why would it? He and his agents were in full hazmat suits, carrying tranquilliser apparatus and riot gear, and shields and weaponry of all shapes and sizes. Mr Spink never took any chances when he was raiding a suspicious property like this one.

And the toddler was a toddler.

Wearing bunny pyjamas.

Not even a scintilla of alarm was aroused in Mr Spink's mind.

He raised an eyebrow, and prodded one of his agents with his elbow.

'Arrest the toddler,' he said.

The agent stepped forward, their tranquilliser apparatus at the ready.

They pointed it in the toddler's direction.

Annipeck narrowed her eyes. She held up her fingers and wiggled them.

At first Mr Spink thought she was *waving*.

It was the sort of inexplicable thing that he had seen children do before, and less sensible human beings than Mr Spink thought was adorably cute. But then, just before Mr Spink's agent squeezed the trigger . . .

. . . a large plastic beach bucket came flying through the air out of nowhere on his right, and landed upside down over the agent's head, completely obscuring their vision. They tried to get it off. It wouldn't budge. And a big plastic beach spade came flying through the air behind it and started bashing the bucket repeatedly, so that Mr Spink's agent was thoroughly disorientated, wandered around in circles for a few seconds, and had to sit down heavily to stop themselves from falling over.

Uh-oh . . . thought Mr Spink, suddenly realising that, unlikely as it might seem, he and his thoroughly well-armed team might be in trouble.

'Get ready,' he whispered, ve-ry slowly pulling down his visor and reaching, terribly nonchalantly, towards his own tranquillising apparatus.

Annipeck had the smug smile of a toddler who knew she was about to really enjoy herself.

She wiggled her fingers again and through the open door of the playroom there waddled, tense-makingly slowly, a teeny-weeny plastic green action figure.

It moved past Annipeck on the floor, waddling from side to side on its straight legs towards an astonished Mr Spink and his gobsmacked agents, like the sheriff in a movie advancing on their foe down Main Street.

What on Earth was going on?

Mr Spink's stomach sank as beyond the sound of the spade banging, he now heard a *tap-tap-tapping* noise. *Tap tap tap*. Masses and masses and masses of miniature *tap-tap-tapping* noises.

Tap tap tap tap tap tap tap tap TAP.

And out of the corner of his eye, he could see, like tiny, brightly coloured mice, streaming out of the playroom, an advancing army of action figures, and farm animals, and toy cars and Lego blocks, and glow-in-the-dark stars, all tapping closer and closer and closer and closer.

TAP TAP TAP.

There were astonishing numbers of the things. The O'Hero-Smiths were, after all, a large family of five children and Aunt Trudie did love a jumble sale. Daniel and Freya were always meaning to have a clear-out, but they had a lot of marking on their hands, and it hardly seemed worth it when you still have a two-year-old, so over the years they had accumulated a truly *bewildering* amount of second-hand plastic toys. Battalions and battalions of them, pouring out of drawers and from under beds, and marching out of dusty corners where they'd lain forlorn for years under large pieces of furniture.

tap tap tap tap tap
tap tap tap tap
tap tap tap cap
tap tap tap cap
tap tap tap tap
cap tap tap tap tap

Mr Spink turned his head, and the little plastic army to his right froze.

And then he turned his head the other way and the army on the left side froze.

But as soon as he did that, he could hear the ones that had frozen behind him now tapping forward again, like a ghastly game of Grandmother's Footsteps.

Mr Spink moved his sweaty hand ever so slowly closer and closer towards his tranquilliser.

The flow of small toys came nearer and nearer . . . and finally stopped, encircling the frozen crew of the Supernatural Intelligence Agency.

The tapping stopped.

Even the plastic spade stopped banging on the bucket.

There was a tense pause.

And then Mr Spink went for his tranquilliser trigger.

In the same blink of an eye, Annipeck wiggled her fingers.

And with bewildering speed a HAIL of plastic Care Bears launched themselves, martial-arts style, at Mr Spink, knocking his hand away from the tranquilliser apparatus, while the farm animals and the small toy cars swarmed up the legs of the other agents. Squeezy bottles of washing-up liquid shot out of the kitchen and squirted all over the floor so that the embattled SIA agents were slipping and sliding on the wooden floorboards, as they tried to prise plastic animals from their ears. Clueless barked madly from the kitchen, just to add to the foamy chaos.

'Get out your riot shields!' yelled Mr Spink. *'We're under attack!'*

There's something a little demeaning about cowering behind your riot shield when you're being ambushed by

swarms of Sylvanian Families and Polly Pockets and Lego Minifigures, but in fairness to Mr Spink and his agents, although these sound not very threatening in themselves, when they are launching themselves at you wildly at considerable speed and in huge numbers, being assaulted by an aggressive posse of them is a lot more scary than it might sound.

It was like being mugged by an entire floor of Toys R Us.

I haven't even mentioned the platoons of Playmobil and the Peppa Pig bath toys pelting from upstairs, and the rowdy gang of Barbies, who were particularly combative (maybe it was the punk hairstyles and military outfits that Izzabird had given them when she was younger), and had a nasty karate kicking action that was surprisingly painful considering how small they were.

Annipeck, who was having a perfectly lovely time, was now wiggling not just the tips of her fingers, but waving her whole arms about like she was conducting some outlandish orchestra, throwing in the odd plastic beach ball and plastic laundry basket full of smelly clothes.

'Retreat!' yelled Mr Spink to his agents, pointing

You can be small, but you can be MIGHTY!

towards the upstairs landing. *'Retreat!'*

Mr Spink and the agents holed up on the first-floor landing, in a hail of Lego, protecting themselves with their riot shields, as large numbers of Playmobil rushed up the stairs, waving tiny pieces of picnic equipment, spades and medieval spears.

They were followed by He-Man and the Masters of the Universe and the Barbies.

Mr Spink rallied himself. OK, the toddler had Magical powers, but she *was* only a toddler after all, and there was only one of *her*, and large numbers of *them*.

He muttered instructions into his walkie-talkie, and one of his crew came creeping out of the downstairs toilet to Annipeck's right where she couldn't see him.

He was closing in on Annipeck . . .

. . . when, out of nowhere, Everest came running full pelt along the top of the bannister. (He was a bit bigger, but still teeny-weeny, it has to be said.) He slid down the bannister towards the ground floor like he was surfing a wave, turned a graceful somersault at the end to land lightly on the carpet, and vaulted into the pilot's seat of a large, vintage 1980s Fisher-Price aeroplane, shouting 'START UP THE ENGINES, ANNIPECK, AND WATCH OUT BEHIND YOU!'

'Efferist!' said Annipeck gleefully, dealing with the man

creeping up behind her by running him over with Izzabird's
bouncing Space Hopper.

And before Mr Spink knew what was happening, that
plastic aeroplane was dive-bombing out of the air, aiming
for Mr Spink's head, with Everest in the cockpit, yelling:

'AN O'HERO HOUSE IS HIS CASTLE! AN
O'HERO KNOWS NO LIMITS! NEXT STOP
ANDROMEDA AND TAKE *THAT*, YOU REVOLTING
BURGLAR!' as he leant out of the window, pelting
Mr Spink with plastic Playmobil luggage.

Mr Spink only just ducked in time, and the plane
swooped on, and turned in the air, taxiing round
to get ready for another attack.

'We have to stop the toddler!' shouted
Mr Spink. 'Tranquillise her! The toddler
is holding up a discovery of historic

international importance!'

Bravely, Mr Spink stood up and pointed his tranquilliser at the toddler again. (I'm being sarcastic. This wasn't brave at all, trying to tranquillise an unarmed baby.)

Annipeck looked back at him.

'Bad, bad man,' she said, wrinkling her nose.

The plastic bits of the tranquillising apparatus melted red-hot all over Mr Spink's hand, and he dropped it with a scream.

'Serve you right,' muttered the agent next to him, even though a toy pirate had just jabbed him in a delicate area with her telescope.

'Imagine trying to tranquillise a TODDLER!' yelled Everest, dive-bombing them again. 'Magic their tranquilliser apparatus, Annipeck!'

Oo, good idea!

Annipeck's sweet little eyes focused on all the SIA equipment, and the tranquilliser guns and darts hopped out of the hands of the agents and started chasing their owners all around the landing.

Mr Spink ran down the stairs, pursued by his own half-melted tranquilliser darts, Everest's plane circling his head dizzily.

'Call them off, you beastly toddler, call them off!'

Armies of Playmobil, scurrying across the floor. Herds of

farm animals getting under agents' feet as they fled. Showers of Lego pelting them.

Clueless running around barking wildly.

Fifteen minutes later, *every single one* of those SIA agents were down.

The kitchen, the hall and the stairs were strewn with Mr Spink and his sleeping crew. All of them punctured by their own tranquilliser equipment.

Annipeck had won.

Chapter 26 Unfortunately, Back on Blink 22, Things Weren't Going so Well...

Unfortunately, we have to return to Blink 22, where things weren't going so well.

If you remember, Blunderbore had placed his giant robot fingers around K2's head.

For a second, K2 felt nothing at all. And then there was an unpleasant sucking sensation, as if all of the thoughts were being drawn out of his brain.

As they were being uploaded, K2 could see them in his mind's eye, all of the worlds where life was possible.

The first slid away slowly, beautiful maps of worlds with trees made of sugar . . . worlds cut in two, worlds mostly composed of ocean, worlds large and small and in between. And then quicker, quicker, until they were flying out of his mind so fast K2 couldn't even comprehend them. There was just a blur of colours and textures and smells and sounds being lost to him forever.

A long, long time, K2 sat, clinging to the Utchimabug for dear life. The screen on the robot's spookily giant head flickered in wild and wonderful colours as K2's thoughts entered its memory banks at breath-taking speed. Until the maps began to go past K2's mind's eye more slowly again, one after another. K2 grasped at them in his head

desperately, one last, lingering look . . .

And then, finally they stopped altogether.

K2 slumped on the throne, exhausted, tears running down his cheeks.

'Oh, K2 . . .' said the other children, stiff with anxiety and sympathy for their brother. His wonderful Gift . . . gone.

All gone.

'*You* no longer have an Atlasss,' spat Vorcxix, flicking gloatingly through the worlds on Blunderbore's computer screen to check they were all there. 'You see what a relief it is to share such a dangerous Gift . . . You are no longer unique, so you are no longer important.'

K2 looked up at Blunderbore sadly.

Within he felt a great tiredness, as if he had had a terrible bout of the flu, leaving him as flat and floppy as a woolly glove with the hand taken out of it. As he stood up from the Throne, Bug still in his arms, he had to concentrate hard on not falling over.

Mabel and Izzabird and Theo rushed to support him. Puck hovered over them worriedly.

'Are you OK, K2?' said Izzabird anxiously.

K2 nodded. He handed Bug back to Mabel.

Before, the Gift had been such a burden to him.

But now he no longer had it, he felt so empty.

K2 forced himself to raise his head and look Vorcxix

in the eye. It took a lot of effort, as if his neck muscles had mysteriously turned to jelly.

'Now you have the Atlas, Vorcxix,' he said fiercely, 'you need to keep your promise and let us go free, back to our own world. You promised not to kill us. You promised not to follow us.'

Vorcxix gave a very nasty smile indeed.

'Of course!' said Vorcxix. 'Technically, you are now free, and when I leave the room, I *myself* will leave the door unlocked . . . but I am afraid that Blunderbore here is a very cautious chap and he may lock it behind us.'

'I follow orders,' said Blunderbore impassively.

'But that's *cheating*!' protested Izzabird.

'Not cheating,' said Vorcxix. 'Merely being precisssse with language.'

He made a *tut-tutting* noise with his forked tongue. 'Who is educating you children? This will be a lesssssson to you, to pay attention to the *detail* when you make a deal. What a ssshame it isss that you will not live long enough to learn from that lesson . . .'

'But you promised not to kill us either!' said Mabel, outraged at this duplicity. Shakily, Theo put his arm around her.

'I promised that I *myself* would not kill you,' said Vorcxix primly. 'It's not my fault if *ssssssomething else* accidentally kills you. *Something else* that might find its way accidentally into this room. Something . . . lethal.'

He opened his eyes wide, and purred.

'Blink 22 is ssssssuch a dangerous place . . . I'm sure your Alternative Atlas will have warned you about the terribly venomous and alarming creatures that live here? I'm not going to give you any more clues, except . . . don't touch anything, that's my advice to you right now.'

The children looked around themselves with wide eyes.

Blunderbore removed all their weaponry. The Murgadroids took the Silver Starwalker.

Hssssssrrrreeeekssssssssss . . .

'What . . . is . . . that . . . sound?' whispered Izzabird.

Above and all around them, there was a terrifyingly eerie distant hissing, coming closer, closer, that tweaked at the

Blunderbore now
had ALL of K2's
Alternative Atlas

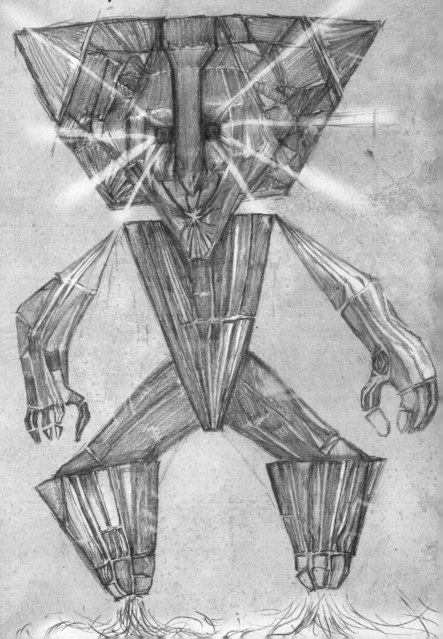

nerves like nails shredding down a blackboard.

'I am taking a little journey now away from Blink 22 and when I return, well, I suspect you will be no longer . . .'

Vorcxix did not tell them where he was going. And perhaps that was a good thing, for there was nothing they could do to stop him.

The door shut behind Vorcxix and they heard him say the word, 'Close'. Then a panel beside the door lit up, and there was an ominous clicking noise.

Hssfreeksssss...

Chapter 27
OH Noooooooo! Indeed

'**N**o, no, no, no, no,' said the children to each other, running to the door.

'Open!' Theo shouted into the panel, but it obviously only responded to orders from Vorcxix.

'Don't panic . . . don't panic . . .' gasped Izzabird, as they gazed around at the Throne Room. No windows. The only door completely locked. Miles underground.

And then just when it seemed like things couldn't get worse . . .

Hssssrrreeksssssssssssssssss . . .

The air was alive with those nerve-shredding icy spitting sounds and if whatever-was-making-that-noise was as dangerous as it sounded, they were in big, big trouble . . .

Hssssssrrreeksssssssssss . . .

'What's that, Puck?' whispered Mabel, gripping the unconscious, floppy Bug.

Panels slid back in the walls, and out of them poured . . . snakes as white as snow, shiningly beautiful, like living, breathing icicles.

Puck searched through his slightly crushed information systems.

'*Snowsnakes!*' said Puck triumphantly. 'Fifty times the

venom of a funnel web spider . . .

if they bites you, just one *squitch* of

a nibble will kill a human being in less

than 0.55555 seconds!'

'Oh, very helpful, Puck, thank you,' groaned Izzabird, supporting a still weak K2.

'We should never have come on our *own*!' wailed Mabel, hugging Bug more tightly. 'We should have told Aunt Trudie!'

'Nonsense!' said Izzabird. 'We can do this, can't we, Puck?'

'Yes, is OK!' said Puck. 'Don'ts you worry yours little humans noddles! Snowsnakes' eyesight very poor, so will only bite you if you *move* . . .'

They all froze, still as statues.

'Does anyone have a Plan?' said Izzabird, super-casually, so as not to further alarm Mabel. As she spoke, the snakes were sliding closer, leaving lines of snow crystals crisscrossing across the floor in their wake.

'I'm working on something,' said Theo thinking about the earlier incident with the Murgadroids.

How had
he made that
happen? 'But
I think we need
to be in mortal
danger . . .'

'We *are* in
mortal danger!'
squealed Mabel,
peering down at the snake
nosing her shoe and turning her
foot inside it numb with cold.

'I mean, I would have thought
this might be enough of a crisis for
you, Theo?' said K2 shakily. 'We're stuck
in this room, if we don't get out we're going
to die, what *extra* danger do you want on top?
Monkeys *with machetes*? Lions with laser-guns?'

Theo could feel beads of sweat on his forehead.
One of the snowsnakes slithered up to him, the heavy
body sludging over his foot, and he had to concentrate
as hard as he could to ignore the cramp in his calf, the itch
in his knee, as the long, languorous body of the reptile curled
coldly around his left leg.

RRRkkkkkkkkkk! More panels opened, this time in the floor, and then there was a scuttering, and a scattering, as teeny bright red things with fiery legs spitting with flames scurried into the Throne Room, in their many-legged multitudes.

'Stinglings!' said Puck, delightedly. 'You sees, I is not only useful but *informative*. Very rare Firecracker Stinglings, born deep in the fire-ice! Now you has to REALLY not move . . .'

'What happens if you move?' asked Izzabird, as a Firecracker Stingling jumped on to the end of one of Puck's tin-opener attachments. He tried to shake it off, and

BANG!

The Firecracker Stingling exploded, sending the tin-opener attachment flying across to the other side of the room.

'Whoops,' said Puck. *'That's* whats happens.'

'Is there anything you can *do* about the Stinglings, Puck?' begged Mabel, one slow tear crawling down her cheek, as the Firecracker Stinglings began to crawl over her sock and on to her calf. Every little fiery footprint was like a lighted match against the skin.

'Not really,' admitted Puck.

Pause.

'Theys repelled by the smell of parsnips, has anyone gots any parsnips?'

No one had any parsnips.

Another pause as violet acid dripping from the snowsnakes' tongues hit the floor and there was an electric hissing sound as bits of the ground burned away.

That's how venomous they were.

'But . . . we . . . can't . . . stay . . . like . . . this . . . for . . . ever . . .' said a statue-like K2, as the burning Stinglings scuttled upwards, sending every hair on his head electrically alive.

'We CAN do this! An O'Hero-Smith never gives up!' said Izzabird staunchly, trying not to quiver when a snowsnake flicked its icy tongue into her ear. 'Remember what Horizabel says about using a little gumption!'

'Oh dear. Things just got worse. Not moving not going to help with the *crabs*,' said Puck.

What crabs?

'The Dead-drop Luminifer Witchet Crabs,' said Puck, pointing to another hatch, opening in the ceiling this time, which luminously bright crabs with one huge waving pincer were pouring through, crawling sideways towards them. 'Most deadly pincers in the universe . . . can cut you to ribbons in seconds . . . they're even more of a problem than the snakes and the Firecracker Stinglings . . .'

More *of a problem? How could they possibly be more of a problem?*

'Dead-drop Crabs hunt by detecting BREATHING . . .' explained Puck.

Very nasty pause indeed.

Yup. This was definitely more of a problem.

'By "breathing" you mean the in-out, out-in, oxygen-inhaling, carbon-dioxide exhaling process by which human beings survive?' said K2.

'That's right! I's suggest everyones stop breathing!' recommended Puck.

'*Whaaaat?*' gasped Theo.

'Humans beings, hold your breath *now*!' yelled Puck.

'But we can't hold our breaths *forever*!' cried K2.

'Don't give up!' repeated Izzabird. 'Don't be negative! *Think!*'

The Dead-drop Crabs turned round, very slowly, pointing their glowing pincers towards the inhaling, exhaling children, and inched their way towards them. 'All right, all right . . .' said K2 hurriedly, and all four children breathed in.

Two minutes passed.

'Mmfff mmff mmmf!' said a red-faced Izzabird, and although she could not speak, they all knew she was saying, '*Think*, everyone, *think*!'

Something odd was happening to the snowsnakes.

They had retreated from curling around the children's bodies, and everyone had a moment of relief, before realising the snowsnakes were intertwining around themselves, in a coiling, wriggling mass, unseaming the sides of their bodies in a perfectly revolting fashion, to slide into each other and form one GIGANTIC snowsnake, gleaming white, with truly enormous fangs, and a neck that was bulging with violet venom glands.

Mabel suppressed a terrified cough with a shudder, and the immense snowsnake reared up suddenly, and swayed aggressively in her face at the sign of movement.

There was absolutely nothing Theo could do to protect her.

If he moved so much as a finger, the Firecracker Stinglings currently crawling all over his arm would explode and blast it off, just like they had with Puck's tin-opener attachment, and *that* wouldn't help either of them.

An O'Hero-Smith Knows No Limits, thought Theo desperately. *The Sky Is Just the Beginning. No Rivers Can Stop Us, No Mountains Can Stand in Our Way . . .*

Another minute passed.

The snowsnake had its mouth wide open now, its icicle fangs glistening. Mabel's eyes were wide.

But the children couldn't hold their breath any longer.

All four of them exhaled at the same moment, and took in a wonderful deep gasp of air, as cool and refreshing as a drink of water.

The Dead-drop Crabs turned in the children's direction, scuttling forward excitedly.

And the snowsnake *LAUNCHED* itself at Mabel, coiling this way, that way, with horrible speed, preparing the death strike, mouth opening wide, venom glands inflating.

You should never give up. However desperate the situation, however impossible the odds, never give up. Even when Firecracker Stinglings are crawling over every single crevice of your body, and a gigantic snowsnake is attacking, and the Dead-drop Crabs are advancing, you can still find help in an unexpected corner.

Just before Mabel had let out that last breath she had remembered the page K2 had drawn in his Atlas about Bug.

Something about how it had a defence mechanism in its tail that it could use against combustible insects . . .

Up until then she had been nobly protecting Bug in her arms. Now, despite her terror, she relaxed her hold, allowing the Firecracker Stinglings to crawl on to Bug's tail, and the automatic defence reaction in

You should never give up.
It is never too late.

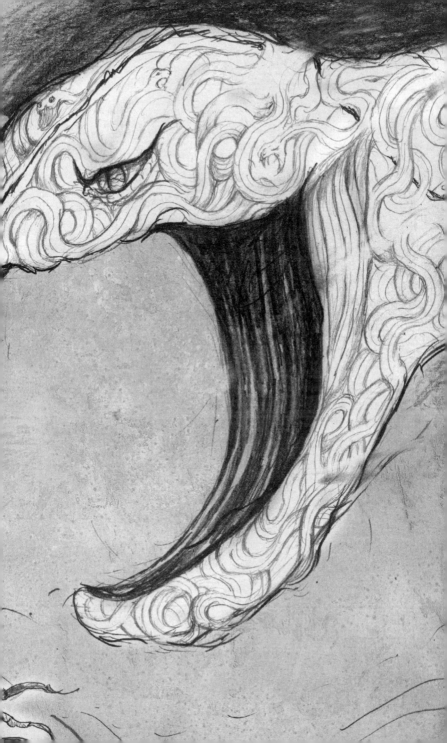

Bug was instant. A puff of rainbow-coloured smoke came out of the end of its tail . . .

. . . *and the strong smell of parsnips wafted through the underground room.*

The Firecracker Stinglings reacted instantly, some of them dropping dead in the smoke, the rest jumping off the children's bodies in a fiery mass, retreating in their many thousands as fast as their legs could scuttle, away to the edges of the room, as far as possible from the parsnip-flavoured smog.

It had no effect on the mammoth snowsnake that was launching itself towards Mabel.

But with the Firecracker Stinglings no longer crawling all over his arm, Theo could now *move*.

He lifted his finger, pointed it at the attacking snowsnake, and concentrated his whole mind on the digit.

He focused on his fear right now, the danger they were in, how cross he was about moving to Soggy-Bottom-Marsh-Place, about losing his mother, how much he had loved her and how much he loved Mabel. And then, as he felt the love and the anger and the fear rising up from the cold-and-hot place within him, making the end of his finger tingle like it had pins and needles, he could see the tip of that finger disappearing, and his finger disappeared up to the knuckle and then up to his wrist, like someone was wiping it off his entire hand with some sort of supernatural vanishing agent.

HSSSSREEKOOWWROORSSS!

With an extraordinary noise like a shrieking, hissing banshee, the mammoth snowsnake made its final death strike, aiming straight at Mabel's head.

'Mabel!' screamed Izzabird and K2 in horror.

If K2 is brave enough to give up his Gift, I can LET GO with mine . . . thought Theo.

And as Theo saw his finger dissolve into the air, he felt something mixed in with the love and the fear and the anger – sheer *joy* in the POWER of it. And instead of resisting, planning, considering, like he normally did, he just *went* with that joy, and . . .

. . . there was a small electric hiss . . .

And the gigantic leaping snowsnake blasted backwards, stunned, right in the middle of its death strike, inches away from Mabel. It EXPLODED into the squirming pieces of individual snowsnakes again, landing in all four corners of the room, and . . .

Theo vanished entirely, like someone had turned out a light from within him.

Izzabird and Mabel and K2 couldn't believe their eyes.

'Theo's turned *INVISIBLE!*' cried Izzabird in bewildered total astonishment.

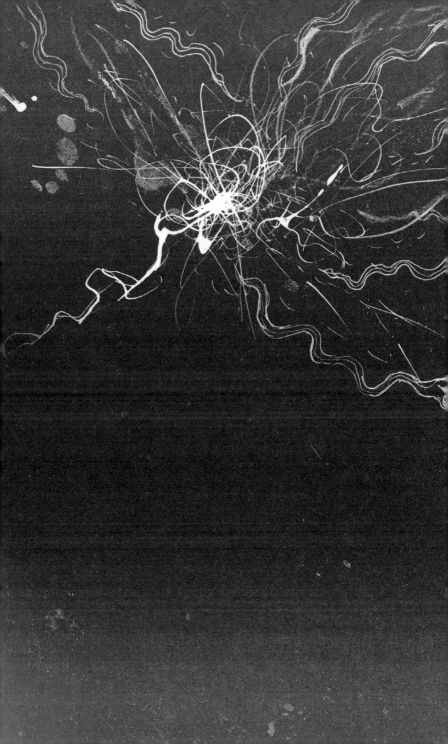

And then everything happened very quickly.

There was no time to take in the relief of a gasping, shaking Mabel being saved, or for amazement at what had happened to Theo, for the Dead-drop Crabs *rushed* them, in a mass of waving pincers.

One crab launched itself at K2's head, in an extraordinary jumping motion.

It was intercepted by Puck, who caught it by one of its legs as it leapt through the air.

'Watch out!' cried Puck. 'These are the JUMPING kind of Dead-drop Luminifer Witchet Crabs!'

Oh, great.

The next one leapt at Izzabird's arm, and in the nick of time, Puck intercepted this one as well, the crab just scraping the end of Bug's nose as Puck whisked it away on the end of one of his corkscrew attachments.

The snowsnakes, now separate ones again, had recovered from the explosion, and were attacking as individuals once more.

Bug, weak as a kitten, opened its eyes with a protesting 'Peep!', and realised its beloved Mabel and her friends were in big trouble.

It drew up its last reserves of energy and scrambled surprisingly speedily out of Mabel's arms, down her leg and on to the floor, PEEPING loudly, its waving tail still wafting out parsnip-flavoured smoke.

'*Bug!*' cried Mabel in horror, as the snowsnakes and the crabs rushed towards the Magical Creature, and the Firecracker Stinglings scattered away, up the walls and across the ceiling.

But Bug was immune to the venom of the snowsnakes, however often they bit it. This world was Bug's home, after all, so its ancestors would have evolved to live alongside deadly creatures such as these. And when the crabs' pincers opened up to snap at it, Bug's deep fur gave them little electric shocks, and they could not get a grip.

Bug's fur lit up rainbow-bright, as it launched itself at its friends' attackers like a round karate-kicking kitten, squealing like a kettle coming to the boil, feather-duster tail blasting rainbow-coloured parsnip-flavoured smoke that swished Stinglings to the corners of the room.

Puck joined in, batting away snowsnakes and crabs with his fork or his screwdriver, the two of them forming a protective circle round the children, for the fangs and the pincers and the bites had no more effect on the metal legs of Puck than they did on the fur of Bug.

But they couldn't hold out much longer.

Puck and Bug couldn't be everywhere at once.

All it would take was for *one* snowsnake to slide through Puck's legs, or *one* crab to scurry out of the weakening Bug's path, and one of the children could be dead in seconds.

'Come to the door!' It was Theo's voice. But it seemed to be coming from BEHIND the locked door.

How was that possible? Theo was invisible but he couldn't walk through doors . . .

Could he???

'I'll open it when you get here!' shouted the voice of Theo.

In a last, desperate push, Puck and Bug cleared a path free of Stinglings or crabs or snowsnakes.

The children made a dash for it, and when they reached the door, astonishingly, it opened, seemingly automatically, as if it were in a supermarket back on Planet Earth, rather than an impregnable locked door in the underground hideout of a Universal-level Grade A super-villain. They ran through it, followed by Puck, gently removing Stinglings and snakes and crabs out of the way while he waited for the toddling, staggering, electric-shocking little Bug, now weakening again after its sudden burst of energy.

Once Bug had tottered through, the door closed behind them.

And the children on the other side of it finally caught their breaths.

I, Horizabel the Grimm, on the other hand, millions of miles away watching this scene, found I was holding my own breath in amazement.

What I had just seen could only mean one thing.
Oh my goodness, oh my goodness.
THIS was another Gift that I had never ever seen before.
Theo Smith had GHOST POWERS.

Chapter 28
Ghost Powers

'How . . . did . . . you . . . do . . . that?' panted Izzabird to Theo with reluctant stunned admiration, for whatever he had done, she so dearly wished she could do it herself.

On the other side of the door, Theo was flashing in and out of visibility like a human traffic light, shivering and sweating, feeling a very odd mixture of absolutely boiling hot and freezing cold at the same time.

'I'm afraid,' Theo said, with a rather shaky laugh, 'I may have a Gift.'

There was the distant sound of running robot feet, and shouting, and the Silver Starwalker came swerving round the corner, immediately followed by the two Murgadroids Izzabird had escaped from in hot pursuit.

The Starwalker has a mind of its own, and would not let itself be used for tracking purposes by Vorcxix so easily. The Murgadroids stopped, astonished to see the human children out in the corridor.

'The humans have escaped!' one of the Murgadroids said into a panel built into the wall of the tunnel beside it. 'Shoot for the kill!'

The children could hear these words echoing out

Ghost Powers

Powers that are supposedly mythical. Powers that allowed their wielder not just to be invisible, but to be GHOST-LIKE, walking through walls and wafting their Magic into corners and places that other Magic couldn't.

of every other panel in the tunnel, and beyond, being amplified on loudspeakers across the army base.

Theo flickered out of sight again, and suddenly the Murgadroid gave a cry of alarm as an invisible force propelled it backwards, and smashed it straight back into the other robot. Both Murgadroids exploded.

'Good shot, Theo!' cried Izzabird in delight in the vague direction of where she thought he might be standing, and forgetting her jealousy entirely. 'Take *that*, you mindless, murderous, steel and plastic *dull-brains*!'

'Oh my stars!' squealed Puck. 'I's finks Theo has *Ghost Powers*!'

'What's "Ghost Powers"?' said Izza, trying to think back to her Magic lessons.

But there was no time for explanations. They could already hear the sound of countless more running robot feet, now the first Murgadroid had raised the alarm. The whole of Vorcxix's army would now be after them.

We need a diversion, thought Theo. *Those panels must be interconnected, so that Vorcxix can give orders across the entire army base.*

He put his finger against the panel and concentrated his mind into it, sending out his Ghost Powers, probing and poking, until sparks shot and ricocheted along the tunnel, exploding all the interconnecting panels as they went, sending out choking, billowing clouds of smoke and flames so hot that Mabel's face was already burning. Sounds of more explosions in the distance echoed down the tunnel, as Theo's Ghost Powers went shooting on, further into the vast cavern.

'Hang on, everyone!' said Theo, gradually growing visible again, helping Mabel – Bug back in her arms – and the others scramble on board the Silver Starwalker, which was hovering expectantly beside them, a foot above the ground.

Mabel and Izzabird and K2 held tight, slotting their feet into the grooves of the Silver Starwalker as Theo kept the orb steady so that the beautiful Flymaster could steer them through the maze of Vorcxix's lair, for she was the one who knew the way, and it was hard for human eyes to see through the clouds of smoke that were filling the corridors.

They met with virtually no resistance from the robots, who were far more preoccupied with trying to contain the chaos that now gripped the soldiers of Vorcxix's gigantic army. As each panel exploded with Theo's Ghost Powers, the robots assumed they were being attacked, so like worker bees whose hive is threatened, the entire robot army was on the move, swarming upwards to the surface to face these unknown invaders.

So the Starwalker swooped elegantly through the confusion of smoke and missiles in the tunnels, every now and then passing the entrance to a room where Workerbots were fighting

Scorpio-cyborgs, or randomly sending off missiles that hit other robots, who then launched counter-defences.

Up, up, they swooped. A lone Murgadroid shot one laser shot at them, but Puck deflected it with his metal umbrella attachment.

They flew out of the entrance to the lair, robots streaming from the underground fortress underneath them, as an ominous rumbling sounded below in the heart of Vorcxix's army base. That shot of Ghost Powers from Theo's finger had crackled its way through the whole of the underground base like wildfire through a wood, and now it had finally reached the gigantic store of ammunition right in the centre. You need to keep a lot of firepower if you're going to take over an entire galaxy.

Great cracks shot out in jagged lines across the ice . . . robots on wheels tumbled into the sea that appeared in between those cracks . . . robots on skis jumped desperately from ice floe to ice floe . . . robots on wings took to the air in retreat.

Now the robot warriors who had escaped streamed back towards what-once-had-been-their-headquarters to try and aid their fellow cyborgs, but even as the children watched, these robots seemed to be deviating from their courses, falling from the sky, or looping in confused circles. The command centre was down, so they all were.

There was a moment of loud silence, as if the planet

sucked in its breath in anticipation and the very atoms in
the fire-and-ice flecked air froze in expectation.

'Fly, Starwalker, fly!' cried Izzabird, and the little
Flymaster put on an extra burst of speed, and then,

BOOOOOOOOOOOOOOOOOOM!!!!

They had escaped in the nick and split of time.

Theo looked over his shoulder as behind them the army
base blasted up into the air like a volcano erupting, and
the mighty ocean rushed into the maze of corridors below
in great swamping tidal waves, and Vorcxix's headquarters
collapsed in on itself, entombing what once was Vorcxix's
army in numberless tons of snow and ice and meltwater, and
an avalanche of clean snow covered it all as if it had never
been there in the first place.

They were witnessing the disappearance of Vorcxix's
entire robot army.

And it wasn't over yet.

As the explosion continued to tremor, great ruptures and
tears spread all the way to a nearby mountain and appeared
in the face of its cliffs. The cliffs quivered a second.

'Wow!' gasped K2 looking back in awe. 'Nice work, Theo!'

Theo stared in shock at his own finger and Mabel gave
him a squeeze of congratulation.

'We DID it! I KNEW we could do it on our own!'
yelled Izza.

But there was only time for one moment of whole-hearted whooping joy before Mabel reminded them, 'We've only done *part* of it, though,' and she pointed to little Bug, floppy and lifeless as an old woollen jumper in her arms.

Even the jubilation of the wild things all around was not waking Bug up now. The effort it had taken to defend them back in Vorcxix's control room seemed to have taken the last sparks of life out of it. It was now a horrible dark ashy grey colour. Its eyes were closed.

'We're losing it!' cried Mabel.

'It needs to get to its parents NOW!' said K2, trying to peer through the hail of snow and fire-ice that was still drifting down on them like the ash from a volcano.

'The Tabletop Mountains are over there,' shouted Puck, and Izza wildly spun the orb of the Starwalker and pointed her in that direction.

They all joined in stroking the little dying creature, saying soothingly, 'Don't worry, Bug, you're going home . . . we're nearly there . . .'

And as they flew on over endless plains of ice, down below, where the ice had cracked, leaping out of the waves like dolphins were pure white horses with long twisting black horns on the end of their noses. And as they leapt out of the sea in perfect, dolphin-like semicircles, the children saw the bottom halves of their bodies were shaped like fish, with gleaming silver scales that winked dazzling peacock colours-of-the-rainbow in the sunshine, before they plunged back into the sea again.

'Unicorns!' gasped Mabel in delight.

'KELPIES,' corrected Puck nervously. 'Thank goodness we'res up in the air . . . Deadly hunters those kelpies . . . if those venomous horns catch you, you're dead quicker than a bite of a rattlesnake.'

But the kelpies were not interested in the little human beings flying above them. They were in pursuit of the Dead-drop Luminifer Witchet Crabs flooding out of the old army base and plopping into the water – a feast for them all.

The Starwalker was travelling so fast that Vorcxix's former army base was way behind them already, and Izzabird pointed to something extraordinary up ahead.

A gigantic table of ice and rock, stretching high into

the sky. At first it looked like they must be manufactured constructions. But as the Starwalker got closer it became clear that they were great thin towers of ice and rock, upon which were balanced, like some great dinner plate, a more temperate plain, where a gentler life was possible.

On the ice floes at the bottom of one of these towers supporting the Tabletop Plains there were the dozing shapes of silver seals, lazily soaking up the weak rays of sunshine.

As they approached, the sea creatures started wriggling frantically. And to the children's shock they squirmed out of their own skins, and out of the discarded furs sprang humanoid creatures, worming their way out like butterflies from a chrysalis, or a person out of a wetsuit, and then they dived into breathing holes in the ice.

Their skins they left on the shore, like abandoned fur coats.

'Selkies,' Puck explained. 'Again, a lot more dangerous than they look.'

The Starwalker pointed upwards now, shooting vertically up one of the vast pillars supporting the Tabletop Plains, and when they finally reached the shimmering rainbow clouds hovering just above, they saw the plains of the Temperate Zone spreading out before them. Mabel gasped as the sudden burst of warmth touched her cheeks, as if it were a spring day in Iceland, perhaps, or the edges of Greenland when the ice melts and life is returning to the tundra.

And in her arms, the little Utchimabug's fur quivered happily.

It opened weak bug eyes, and O, how wonderful it was for Mabel to see the sheer joy in its expression as it gazed out on the wide grassland plains that were its home. 'Peep!' squeaked Bug longingly. 'Peeeeeeeeep!!!!!'

Its fur gradually turned a very faint primrose, the beginnings of warmth and life returned to its little frozen nose, wrinkling and sniffing the milder air delightedly. Bug snuggled in Mabel's arms as the Silver Starwalker swooped down over these plains, past wind-blasted trees, growing horizontally, for the wind was still so strong on the edges of the Tabletop Plains that the trees grew not vertically but sideways.

And as they flew the Utchimabug squeaked more and more urgently.

'It's coming to life!' breathed Mabel gleefully.

On they travelled, past drifting herds of rock-like beasts, that looked from far away to be dinosaurs of some kind, but when they got closer, were a strange mixture of boulder and plant, a rock with vegetation sprouting from its cracks, moving on long slow legs of knotted grass.

Down on the ground, a small pride of snowcats, long lost from Planet Earth, but thriving here, fur thick as powder snow, slinking unctuously through the grasses.

'PEEP!' squeaked the Utchimabug, wildly overexcited. 'PEEP! PEEP! PEEEEEEP!!!!'

The heart ached to hear the joy in its voice. The pure happiness of a creature coming *home*.

Mabel was crying, now, for she knew the moment of parting was coming, but how can you cling on when you know that the thing you love is wanting to be free, is wanting to go *home*?

Its fur now rippling rainbow colours, it squirmed its way up to look right into Mabel's face.

It gazed deep into her eyes and although the language of Utchimabugs is hard to comprehend, Mabel understood that look, for the look is universal and needs no words.

'Thank you,' said the look.

And all around the waking, joyful, springtime world echoed the blessing.

'Goodsbye, little Utchimabug,' said Puck sadly.

'Goodbye,' said Theo and K2 and Izzabird.

The Utchimabug leant forward and bit Mabel very gently on the nose.

It didn't really hurt, but it was enough of a surprise for her to release her grip a little.

And with a final joyful, wriggling squeal, the Utchimabug launched itself right off the edge of the Starwalker, like a diving lemming.

Goodsbye, little Bug

'Nooooooooooo!!!!!!' cried the O'Hero-Smiths,
holding out their hands in a vain attempt to catch it as it
somersaulted downwards through the air.

But after a few heart-stopping seconds . . .

. . . a couple of titchy bee-like wings sprang from its
shoulders and started flapping wildly.

'It's got wings!' said Izzabird in surprise. 'None of the
books said they had *wings*!'

Well, maybe that was because these wings didn't really
count as actual *wings*. Only the most optimistic of observers
could say that they worked as effective airborne aids.

Creatures that plump and hairy aren't built for gliding.

Bumblebees do manage to baffle scientists by staying airborne in apparent defiance of the laws of physics, but whatever *they* do with their wings, they certainly hadn't explained their secret to the Utchimabug. The way it was using its little appendages was never going to keep it up in the air, however hard it flapped them – but maybe they slowed its plunging descent a little.

'I can't look!' said K2, putting his hands over his eyes.

'What colour is it?'

I can't look...

I can't look...

'Purple,' said Izzabird, as the Utchimabug vainly tried to get control, somersaulting wildly. 'Very, very purple . . .'

The Utchimabug made a crash-landing . . . and at least its very thick coat would have cushioned the fall somewhat . . .

. . . but it landed right in front of a prowling snowcat.

The snowcat stiffened in surprise then crept forward towards the dazed Utchimabug, licking its lips.

'Pee-iip!' said the Utchimabug in a friendly, disorientated sort of way, wagging its wings at it.

'Ru-u-u-u-uunnnnnnn!' shouted the O'Hero-Smiths from above.

OOOOOooo-er. The Utchimabug stopped wagging.

It staggered unsteadily to its feet and dashed off through the grasses, squealing madly, followed by the leaping snowcat.

And the unluck was already doing its work for the Utchimabug's hunter. The pursuing snowcat, hot on its tail, must have suddenly put its paw into a small creature's burrow. Because it tripped and tumbled head over heels, and turned in one unsteady second from a magnificent prowl of a predator into a rather undignified yowling mess of furry muscles and talons and teeth.

On the little Utchimabug scrambled, running unsteadily out of their lives, just as wobblily and haphazardly as it had run into them, several weeks and chapters ago.

'It's turning yellow again!' cried Theo in relief, just glimpsing a plump, bright buttercup-yellow flash of colour bumbling through the grasses.

'Look!' said K2, pointing excitedly.

Running towards it, two unsteady furry forms staggering through the grasses, rainbow colours shifting happily across their faces.

'That must be its PARENTS!' cried Izzabird.

'It's going to be *fine*,' smiled Mabel, tears running down her face, watching the little Utchimabug below falling into the arms of its Utchimabug parents. 'I'm not sad, because I know it's going to be *just fine*, now it's home.'

They watched the little family as they disappeared into the undergrowth.

Stayed watching the grasslands, brimming with life, a few moments more.

Another beat of benediction, another moment of gratitude, another breath taken in the midst of the adventure.

All four of the O'Hero-Smiths gave a sigh of satisfaction.

'Theo and I TOLD you we could do it, K2,' said Izzabird jubilantly. 'All on our own, the grown-ups would never have let us come, and we *did* it! Our first mission!'

'Those grown-ups should have trusted us,' said Theo. 'We can do this. A few Risk Assessments . . .'

'Some proper Planning,' said Izzabird, tapping her Plan Book confidently.

'And Ghost Powers.' Theo grinned.

'And we are Starcrossers-in-the-Making!' said Izzabird. 'Operation Blink 22 and Back Again, the first mission of the new Magical Escape Service, is COMPLETELY SUCCESSFUL!'

The two older O'Hero-Smith children high-fived each other.

And then Mabel made a very good point.

'But we haven't got back home yet,' said Mabel, 'and how on Earth are we going to do that, when K2 doesn't have his Gift any more?'

Well, *that* brought the older two back down to Earth with a bump. All the Ghost Powers in the world wouldn't get them back home without an Atlas.

'I hadn't thought of that,' admitted Izzabird, very gloomily indeed.

Oh dear, oh dear, oh dear.

They really didn't want to be stuck on Blink 22 *forever*, however beautiful it was, and even now it was no longer ruled by robots, and the world was returning to the wild. It was still an alien planet, after all.

The reality of what they had done finally struck, and they all looked at each other in slowly dawning horror. They had rescued Bug, only to maroon themselves millions and millions of miles away from everyone they loved.

'Ah, well *about* that,' K2 coughed cautiously. 'I *did* have my *own* Plan . . . it was a BIG gamble, but that's why I asked to hold the Utchimabug when I was having my brain uploaded. I thought the Utchimabug might make everything go wrong, and that might mean . . .'

Izzabird looked at her twin in growing admiration.

'Oh, WELL DONE, K2!' said Izzabird, rising from the depths of despair to joyous relief in an instant. 'That's BRILLIANT! *So* . . . I wonder if that means that . . . whatever Blunderbore now has on its systems, it might not have taken your entire Gift after all . . . ? Quick, try drawing something!'

She landed the Starwalker on one of the thickest branches of a nearby tree.

'Well, I'm not sure whether my Plan worked,' warned K2, 'but I think the upload didn't work as well as Vorcxix thought it would and *maybe* the maps are still in there after all . . .'

'Of COURSE they're still in there!' said Izzabird, tearing out some pages from her Plan Book so that K2 could draw on them.

And then there was a very uneasy silence *indeed*, as they waited to see whether K2's Gift was still there. None of them looked at K2, so as not to put any pressure on him. Izzabird made furious notes, while Mabel hummed happy music to help relax K2, and Theo kept an eye out for snowsnakes, or any other undesirable creatures that might be able to climb trees.

K2 put his pencil on the paper, heart trembling with anxiety.

Had his risk worked? Had he lost his Gift forever?

He made a few clumsy strokes with the pencil.

Oh my goodness . . . I've lost it . . . it's not coming back . . .

The pencil made so many mistakes, K2 trying not to worry, trying not to panic . . .

. . . until the empty feeling inside K2 disappeared, a door seemed to open deep inside himself, the pencil gave a final contrary wriggle . . .

. . . and relief flooded through every single particle of K2 as the pencil took on a life of its own, sketching out the ice deserts beneath them, the Snowy Mountains, the extraordinary Tabletop Plains of Blink 22, first faintly, and then stronger and wilder and with more and more detail.

It's come back!!

'I KNEW IT!' said Izzabird, unable to resist looking over K2's shoulder.

'So where's the Which Way back, K2?' asked Theo, clapping him on the back in congratulation.

'It looks like the Which Way in the treehouse hasn't moved yet,' said K2.

'Excellent! You see, Mabel? There was nothing to worry about after all,' said Izzabird, scrambling downwards from her tree branch, for all the world as if they hadn't been in

danger of never seeing the rest of their family ever again, just five minutes earlier. 'All aboard the Starwalker!'

But they couldn't get the Silver Starwalker to start.

'Why won't it move now?' worried Theo, spinning the orb at the back for the seventh time.

And then a voice behind them made them jump out of their skins.

A voice colder than the bright frost-wind currently biting at their cheeks.

'Because YOU are not its owner,' said the voice. '*I* am.'

It was the voice of Horizabel the Grimm.

Chapter 29 Horizabel Is More Than a Little ANNOYED

ap tap tap on the tree trunk, went the pretty little foot of Horizabel the Grimm, who was balanced perfectly, as relaxed as if she was down on the ground.

'Greetings, little human beings,' said Horizabel, her normally good-humoured face looking like thunder and her arms crossed with irritation. 'You can stop gawping at me like four goldfish. It is indeed me.'

Mabel and K2 and Theo and Izzabird carried on staring at her in guilty and gobsmacked astonishment. Even Izzabird was a little abashed to be caught red-handed by an extremely irritated Grimm whose Flymaster she had recently stolen and carried out an entire adventure on without asking permission. Not to mention not letting her into Planet Earth through one of the Which Ways at her explicit request.

'I'm waiting,' snapped Horizabel, still tapping her foot.

'Er . . .' said Mabel, the first to collect herself. 'Greetings, Horizabel, it's lovely to see you, and we're so very, very sorry . . .'

'As usual, the only one with some manners, Mabel,' sniffed Horizabel, 'but apology NOT ACCEPTED.' Oh dear. Horizabel really was very annoyed indeed. She examined the fingertips of her robotic hand. 'I suppose you all think you've been terribly clever.'

'Well . . . we've been *quite* clever, you have to admit, Horizabel,' said Izzabird proudly. 'You're the one who's always telling us to grow a little gumption and to look out for ourselves, so you can't start complaining when we do actually *do* that. And look what we've done! We've returned the Utchimabug to its home planet, we've broken out of Vorcxix's lair, destroyed Vorcxix's army, we really must tell you all about that, and Theo has a Gift, so you've got to admit, we are Starcrossers-in-the-Making! I mean, before we even got here, we managed to break out of a pretty scary situation on another planet . . .'

'Ah yes, you may be interested to know exactly where that was?' said Horizabel, narrowing her eyes. 'You know, the location where you so rudely broke in, entirely without permission, and proceeded to cause chaos? *That* one . . . You're quite right, *that* place *is* pretty scary.'

Suddenly the O'Hero-Smiths weren't sure they did really want to know exactly where that was.

'*That* was the Planet of the Evergods, the centre of the Universal Government,' said Horizabel. 'The same government that has been hunting your family for, ooh, the last couple of millennia or so. The same government that up until that moment were not completely sure of your existence, until you flew around smashing their windows and smearing your DNA over their broken crystal and giving them an excellent view of all of yourselves on their security cameras on the Dark Side . . . well, you're on their radar *now*, little human beings, I can tell you that, you're on their radar *now*, and there's a bounty on your heads that makes the bounty on Everest's head look like chicken feed . . .'

Whoops.

'What's more, Vorcxix the Vile is making his way back to Planet Earth with THE EXCORIATOR and Blunderbore through the Which Way that you have very helpfully reopened,' said Horizabel. 'And all I can say is that Vorcxix is probably not heading in that direction to read your baby sister a bedtime story . . .'

OH
MY
GOODNESS!!!

Annipeck! Daniel! Freya! The
aunts!

The children's hearts
descended into their sneakers at
the thought of the danger their
family was in – and it was all
THEIR fault!

You see, however far you
travel, you still have to think about
what might be going on
at home.

'What's going to happen now?' whispered K2.

'Well, looking into the future is a tricky business, as you've probably found out from living with your mother,' said Horizabel. 'However, this close up it's not really all that difficult. Anyone in that house is going to DIE. Or get abducted by Vorcxix. Unless you have a little help from me. And even then you could be too late.'

'Help us, Horizabel, help us!' cried Mabel. 'Please, please help us!'

'I thought you didn't need any help,' said Horizabel, still in a big huff. 'And just tell me *why* I should give you my most valuable assistance? Back there in my bosses' HQ I just

Horizabel was still in a very bad mood.

got myself out of a black hole's worth of howling life-ending disaster through trying to protect you from the Universal Government, and I don't even want to go into what I had to do to get myself out of it. Only *I* could have talked myself out of that situation. So why should I help you now, when you appear to be absolutely nothing but trouble? Give me one good reason.'

'Help us, Horizabel, help us,' begged *all* the O'Hero-Smith children. 'Please, please help us. We need you to help us get there in time.'

'That is not a reason,' said Horizabel coldly.

But in fact, all unknowing, the O'Hero-Smith children *had* accidentally given Horizabel a reason to help them.

For Horizabel suddenly realised that she herself had been wrong about something.

It doesn't happen often.

When she told them not to go deal with Bug themselves, well, it was actually really rather helpful that the O'Hero-Smiths were so disobedient and ignored her advice in the end, because following them there had alerted Horizabel to the fact that Vorcxix was building an illegal robot army. Which was useful information, whatever the outcome of this particular little disaster. Especially as they had managed to destroy it too.

And to tell you the truth, Horizabel had always intended

to go back to Planet Earth anyway, she just wanted to punish the cheeky little human beings a smidgen, and put them in their place.

There could have been no other reason that Horizabel made the decision to help them at this point.

Could there?

Well, there was also the fact that this was going to give Horizabel the excuse to travel really really *fast*, and she completely loved doing that.

Chapter 30 Horizabel Goes Very Fast

'All right, then,' said Horizabel, sniffing. 'I know I'm going to regret this, but I'll help you – *again*. As long as you're a little more grateful this time and do exactly what you're told.' She paused. 'Actually I don't even know why I'm saying that, I already know that's not going to happen.' She gave a martyrish sigh. And then a delicious grin as she took over the running of the Silver Starwalker.

Her bad mood had completely disappeared now that everything had got wildly complicated and she had the opportunity to travel considerably faster than was either safe or sensible.

'So many web-lines crossing!' she said with joyous relish. 'So many star-paths leading to the same place in such a chaotic way that there's bound to be some sort of BOOM!'

'Hey, that's our baby sister and our family and our house you're talking about!' said K2 furiously, his teeth *aching* with anxiety. 'This isn't some sort of video game you're playing here, Horizabel.'

'Yes, I'm so sorry,' said Horizabel, and she genuinely sounded regretful. 'Us Grimms aren't very good at the heartfelt touchy-feely stuff. But you're ever so lucky that I'm here to save the day,' she added chattily. 'Or I might not, I'm not sure, isn't that exciting?'

Mabel didn't think that was all that exciting, what with one thing and another. She could have lived without this particular thrill.

'Hold on to your thinking-caps,' Horizabel advised them all now. 'Apply the leg shackles in case we hit turbulence. I'm going to have to UP the speed here a little. Blinkers, go into Bulk Mode and then you can help pull us? We're going into Hyper-exceleration Overdrive, which is the fastest speed we can go without anybody actually *melting* . . . Oh, don't look so disapproving, Blinkers, you know I only get to do this when it's absolutely necessary, let me enjoy the moment . . .'

Horizabel put down her hood and her breathing apparatus. She removed the power orb from the back of the Flymaster. She spun it once, twice, three times, levitating it above the end of her finger until it was darker than night and had lightning shooting across it and was so hot it was giving off spitting sparks and a thick choking smoke that made Mabel cough.

Oh, for the stars' sake, she is so cool, thought Theo longingly.

Horizabel threw the power orb up in the air, where it spun even faster, so quick you could barely see it, caught it again in her expert robot hand and then fixed it back in the

Power Orbs

Magic energy is stored in these orbs and then used to power rockets, space bikes or any other technology. The Power Orbs can also be used as tools for looking back or forward in time, or across vast space distances. Any spell, omen or prophecy that is cast into a Power Orb is greatly magnified in strength.

hole at the back of the Flymaster.

An Airbag inflated above them, assuming the shape of a tiny weeny flattened Airship, with the Starwalker at the bottom of it. Blinkers transformed into Bulk Mode, charged her rockets and latched on to the front of the Starwalker. Everyone inside the transparent Airbag attached the leg shackles. Horizabel then climbed out through a hatch and sat cross-legged on the top of the Airbag, her star cowl swooping out behind her.

'Let's go!' cried Horizabel enthusiastically. 'Hyper-exceleration Overdrive warp thirteen something or other? Not actually sure of the name of this mode, but whatever it is . . . I LOVE IT!! Here . . . we . . . *go*!!!!!'

She snapped her fingers, and Blinkers and the Starwalker rocketed forward, a sheer torpedo of white-hot wild flame torching out behind them. Apart from the inevitable first nausea-inducing lurch when it took off, during which K2 felt he had left his stomach so far behind that it would take a fair few weeks for it to catch up again, the situation inside the Airbag normalised remarkably quickly considering the astonishing velocity at which they were travelling.

Once they got going, they were travelling way too fast for turbulence, and way too fast for noise, so inside the Airbag of the Starwalker they almost got the sense they weren't moving at all, until Izzabird looked outside and saw the heady blur of the landscape below in a smudging smear of speed.

'Are we going to get there in time?' said Mabel anxiously.

'Well, we're certainly going as fast as we can . . .' said Theo.

Izzabird tried rapping on the top of the Airbag to ask Horizabel how long they would be, but Horizabel couldn't hear what Izzabird was saying, what with all the goodness-knows-how-many miles per hour winds and everything. Besides, the rap distracted her for a second, causing the Starwalker to swerve so violently that they nearly exploded into an inconvenient mountain, so Mabel suggested that asking Horizabel questions probably wasn't a good idea when they were going at this speed.

'Can we work out some way of warning our family they're about to get attacked?' asked K2.

'Oh, *that'll* be easy-peasy, won't it, sending a message to another world across the other side of the universe?' said Theo sarcastically. 'I just have this feeling that we're not going to get a mobile signal.'

'Can you send messages by Atlas?' asked Mabel. 'There must be some way the worlds communicate with each other . . .'

K2 adjusted his thinking-cap to its jauntiest angle.

He knew that a thinking-cap couldn't really help you

think, but somehow he always seemed to be wearing one when he had his best ideas. There was bound to be some sort of universal communication system, an intergalactic version of the World Wide Web, but it was too late to find out what that was, let alone hack into it.

'What about Annipeck's phone?' said K2. 'That wasn't using mobile signals, was it? It was using Magic?'

It was worth a try. With shaking hands, Izzabird got out her phone and scrolled through the contacts.

She pressed on Annipeck's name.

pick up
pick up pick up!

Chapter 31 However Fast Horizabel and the O'Hero-Smiths Are Travelling, It Really Isn't Fast Enough

Meanwhile back on Planet Earth, in the House of the O'Hero-Smiths, five minutes earlier, Annipeck and Everest had parted ways.

'You really are the most wonderful baby,' admired Everest, shaking her by the hand, almost tearfully. 'A true O'Hero! It has been an honour to go into battle with you.'

'O'Hero-*Smiff*!' corrected Annipeck.

She patted him kindly on the head. He was small, but he would learn.

'Parting is such sweet sorrow, but it is time for me to get on with my Quest, at last,' said Everest. 'I think I'm big enough to carry the Infinity Clock now, and Freya and the aunts should be back any minute.'

So Everest ran off to collect the Infinity Clock, and Annipeck toddled off to get breakfast. She was sad to part with Everest, but right now, Annipeck was *hungry*.

Annipeck poured herself some cereal, bowl on the floor, and generously allowed Clueless to slurp some of it.

She climbed up to the table to eat the rest of the cereal, only losing about half the cereal and milk in the process. The toothbrushes cleared up the mess.

Ring! Ring!

Annipeck's toy telephone took a big run-up, zoomed vertically up the kitchen table leg, and across the table, to park in front of Annipeck, the receiver vibrating in time to the rings.

Annipeck looked in surprise at her telephone, spoon halfway to her mouth. *She* hadn't made it do that.

Ring! Ring!

Annipeck put down the spoon and picked up the receiver.

'Hel-*lo*?' she said politely, if a little warily.

Crackle crackle . . . the line was very faint, but there was a surprisingly short wait for the reply considering the stupendous distances involved.

'Annipeck!' The excited, relieved voices of K2, Izzabird, Mabel and Theo drifted down the line. 'Oh, for the stars' sake – it worked!'

'K2!' Annipeck replied delightedly. 'Iz-bird! Feo! Mabel!' And then she frowned. 'Where is you? Are you ANYWHERE? Annipeck COME TOO!'

'Annipeck,' said K2, trying not to sound panicked, 'we can't explain now, but some bad people may be trying to get into the house. Get Mummy, quickly!'

'No Mummy!' Annipeck informed him, shaking her head solemnly, very proud of herself, for as the youngest in the family, she was always pleased to be the first to provide important information.

'*Where is she??* What about the aunts?? Surely they've got back by now? What have they been doing?'

Puck gave a small helpful cough. 'Time *mays* run slower on Planet Earth than it does here . . . Blink 22 is probablys closer to a blacks hole or something . . .'

'Oh, for goodness' sake!' exclaimed K2. This Starcrossing business took a little getting used to. 'Is Daniel there, though?'

'No Mummy! No Aunt Vile-let, no Aunt Trudie, no Daddy . . .' said Annipeck.

'Anni, you're not in the house ON YOUR OWN, are you?' howled Izzabird.

'No, no, *no*,' said Annipeck reassuringly. 'Annipeck not on her OWN . . .'

'Oh, thank goodness . . .'

'With *Clueless*!' said Annipeck sunnily, waving her spoon in the dog's direction for emphasis.

Clueless gave a loyal bark when she heard her name and a few drops of milk from Annipeck's spoon landed on her nose. 'And the toofbrushes . . . and the Lego . . . and the phone . . .'

But her siblings didn't seem to think that the dog or any of these other companions really counted.

'Where's Dad? Don't panic, Annipeck,' said Mabel. 'We'll be back as soon as we can . . . DON'T ANSWER

THE DOOR TO ANYONE HOWEVER HARD THEY KNOCK . . .'

'Annipeck BEAT the bad people!' Annipeck said proudly. 'ALL ON HER OWN.'

What *was* she talking about?

'OK, Annipeck,' said Izzabird, grabbing the phone from K2. 'You can't stop the bad people on your own, you really can't!

Annipeck, you need to hide NOW!!!

We're going to try and get there as soon as possible to help you, but in the meantime, I want you to *hide*.'

'But I is eating my cereal . . .' said Annipeck crossly. 'Annipeck hasn't had *breakfast* . . .'

'This is important!' yelled Izzabird. 'You need to hide NOW!!!' She desperately tried to imagine somewhere

Annipeck could hide in a hurry. 'The bottom shelf of the kitchen cupboard! You know the cupboard behind the kitchen door? Crawl in there, curl up at the back very, very small so they can't see you, hide all your Magical objects and Clueless, and DON'T MAKE A SOUND. These are

But I is eating
my cereal...

BAD PEOPLE, Annipeck. BAD, BAD PEOPLE. And they mustn't find you.'

Pause.

Thoughtful *munch munch munch*ing from Annipeck. *Why do they never listen to me?* she thought. *I've already beaten these bad people.*

But Annipeck was an obliging child, and Izzabird was clearly concerned.

'O-*kay*,' she sighed eventually, still a bit cross, but resigned.

She added a polite 'Thank-*yoo*! Call again soon!' in a bright, sing-song voice, because Annipeck knew that was the right way to end a telephone conversation.

She put the phone down, and got back to eating her cereal.

And a million gazillion miles away, on the planet of Blink 22, the line went dead.

'Annipeck? Annipeck??? Annipeck, you don't understand, this is *VORCXIX THE VILE we're talking about,* you really do have to HIDE!!'

But however many times they rang back, they just got the engaged tone. Either Annipeck hadn't put the receiver back on properly or they had lost the connection.

The O'Hero-Smith children looked at each other in Absolute Total Horror.

You see, sometimes you think the end of your Quest is some great battle on a distant planet inhabited by millions of war-like robots.

When actually the end of the Quest is right back at home.

As one, the O'Hero-Smith children banged on the ceiling of the Airbag, shouting 'Horizabel! Horizabel!' and *this time* Horizabel heard them.

Horizabel switched the Starwalker on to automatic pilot, pretty dangerous frankly when you're going that speed, but there you go. The O'Hero-Smiths needed cheering up. She looked horribly cheerful herself as she thrust her head down through into the Airbag. 'Hello, everyone, how are you all doing down here? How's morale?'

'Really, really bad,' said K2 hollowly. 'Mum and the aunts are still off fighting Mr Spink at the laboratory . . . and Daniel doesn't seem to be there either . . .'

'We should never have left!' cried Mabel, wringing her hands. 'This is all our fault!'

'Corr-*ect*,' said Horizabel sunnily. 'I'm not going to say "I Told You So", because that's always really irritating. But I did. To sum up the present situation, the current defence of the House of the O'Hero-Smiths at the Crossing of the Ways in Soggy-Bottom-Marsh-Place is now in the hands of two-year-old Annipeck. Thrilling, isn't it? I thought *I* was a Bad Babysitter, but you guys . . .

Personally I wouldn't worry too much, though, there's absolutely nothing you can do.'

Horizabel's head disappeared as she went back to the rather important task of steering the nearly-out-of-control Starwalker.

Not worry too much?

Not worry too much?

How do you not worry too much when your heart is so many miles away and there is nothing you can do?

Chapter 32 The Defence of the House of the O'Hero-Smiths is Depending on Annipeck (and also teeny-weeny Everest)

Meanwhile, in the hall, teeny-weeny Everest finally had the chance to complete his mission at the House of the O'Hero-Smiths. From its hiding place in the cellar, he had fetched the Infinity Clock, and although it was only pocket-size for an averagely proportioned human being, Everest was still *only slightly* larger than that. So he was having to carry it balanced precariously on the top of his head, while weaving his way between the sleeping bodies in the hall.

beep beep

Everest carrying the Infinity Clock

But as teeny-weeny Everest O'Hero picked his way through this ghastly mess, checking his teeny-weeny copy of the Alternative Atlas for the Which Ways that would lead him to the next part of his Quest at last, thanking his lucky stars *he* wasn't going to have to clear it all up, I mean he loved children with all his heart and soul but he'd forgotten what chaos they caused – he happened to notice the front door was ever so slightly ajar.

Bother it!

If the door was ajar, it was asking for trouble, for it meant the house wasn't Magically protected as nobody had to knock, they could just walk right in. He'd seen enough of Annipeck to realise she was well able to defend herself, but she *was* only a toddler after all, he couldn't get on with his own mission without making sure she was as safe as possible.

Everest put down the object he was carrying, and ran to the door.

He'd forgotten how small he still was. Even he-e-eaving as hard as he could, he couldn't make the heavy old door budge. And as he was straining away, sunlight glinted on something emerald-green in the old treehouse in the garden, dazzling him for a second, so he looked up to see what it was.

And there . . .

. . . right in the middle of the treehouse, which appeared

to be smashed to pieces, and half hanging out of the tree, was a spinning green *something* . . .

What was it?

It looked like Aunt Trudie's colander for draining lettuce, spinning round and round, and gradually emerging like a great big green woodpecker from the middle of the treehouse, and as it pushed its way out, he saw that it wasn't a colander at all, or a woodpecker, but a gigantic robot head.

Oh. My. Stars.

Everest's heart disappeared into his boots as he realised what it was.

A robot coming through a Which Way.

And his heart sank even lower, if possible, than that, as he recognised the figure following it.

Vorcxix the Vile! He knew all about what a villain he was, from his own encounters with him alongside the children a few months ago.

Even Annipeck wouldn't be able to deal with *him* on her own.

He could now see the feet of Daniel, who was still unconscious on the front lawn, so *he* wasn't going to be much use.

With all his weeny mouse-like strength Everest tried even harder to close the door.

But Everest, also known as World-Walker, the

Uncatchable One, who had once tracked the motion of the stars beyond the Outer Limits, was now in a very different stage of his life than he had been in his glorious youth.

Too small and weak in his present incarnation, to even shut his own front door.

The Hero laid his head on the door frame in despair.

He couldn't budge it.

He knew that this was perhaps the last chance he would have to escape and complete his Quest, and return his life to its former glory with the help of the Infinity Clock, and that key that he'd soon track down, if he could only be on his way now . . .

But once a hero, always a hero.

Everest didn't hesitate.

He gave one, brief, regretful look at the precious object that he had come so far to collect, and then he abandoned it, because he knew it would slow him down. Running full pelt, weaving through the prone plastic toys, back towards the kitchen to warn Annipeck.

There would be no time for Annipeck to toddle through and shut the front door herself now. Vorcxix and his robot companions would be across that garden in a couple of strides and straight into the house before that could happen.

Annipeck was happily finishing her bowl of Snak-O-Pops when Everest ran into the kitchen.

'Vorcxix the Vile is here!' shouted Everest O'Hero in his loudest voice. '*Hide*, Annipeck, *hide!*'

For the first time so far in this whole adventure, Annipeck was afraid.

Annipeck had met Vorcxix the Vile in person some six months earlier in the world of Excelsiar, so she knew who she was about to face.

His was the kind of badness that made Mr Spink and his SIA agents look like dear little fluffy lambs or toddlers in birthday dresses in comparison.

Annipeck was made of stern stuff.

But her little lip trembled.

She clambered straight down off the high chair and followed Everest, who led her not to the cupboard behind the kitchen door, as Izzabird had suggested, but to the 'secret passageway' inside the kitchen fireplace, because Everest, being older than Izzabird, knew a few more of the House's secrets.*

Annipeck and Everest and Clueless and the toothbrushes had only just scrambled through the secret door in the fireplace and shut it behind them when . . .

WHAM!

---

* 'Priest-holes' were built in many old houses in the 16th century to conceal Catholic priests being hunted down by the authorities in Protestant Britain. In the House of the O'Hero-Smiths they were constructed to hide Magical Beings from similar persecution.

The ancient front door was slammed right open with such violence that it shivered on its venerable hinges, and our old enemy THE EXCORIATOR, followed by Vorcxix and Blunderbore, stalked into the House of the O'Hero-Smiths.

And the first thing that Vorcxix clapped eyes on when he strode through that door was the precious object that Everest had abandoned so he could warn Annipeck.

Vorcxix blinked at it for a second, concerned that this might be a trap, or a bomb. It's an outstanding coincidence, to find such a universally significant and well-known object just lying there waiting for you on the doormat.

'For the stars' sake!' gasped Vorcxix, picking up the little object and turning it over in his hand. 'The tales of Everest were true after all . . . *the Infinity Clock, as I live and breathe . . .* !'

The story of 'How Everest Stole the Infinity Clock' is too long to go into here, but it was one of those tales that had long been the gossip of the galaxies. Most people thought that the story was made up, and the Infinity Clock had been lost much earlier, somewhere in the mists of time, if it ever existed at all . . . but it was still one of the many reasons that Everest was top of the Twelve Bounty Hunters' List of Most Wanted Outlaws, and the Universal Government's Public Enemy Number One.

So this was a bit like turning up at King Arthur's castle

in Camelot to find a big sword with 'Excalibur' written on the hilt lying on the doormat, as a sort of welcoming hello.

You know you're in the right place, at least.

Vorcxix smiled a very nasty smile, pocketing the precious object as he did so.

'At lasssst . . .' he hissed. 'The lair of the O'Hero-Smiths . . . What a falling-down old dump! And in this total backwater of a world . . .'

Vorcxix wasn't impressed by Planet Earth – why would he be?

The wildwood world of Witchmalkin is blanketed with trees higher than skyscrapers that make Borneo's jungles look like pleasant groves. You get lost out there, you could be gone for decades, hunted by Howling Horrillagos and Sabre-toothed Werewolves. The cracked planet of Degrxxilxx is split all over with gorges so deep that if you dropped a stone off the edge of one of them, it would take four or five days to reach the bottom. What is the Grand Canyon compared to *that*?

And don't even get me started with *weather* . . . The whirlwinds of Torcoririm make it an intergalactically famous tourist attraction. The truth is, Earth's inhabitants may be fond of their birthplace – although that isn't always as clear as it should be from the careless way they look after it – and it is, admittedly, very pleasant and temperate compared to a lot of places where life has to cling on to survive, but to the casual visitor it really isn't all that impressive.

Vorcxix chuckled, pointed his Spelling Finger at a photograph of Everest bungee-jumping off the Golden Gate Bridge, and it burst into silver flames. The metal of the frame dripped like candle wax down the edge of the side-table.

And then he looked around the plastic apocalypse in the hall with interest.

What on Earth had happened here? Some sort of battle, clearly, unless the O'Hero-Smith family was terribly untidy.

And even *that* wouldn't explain the corpses.

Vorcxix gave the body of the nearest SIA agent a contemptuous kick. They appeared, on a closer look, to be *sleeping*, actually, not dead, but who on Earth were they? People of no importance. Vorcxix needed to be quick here. He had to get back and find out why he'd lost contact with his forces in Blink 22. Vorcxix knew who he was looking for. As the Witch said, he needed the child who had Magic-That-Works-On-Plastic, and from the sheer amount of plastic equipment in that hall, still quivering slightly and warm to the touch, he knew that person couldn't be far away.

There was only one person Vorcxix had ever met who had THAT Magic.

'Annipeck!' cooed Vorcxix. 'I know you're in here somewhere! Oh, Annipeck!'

No answer.

Vorcxix clicked his fingers at THE EXCORIATOR and Blunderbore. 'Search the house before we destroy it and anyone in it . . .'

His keen reptilian eyes narrowed, as he noticed among the astonishing debris of plastic, so thickly encrusting the hall that it might have been some sort of multicoloured beach . . . footprints.

Little running footprints.

One of the tranquilliser guns had leaked tranquilliser fluid on to the floor, and Everest had stepped in it, in his rush to warn Annipeck.

The footprints were the very palest of violet in colour, but the eyes of a Were-dread Enraptor are more acute than the eyes of a human.

Into the kitchen, Vorcxix followed the little footprints, growing fainter and fainter.

Blunderbore came through the kitchen doorway behind him, saluted.

'The house appears to be deserted. No living beings I can detect, apart from some Magical Creatures in the attic . . .'

Well, this wasn't quite as planned, he had hoped to wipe out the entire O'Hero-Smith family in one go, but in some ways this was better. In fact, everything was turning out in a way that was almost too good to be true.

The door to the house left wide open.

And the two things he had come here to look for, above all else, left for him undefended.

The Infinity Clock.

And Annipeck.

He could come back for the family with his entire army another time.

Vorcxix placed a finger to his lips to tell the robots to be quiet.

The faint footsteps stopped at the fireplace.

Vorcxix focused his laser eyes on the chimney, and the outline of a secret door appeared in a shimmering red.

Vorcxix pointed his Spellfinger, but the electric energy of the Spell fizzled out as soon as it met the surface of the secret door. Bother, it was Magically sealed. He couldn't get in. He'd have to *trick* the baby out by bribery. Vorcxix took out his computer Atlas, scrolled through to Planet Earth, and clicked on the page about infant Human Beings. Habitat . . . *no* . . . Dress . . . *no* . . . *Aha!*

Diet.

Most baby living beings would do pretty much anything for their favourite food.

'I've found you, Annipeck!' cooed Vorcxix. 'Come out, dear little toddler . . .'

Behind the door, in the darkness of the secret corridor

of the chimney breast, Annipeck was holding on tight to the sleeping, shaggy body of Clueless, who had got tranquilliser fluid on her paws and had now passed out beside her. Even Everest O'Hero, who might have been able to advise her in this perilous moment, was unconscious. He had made it through the door beside her, but unfortunately he had holes in his boots, so his feet were soggy with the tranquilliser fluid he had stepped in, and it didn't take much to knock out a Hero that small. He was snoring away, out for the count, the toothbrushes trying to revive him.

So now baby Annipeck really was all on her own.

'Bad man . . .' she whispered through the door. 'Very bad man.'

Aha! said Vorcxix to himself. He knew it! The toddler was there.

'Yessssss, I'm afraid so,' he said out loud, regretfully. 'But I'm a bad man . . . *with lollipops . . .*'

Now, Annipeck was a baby of some considerable splendidness, but she *was* only two and a bit, after all, and, it would take a truly *superhuman* baby to resist lollipops.

Annipeck's face on the other side of the door took on a thoughtful expression. 'Lollipops?' she said consideringly.

'Hundreds and hundreds and hundreds of lollipops, Annipeck. Strawberry ones! Orange ones! Stripy ones!' said Vorcxix.

The terrified little toothbrushes shook their heads at her.

Not just because lollipops were extremely bad for your teeth. But because they knew, deep in their toothbrush beings, that it wouldn't be a good idea for Annipeck to open up this door.

Don't open the door, Annipeck!

Don't open the door.

Annipeck couldn't see the toothbrushes in the darkness, but she could feel them shaking their heads.

Her lower lip wobbled again.

'Mummy . . .' she whispered.

She tried to be strong, she *shook* with the effort of it, but she couldn't hold on any more.

'Mummy!' wailed Annipeck. '*Daddy!* I . . . want . . . my . . . daddy!'

And she began to sob.

Bother. Bribery wasn't working. He'd have to try threats.

'I don't have your daddy, Annipeck,' hissed Vorcxix. 'But I do have . . .'

His eyes alighted on a single piece of Lego that hadn't made it through the secret door in time with Annipeck and Everest.

'. . . a piece of your Lego . . .'

356

Vorcxix picked up the red Lego brick, and it trembled in his hand.

'And I may not have Magic-That-Works-On-Plastic,' said Vorcxix grimly. 'But I can still MELT it with fire.'

THE EXCORIATOR stepped into the kitchen.

Annipeck could hear the roar of his flame thrower igniting.

'If you don't open the door by the time I count to three,' said Vorcxix, 'I'm going to melt your Lego.'

Annipeck stiffened.

'One . . .' said Vorcxix.

'Two . . .' said Vorcxix.

And . . .

Annipeck opened the door. Vorcxix reached in and hauled her out.

Chapter 33 Annipeck Opens the Door

Wriggling in Vorcxix's grip, Annipeck held out her little arms to try to Magic her enemies. Vorcxix was holding her from behind, so she pointed her fingers at THE EXCORIATOR.

She had met THE EXCORIATOR and defeated him once before.

The Spells came whizzing out of Annipeck's palms and hit THE EXCORIATOR right in the chest.

And nothing happened.

Annipeck was so surprised she did it again.

And nothing happened once more.

Vorcxix was delighted.

After his last disastrous confrontation with Annipeck, Vorcxix had gone to some considerable trouble to rebuild THE EXCORIATOR, removing any plastic components.

So Annipeck's Magic did not work on him any more.

The little girl burst into tears.

And Vorcxix prevented Annipeck from doing any more of her Magic by the simple expedient of closing his hands over hers to stop her wiggling her fingers.

'EFFERIST!' shouted Annipeck. 'Help Annipeck, EFFERIST!'

Beside the sleeping body of Clueless, in the secret passageway, Everest awoke and sat bolt upright. 'Annipeck!' said the Hero. 'Oh my goodness, the villain has got Annipeck!'

He shook Clueless awake, got to his teeny-weeny feet, and belted across the floor.

Vorcxix had the Infinity Clock, and the child with this interesting new Gift. If he could give his army Magic-That-Works-On-Plastic, it would be pretty much invincible.

So now Vorcxix had what he wanted, it was time to destroy the House of the O'Hero-Smiths.

Vorcxix tossed the little Lego brick on to the kitchen table and THE EXCORIATOR set fire to it with his flame thrower, and they bolted with Annipeck to the door, followed by a madly barking Clueless.

Everest belted after them at full speed, and launched himself in one desperate leap at Vorcxix's ankles. He just managed to grip on to the right-hand spur at the back of the villain's boot, but he could not reach for his teeny-weeny Spelling Stick because he was using both hands to hang on.

The rest of the O'Hero-Smith family really needs to hurry now. Everest is too small to save Annipeck on his own.

Annipeck is in deep, deep trouble.

Chapter 34 Unhand the Toddler, You Villainous Burglar!

Vorcxix, with Annipeck in his arms, and Everest clinging to his spur, ran across the devastated hall, followed by THE EXCORIATOR and Blunderbore.

Out of the open door they ran, and across the lawn, towards the Which Way in the treehouse . . .

Now, all could have gone very badly indeed, with Annipeck stolen by Vorcxix the Vile, who was a considerably more unpleasant Being than Cyril Sidewinder, the man who stole her on the previous occasion. And the House on the Which Way burnt to the ground.

But the delay caused by Everest nobly dropping his own mission to save Annipeck meant that Vorcxix was a little later than he could have been.

So . . . just as Vorcxix and his robots were halfway across the lawn, within five or six robot strides of disappearing through the Which Way . . .

Aunt Violet, battle-scarred but triumphant, soared over the garden wall on her 1970s Hoover, the sidecar stuffed with Magical Creatures, shouting:

'UNHAND THE TODDLER, YOU VILLAINOUS BURGLAR!'

Aunt Trudie and Freya swooped down after her, on their own Hoovers, and landed beside Aunt Violet, all pointing their Spelling Sticks straight in Vorcxix's direction.

'*Mummy!*' cried Annipeck joyfully, trying to wriggle out of Vorcxix's grip and holding out her arms towards Freya. 'Oo . . . a *unicorn*!' Annipeck was momentarily distracted by one of the animals in the sidecar. 'And *Daddy*!'

For Clueless had run to Daniel's body, unconscious in the long grass, nudging and tugging at his pyjamas, finally waking Daniel up. He had staggered to his feet, and was now limping towards the scene.

'Yes, give us back Annipeck, you scoundrel!' cried Daniel.

Excellent! thought Vorcxix, *Now I can get rid of almost all of the rest of them in one go, after all.*

A hissing noise sounded as Vorcxix activated a protective Spell Dome around himself. 'EXCORIATOR! Take out the mother and father! BLUNDERBORE! Take out the aunts!'

The two robots were just reaching for their Spellblasters when . . .

Theo and Mabel and Izzabird and K2, and, most importantly, HORIZABEL, and the accompanying Blinkers in Bulk Mode, *finally* burst through the Which Way from Blink 22 in Everest's old workshop tower, streaked across the garden on the Starwalker, landing on the lawn beside Freya and the aunts.

Horizabel pointed all of her fingers at Vorcxix.

'CALL OFF YOUR ROBOTS, VORCXIX!' cried Horizabel.

Curses! raged Vorcxix. His Spell Dome wouldn't entirely protect him from the spells of as powerful a Grimm as Horizabel.

'Halt, Blunderbore and EXCORIATOR!' he snapped reluctantly, but now pointing his own laser finger at Annipeck.

'One TWITCH of your SSSpellfingers, Horizabel,' snarled Vorcxix, 'and the toddler gets it!'

K2 and Mabel gave gasps of horror.

'Don't move, Horizabel, please don't move!' begged Mabel.

Vorcxix's eyes were nearly falling out of his head as he took them all in.

'How in the stars did you essssscape my murderous Stinglings, my invincible crabs, you ridiculous little wriggles of humansss?' he marvelled, in furious disbelief. They looked so small, so helpless. 'I suppossse this treacherous Grimm here set you free . . .'

'We got out on our OWN!' yelled Izzabird. '*And* we destroyed your entire robot army into the bargain, you great crocodile HANDBAG of a villain!'

'Fairy talesss, you little liar . . .' gasped Vorcxix. 'Even *Horizabel* couldn't do that . . .'

But a horrible feeling of doubt was beginning to nag at him. *What if . . . ?*

The air positively prickled with tension, the suppressed angry Magic on that lawn roaring in Izzabird's ears, swirling round them like a thunderstorm about to break.

Vorcxix ground his pointed teeth. 'Whossse ssside are you on, Horizabel?' he hissed.

'Whose side are *you* on, Vorcxix?' hissed Horizabel right back.

'Why are you helping thessse enemies of the Government?' hissed Vorcxix.

'Why are you building armies behind the Government's back?' hissed Horizabel.

That was a question to which Vorcxix had no satisfactory answer.

'None of your businessss, Horizabel the Grimm,' hissed Vorcxix.

As Vorcxix stared at the family gathered together, Spelling Sticks at the ready, he was changing his mind about wanting a fight.

A fight with Horizabel might put Vorcxix in mortal danger.

And Vorcxix had begun to have an uneasy feeling about what might have happened back on Blink 22. He had lost communication with his forces there, but that sometimes happened when you travelled through the Which Ways.

He needed to deal with Horizabel and all these O'Hero-Smiths at some point. But right now, he needed to get away, ALIVE, with the Infinity Clock, and check his army back on Blink 22 was safe.

Besides, a fight in the garden of a Magical house where you've just set fire to the kitchen table is never a good idea.

So Vorcxix pinned a serpentine smile to his face.

'We are both breaking the rulessss here, Horizabel . . . I suggesssst we come to sssssome arrangement . . .'

'What is your proposal?' said Horizabel briskly, her Spellfingers still pointing unwaveringly at Vorcxix, eyes flickering, this way, that way, to the robots, and back.

'I *could* kill the toddler . . .' said Vorcxix.

'Noooo!' cried the family.

'But if I give you thisss toddler, here, unharmed,' said Vorcxix, 'in return, you must let the robotssss and me escape through the Which Way in the treehouse, without a battle.'

'Hmmmmmm . . .' said Horizabel, considering the offer.

'Save Annipeck, Horizabel!' chorused the whole family.

'But it's not a very fair offer is it?' said Horizabel thoughtfully. '*We* keep one little toddler, and *you* have Blunderbore, who contains the whole of K2's Alternative Atlas . . .'

Freya and Daniel and the aunts looked worriedly at K2.

Horizabel deliberately didn't mention the Infinity Clock.

Maybe Vorcxix didn't know that *she* knew that *he* had that as well.

And if he *did* know, her not mentioning it would confuse him.

Their two tricksy pairs of eyes met, trying to see into each other's minds.

Why did she not mention the Infinity Clock? Vorcxix was thinking. *She must know that I know that she knows that I have it.*

Does he really not know that I know that he knows that I know he has the Infinity Clock? thought Horizabel. *Why, then, does he think I didn't mention it? Maybe he's going to guess that I did that deliberately . . .*

'But the toddler hassss a very powerful and unusssual Magic,' Vorcxix pointed out, 'and *you* have far more to losssssse from a battle than we do, Horizabel. Robots are robust, particularly the ones I have here . . . *human beings*, however, are as fragile asss a candle-flame. One stray laser bolt, one little blast of Magic and . . . pfffft! Their light isss out!'

'Save the human baby,' cried Puck, in great distress. 'Horizabel, save Annipeck!'

'*I* do not care for human beings, though, Vorcxix,' said Horizabel, ignoring Puck, voice colder than an icicle. 'Because bounty hunters have no hearts . . .'

Vorcxix's eyes narrowed still further. What game was Horizabel playing?

Was she playing for *time*?

Vorcxix didn't know *why* she was playing for time, maybe she was expecting reinforcements?

But he *did* know it meant he should DEFINITELY close the deal even faster, just in case.

'Quick! Quick!' he snarled. 'The offer only ssstandss for one more second! Otherwissse Annipeck gets it!'

'I accept your offer,' said Horizabel, with sudden promptness (the whole O'Hero-Smith family sagged with relief), before adding: 'With the usual conditions, of course.'

'Usual conditions, all right!' barked Vorcxix. 'Quick! Quick! Quick! State your conditions!'

Now, Vorcxix could hardly complain, could he, if the usual conditions were rather lengthy, because Vorcxix's general deviousness had made such elaborate conditions necessary.

'*You* hand over the baby unharmed,' began Horizabel, 'and *I* will let you escape without me or my companions, or anyone here associated with me, either seen or unseen . . .'

'Yes, yes!' said Vorcxix impatiently. 'Hurry up!'

'. . . firing a single shot at you or your robots,' continued Horizabel, 'and in return you and your robots will not fire at, poison, assault, obliterate, strangle or in *any way* harm either me or any of the human beings, or Blinkers here, either right now or in the course of your escape, and that this deal should be in accordance with intergalactic law, and any breaking of said deal should be dealt with in the Highest Courts of the Universal Government or UG for short and . . .'

'Yes, yes,' said Vorcxix, shaking her hand and handing Horizabel the baby, who handed her on to Freya. 'Hurry up! Hurry up! I agree to those terms. Let us conclude and sign the deal.'

Now.

I know what you're thinking . . . this doesn't seem like a very, well, *Horizabel* thing to do – to strike a deal with a villain like Vorcxix just to avoid a fight. There's nothing she likes more than a good Spelling battle after all.

But Vorcxix was right in his earlier guess.

Horizabel *had* been playing for time.

For what no one but Horizabel had noticed, so transfixed were they by the magnetic confrontation between Vorcxix and the bounty hunter, and the peril of Annipeck's plight, was the clandestine operations of teeny-weeny Everest.

Who in the course of their conversation had been stealthily climbing from Vorcxix's spur, which had finally stopped revolving, up Vorcxix's leg, sneaky as a spider.

You should always pay attention to the small things in life.

And while Vorcxix was wondering whether Horizabel knew he had the clock, Everest was realising that, unlikely as it might seem, Horizabel was intending to save Annipeck, so he, Everest, didn't have to rescue her after all. So he changed his plan, mid-climb, back to his original Quest, and carefully entered Vorcxix's pocket, to steal back the clock himself.

And as Horizabel was setting out the lengthy conditions of the agreement between her and Vorcxix, Everest was descending perilously from Vorcxix's belt, the Infinity Clock dangling underneath him, and softly, gently, landing on the lawn, without a soul or a robot brain realising he was doing it, other than Horizabel. And when Vorcxix shook Horizabel firmly by the hand, Everest was already tiptoeing through the long grass of the lawn, the Infinity Clock balanced on his head, off to the Which Way in Aunt Trudie's greenhouse that would take him out of here, thanks to his own teeny-weeny Atlas safe in his pocket.

So Everest, at least, had completed his Mission and Horizabel let him get away with it, because she would rather *Everest* had the clock than Vorcxix did. She could catch up with Everest later.

And Vorcxix wasn't going to get quite the deal he thought he had bargained for.

Too late now, though! The deal was made, and just

needed to be signed.

And something peculiar was happening to Horizabel and Vorcxix.

The O'Hero-Smith family had seen this happen once before, but that didn't change how strange it was.

Hissing like two cats, Horizabel and Vorcxix circled each other, growing in size as they did so.

As the family watched, they hardened like wood, like metal, like stone, before becoming all fire, growing even larger and so bright that everyone else, even the robots, had to fling up their arms to defend their eyes from the fierce and terrible light. From both of their shoulders, dark wings slo-o-owly unfolded.

Into the air, Horizabel and Vorcxix rose, still circling each other, their hisses growing louder, the wind from their wingbeats so strong that it blew everyone's hair back.

'Don't look at them,' whispered Freya, hunched over Annipeck, protecting her.

Everyone was crouched over, blinded, hands over their ears, scorched by the heat of the lightning burning through the air, even though moments ago it had been the brightest of summer days.

Horizabel and Vorcxix sized each other up knowingly, Vorcxix pointed his Spellfinger, Horizabel braced . . . but Vorcxix simply slashed a great shining 'X' in the air, marking his signing of the deal as promised.

SWOOSH-SWISH.

Horizabel paused only a second before responding with her own Spellfinger the other way.

Vorcxix gave a great shriek in a strange language, and flew towards the treehouse.

And as he flew he felt in his pocket . . .

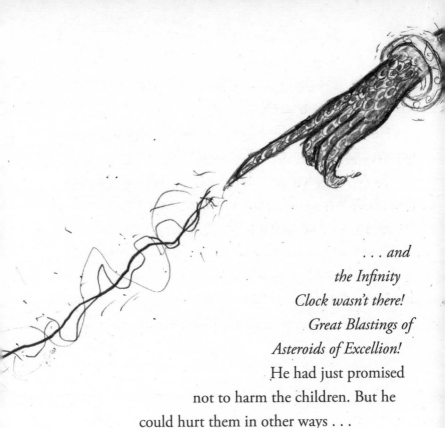

*. . . and
the Infinity
Clock wasn't there!
Great Blastings of
Asteroids of Excellion!*
He had just promised
not to harm the children. But he
could hurt them in other ways . . .

In a fit of PURE spite and rage, he let out a
deadly silent Spell Bolt aiming straight at the little robot,
Puck, whom he knew they were all so fond of.

It all happened so quickly and silently that no one
noticed but Horizabel.

As Vorcxix threw open the Which Way and tumbled
through, THE EXCORIATOR and Blunderbore leapt
after him.

Vorcxix was going to be even angrier when he got back to
Blink 22, to find his robot army destroyed . . . Serve him right.

'Close the Which Way!' screamed Whatever-Horizabel-Had-Turned-Into, in an odd, unnatural voice.

Bemused, befuddled, blinded, but coming to their senses, the aunts and Freya lifted up their shaking Spellsticks. Together they invoked the ancient Spell that closed the Which Ways at the House at the Crossing of the Ways.

And the Which Way that K2 and Izzabird and Theo and Mabel had ill-advisedly opened, while on the back of Horizabel's Starwalker, carrying the Utchimabug, in what seemed like a lifetime ago now, *finally* was closed.

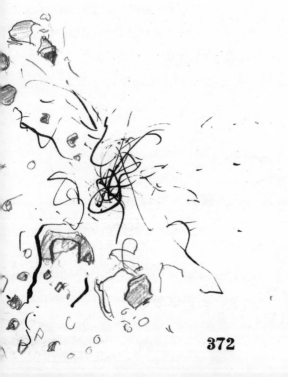

It all happened so quickly
and so silently that no one noticed
but Horizabel.

Chapter 35 Every Story Has a Reckoning, a Price to Be Paid

orizabel let out three great shrieks, beating her wings in triumph.

And then she shrivelled in the air, back to her more humanoid form of Horizabel the Grimm.

She landed gracefully on the ground, where the O'Hero-Smith family was still mostly kneeling or cowering, staring awestruck up at her.

Her wings folded with a gentle rustle, and disappeared beneath her star cowl.

She composed herself again.

'Well, what are you all doing, lying there gawping?' she snapped. 'Shouldn't you be putting out the fire in the kitchen? Oh, for Andromeda's sake, *you* do it, Blinkers!'

As one, the O'Hero-Smith family gave a collective start and turned to look at the house.

Clouds of billowing smoke were drifting out the kitchen window. Blinkers was already at the door.

'Annipeck! The hoses!' shouted Izzabird, running to turn on the big taps by Aunt Trudie's greenhouse. Annipeck brought the hoses to life. Squirming like pythons, they slithered across the lawn and up through the open window.

Everyone else ran in the front door as Blinkers brought

out her fire extinguisher fixings, and what with her foam and the water spraying liberally through the windows they extinguished the blaze from the kitchen table. To Annipeck's joy they even managed to save her little block of Lego. It had melted from the heat, and was now slightly flatter and rounder than it had been before, but was nonetheless her old friend, and she and her toothbrushes greeted it with delight.

'The fire is out, and they've gone,' gasped Izzabird. It felt like she'd been holding her breath for a very long time. 'He's gone, and we did it!' She punched the air. 'Bug is home, we stopped an army, we saved K2's Gift, we got back in time, we closed the Which Way, we're all here, we saved the house and we DID IT!'

'We did it! We did it!' Theo grinned.

'We did it too!' guffawed Aunt Violet. 'We rescued the Magical Creatures and shut down Mr Spink's lab!'

Everyone hugged each other, and gave astonished laughs. Aunt Violet jumped up and down in a jig of celebration.

Freya hung on tight to Annipeck. 'Thank the stars you're all right! But . . . but . . . why was that fiend here with Annipeck . . . and . . . and . . .'

Freya and Daniel looked around at the truly epic devastation surrounding them in the House of the O'Hero-Smiths. The kids suddenly felt meek and horribly guilty as they surveyed the burnt-out soggy mess of the kitchen table, the kitchen now ankle-deep in foam and water, the plastic apocalypse in the hall, the sleeping bodies of Mr Spink and his agents looking alarmingly like corpses, the scorch marks of battle everywhere.

'. . . and . . . *where have you been*? You broke the rules and left your sister unprotected!' said Freya.

'. . . and *what on Earth has happened to the house???*' finished Daniel.

Horizabel marched into the hall behind them.

'Before *I* answer that question,' she said, 'Blinkers, hand me the Amnesia Canisters.'

'What are you doing?' said Aunt Violet in bewilderment as Horizabel clamped the Amnesia Canisters on to her Spelling Stick.

'I'm assuming you're wanting *me* to clear up some of this mess for you?' snapped Horizabel. 'That you don't want these sleepy agents to wake up and remember what happened in the past hour or so?' She pointed round at the limp bodies of Mr Spink and the rest of the SIA. 'So I'm very helpfully wiping their memories for you . . .'

'*We* can do that, Horizabel, really we can,' said Aunt Trudie guiltily.

'No, no, it's absolutely no trouble . . . let *me!*' said Horizabel sarcastically, zapping the snoring body of Mr Spink with her Spelling Stick as she spoke. 'I *love* clearing

up great howling disasters that other people have created . . .
Blinkers, hand me another Amnesia Canister . . .'

Zap! She shot off four more Amnesia Bolts.

'And while I'm explaining to the O'Hero-Smiths how
they got themselves into this mess, could you take these
rather unpleasant people,' Horizabel waved her robot hand
at the sleeping SIA agents, 'a nice distance from here and
maybe along the way whisper something in their ears about
the House of the O'Hero-Smiths being nothing to do with
whatever just happened to them. Be quick about it . . . we
need to get going as soon as is Grimmly possible . . .'

As Blinkers got to work, Horizabel turned back to the
O'Hero-Smiths.

It was time to give these wretched human beings a piece
of her mind.

'So I'll *tell you* what the little human beings have been
doing!' raged Horizabel. 'They've been breaking the solemn
promises that you all made to me only *six months* ago! I
mean, I ask you to make me a *few* little commitments, and
you open up your big human eyes and you swear.' Horizabel
did her best imitation of the O'Hero-Smiths. '"Oh *yes*,
Horizabel, of *course*, Horizabel, we promise we'll never let
K2 use an Alternative Atlas *again*, Horizabel . . ."'

K2 and Izzabird hung their heads and muttered, 'We're
so sorry, Horizabel . . .'

Horizabel ignored their apology, she was in full flow. 'You shake hands on those promises, in the name of True Love and Beyond, you're expecting everyone to keep their vows like normal, civilised, intergalactic gentle-beings, and what happens? K2 not only starts drawing Alternative Atlases like there's no tomorrow, but Izzabird steals my precious Silver Starwalker and all four of them come careering through the Which Ways right bang slap into the heart of the Universal Government, while I'm having a very delicate meeting, practically wearing a big sign on their heads saying "We are the O'Hero family, put a bounty on our heads right now"!'

'Oh, K2, Izza, you didn't?' gasped Aunt Trudie.

'Don't *you* start!' roared Horizabel. 'You adults are as bad as the children! Aunt Trudie and Aunt Violet have been sneaking escaped Magical Creatures into the house behind everyone's backs and hiding them in the loft *for the last six months*! Something that not only drew dangerous attention to yourselves –' Horizabel indicated the unconscious SIA agents at their feet – 'but if you'd had the good sense to share with me, I might have been able to investigate . . . it *means* something, you know, the fact that the most sensitive creatures among us are on the move again – and it's not good . . .'

Revelation!

Aunt Trudie and Aunt Violet turned very pink.

'Aunt Violet! Aunt Trudie!' exclaimed Freya. 'How could you be so irresponsible?'

'You're one to talk, Freya!' stormed Horizabel. 'Leaving the House of the O'Hero-Smiths in the sole charge of a two-year-old? What were you thinking? And people call *me* a Bad Babysitter!'

'Well, technically *I* was supposed to be in charge,' said Daniel miserably.

'And as for YOU,' snapped Horizabel, squaring up to Daniel. 'I know you're not Magical, but can't you at least stay awake for one measly minute?'

To do Daniel justice, even the most Magical of beings might have had some difficulties keeping their eyes open after being zapped by Mr Spink's tranquillising equipment, but Horizabel was in an unforgiving mood.

'Worse than that, you're supposed to be a *headteacher*!' scolded Horizabel. 'Yet I see very little advances in your children's Magical education . . .'

'They're too young to use Magic properly,' protested Freya.

'They don't seem to be too young to go through the Which Way and Starcross to Blink 22 and back again and defeat Vorcxix's *entire army*!' retorted Horizabel. Freya and Daniel and Aunt Trudie and Aunt Violet hung their heads as if they were being told off in Year 2, and Horizabel relented a little.

'You're working together better, admittedly,' acknowledged Horizabel, 'and there's quite a bit less arguing between you children, but you all need to learn from this adventure that the children must be taught about Magic, and to stop keeping so many secrets from one another!'

Everyone in the O'Hero-Smith family looked really rather thoughtful at this.

Horizabel's voice turned from red-poker hot to polar ice-cap cold.

'I'm going to repeat what I have said to you before,' said Horizabel grimly. 'In my job as a bounty hunter, I am supposed to eliminate K2. I ought to be telling the Universal Government where the O'Hero-Smith family hideout is, and probably eliminating that too. And the more you disobey me, the harder it is for me to protect you. Don't underestimate me, O'Hero-Smiths, my patience may run out.'

Horizabel was a bounty hunter, so she didn't have a heart, of course she didn't – but where the O'Hero-Smiths were concerned she had an inexplicable kind of *itch* where her heart might be if she had one. She was hoping she would grow out of it.

Blinkers returned from dropping off Mr Spink and his agents. She had laid the agents down in the middle of a field of corn, at a goodly distance from the House of the O'Hero-Smiths, tucking their equipment gently around them.

And then, on Horizabel's instruction, she gently dragged the body of sleeping Mr Spink in a wide circle around the others, before placing him carefully in the middle of it, along with everyone else. Lovingly, into Mr Spink's arms she put a single piece of rock, an asteroid, so when the dreamers awoke, in the middle of this 'crop circle', Mr Spink would be cradling a strange sphere made of a material as yet unknown in this part of the universe . . .

. . . and *that* would keep all those secret governmental organisations puzzling for decades. It would keep their nosy attention away from the hunt for Magical Creatures.

'Should we be off?' asked Blinkers.

'One second!' said Horizabel. 'And another thing—'

'Horizabel!' interrupted K2. *'Where's Puck?'*

They all looked around. There was no sign of the little robot. How could they not have noticed?

There was a nasty pause.

Horizabel had a stern look in her starry eye.

'Where is he?' said Mabel in bewilderment.

'Didn't you notice?' said Horizabel, in a strange, severe voice. 'Just before Vorcxix went through the Which Way he shot the little robot . . .'

'But that's *cheating*!' gasped Theo, outraged. 'Vorcxix

signed a Universally binding deal saying he wouldn't harm any of us!'

Horizabel shrugged her shoulders.

'I mentioned all of US, but I forgot to include Puck,' admitted Horizabel.

Mabel tugged Horizabel's sleeve. 'But Puck is all right, Horizabel, isn't he? Tell us he's all right? And *where is he?*'

Horizabel shook off Mabel's hand.

'You see, here's the thing about stories,' said Horizabel bleakly. 'There is often a price to be paid if you go on a wild adventure. The forces you are facing are real live dangerous ones, O'Hero-Smiths. And sometimes there will be a reckoning for that. Have you heard of the story of the River Styx? If you cross that river, just once too often, or if you pass through those Which Ways just one too many times, there will be a price to pay the Ferryman, or in this case, the Story Maker. Puck is out there, in the garden . . .'

Noooooo!

The O'Hero-Smith children looked at Horizabel in horror.

And ran out into the garden, where Horizabel was pointing.

Chapter 36
The Reckoning of a Story

Vorcxix's Spell Bolt had been so violent that it had blasted the loyal little robot into millions and millions of tiny pieces.

The children fell to their knees in the grass, trying to pick them up, but there were just so many of them, the task was impossible.

Dear faithful Puck! Who was always getting things wrong and muddling things up . . . who may not have been mortal, and may not have had a human heart, but on so many previous occasions proved that he had love enough inside him to lay down his heartless existence to protect the life of a friend.

'Aunt Violet, can you mend him?' asked Mabel, holding up a few pathetic crumpled pieces of the robot's corkscrew attachment.

'Mabel, I'm a brilliant robot-maker,' sighed Aunt Violet. 'But even *I* am not a miracle-worker. Vorcxix is a member of the High Council, so this is an immensely powerful Spell of destruction. And a lot of these pieces are so small they will have blown away on the wind.'

'Horizabel, you could do it! You can do anything!' cried Mabel.

But Horizabel shook her head, standing there, arms crossed, cloak blowing in the wind.

'Should we be off?' said Blinkers again softly.

Horizabel got ready. Placed her Starwalker on Blinkers's back. Unfurled her wings.

'Please, Horizabel, don't leave us!' begged Izzabird. 'Tell us what to do! How do we mend Puck?'

Horizabel would not look at them. 'I told you there would be a reckoning to pay,' she said, still in that strange voice. 'At least he's only a robot. Let it be a warning to you. I can't keep on giving you chances. You need to learn your lesson. It could have been one of *you*.'

'Puck *isn't* "only a robot"!' said K2 in a choked passionate voice. 'Puck is one of US!'

'You cannot take away a life that was never really there,' insisted Horizabel. 'Puck was never mortal.'

'What about Blinkers here, is *she* "only a robot"?' said Theo.

Horizabel flinched.

And thought about another time, another child, for whom Blinkers was their only friend.

Blinkers stared straight at Horizabel, blankly. Blinked once, twice.

Blink, blink.

'Please, Horizabel, please!' begged the children.

Horizabel paused, and there was a little tug on her star cowl.

She looked down, and there was Annipeck, crying, holding up her melted piece of Lego.

'What are you doing?' hissed Horizabel, pulling her star cowl away as if Annipeck was trying to bite her.

'She's offering you a reckoning,' said Aunt Violet grimly. 'A coin to pay the Ferryman, in lieu of Puck's life. It's a single piece of Lego but it means a lot to Annipeck.'

It's a gift...

Horizabel stared.

The little piece of melted Lego *did* look something like a coin, vaguely round and rough and stomped on as it was. Particularly through the eyes of a toddler. Annipeck pressed it into her hand.

Oh, these humans!

These infuriating little humans!

What *was it* with these humans?

'*I . . .*

cannot . . .

be . . .

BOUGHT!*' the great Grimm hunter hissed at the

heavens, fist clenched in rage around the Lego.

She strode back and forth indecisively.

Thundering moons and setting suns and shooting stars and by the toenails of Hairy Aquarius!

Finally, Horizabel knelt down and whispered kindly in a trembling Annipeck's ear.

'Thank you, Annipeck. *You* have paid the reckoning. Perhaps you CAN put Puck back together again . . . by yourselves.'

Annipeck smiled delightedly.

Horizabel regretted her weakness instantly.

What was she doing? *Growing soft?*

Time to go!

Horizabel composed herself once more. Even managed a small, wry smile.

'I won't ask you to make more promises, mortals,' she said drily. 'For it appears you cannot keep them. But in return for Annipeck's payment, I will give you some advice. Remember the O'Hero-Smith motto . . . *And you MAY have one among you who has the Magic you need to do this* . . . You are small but you are mighty . . . and if you're going to cross those Which Ways, if you're going to draw the Atlas, make sure you know the terrible risks that you are taking. Adults, teach these children how to find or use their Gifts, for I swear by the whiskers of Aries, *these children are going to need them*. And,' she paused, before continuing grudgingly, 'they do show SOME potential . . . Besides that, be careful what you wish for, trust each other more, and for heaven's sake . . . GROW A LITTLE GUMPTION.'

With a swirl of her cloak, Horizabel checked her Alternative Atlas. She needed to get back that Infinity Clock. Everest had been headed in the direction of Aunt Trudie's greenhouse. Aha. There it was. A Which Way. She spread her wings a bit wider, Blinkers beside her. She sprang up into the air, so high, that even when squinting, they couldn't really see her. And then folded her wings like a great peregrine falcon, and dived down with the sound of a rocket descending, changed path the second that she was about to hit the ground, slashing the air below her into a gigantic 'X' of a Which Way as she flew straight into Aunt Trudie's greenhouse with a huge

CRASH!!!!

Followed by an even larger one created by Blinkers.

And then they were gone, showering the O'Hero-Smith family with little pieces of broken glass.

In the garden with the bright sun shining on the millions of tiny broken fragments of Puck, Aunt Trudie shook her head as she stared down at the Impossible Task in front of them. It wasn't fair of Horizabel to get the children's hopes up.

Freya and Aunt Trudie and Aunt Violet pulled out their Spelling Sticks, motioning them above their heads in a circle, and then joining the three lightning blasts buzzing out of the ends of them to create the Power of Three.

But however many Spells they tried, however many incantations, Puck had been hit by such a powerful Spell of destruction that the little pieces remained inert and would not resurrect.

'I'm so sorry, everyone,' said Freya sorrowfully.

Izzabird longed with all her heart to be able to step forward and say, 'I can do it!' When was it going to be HER moment?!

Reluctantly but nobly she turned to Theo instead. This *was* an emergency, after all.

'Horizabel said: *you MAY have one among you who has the Magic you need to do this*. Maybe it's *you*, Theo,' said Izza.

Mending things is far harder than destroying them.

'Puck said you had "Ghost Powers". And whatever *they* are, they seemed to work well on Vorcxix's robot soldiers back on Blink 22 . . .'

Aunt Violet and Aunt Trudie and Freya and Daniel looked very surprised indeed.

'No offence, Theo,' said Aunt Trudie kindly, 'but you're not from a Magical family, so it's highly unlikely you have a Magical Gift . . .'

'Even if such a thing as "Ghost Powers" exist . . .' finished Aunt Violet. 'Which they don't. "Ghost Powers" are a myth.'

For an answer, Theo stretched out his hand with all five fingers pointing as widely as possible, and tried not to think about how foolish this probably made him look if the Magic didn't work.

Theo's fingers began to disappear, and as he slowly turned invisible, he could feel the coldness of the power within him, starting from a wintry stone in his stomach and then growing and building inside him, until it prickled on his skin like pins and needles.

Aunt Violet and Freya and Aunt Trudie and Daniel watched, now absolutely gobsmacked.

'I'll be hornswoggled!' said Aunt Violet, excitedly pointing her Spelling Stick up in the air and sending Magical blasts out of the end of it. 'The boy DOES have Ghost Powers!'

Theo slowly pointed his fingers down towards the little pieces of Puck that lay motionless in the grass.

'Think about Puck, Theo . . .' suggested Aunt Trudie eagerly. 'Every single thing that you can remember about him . . .

Theo concentrated as hard as he could, focusing on the little pieces of Puck in his mind. Imagining Puck getting things wrong and muddling things up. Puck's Not Very Relaxing Bedtime stories, how he always tried his best to help even if everything went pear-shaped as soon as he was involved.

'Horizabel said to remember the O'Hero-Smith motto!' said Mabel.

An O'Hero-Smith Knows No Limits . . . thought Theo. *The Sky Is Just the Beginning. No Rivers Can Stop Us, No Mountains Can Stand in Our Way* . . .

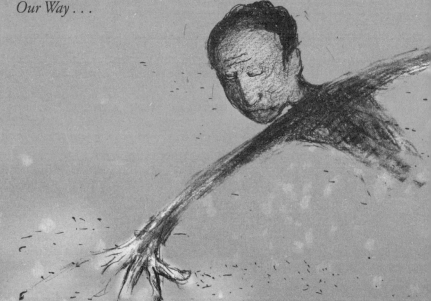

And as his thoughts converged on the idea of 'No Limits', Theo could feel his Magic misting its way into all the robot particles, and it was almost as if he could even sense bits of Puck's personality still residing in them . . .

And then Theo didn't know why, but his mind shifted to his mother. He could remember everything about her. Her eyes, the smell of her hair, the songs she used to sing him and Mabel, the stories she would tell. *She* could never come back, but he thought about how much he wished she could, how he longed for it, an ache in the middle of him. And how much she loved him and Mabel even if she was

The power of
creation took so
much more concentration
than the power of destruction

currently as invisible as Theo was
now. He imagined how wonderful
it would be if he could hear her saying
that in real life.

And the tiny dusty fragments of Puck
lifted themselves off the lawn and shot through
the air at high speed . . .

. . . And whizzed around making a strange tinkling
out-of-tune noise with all the notes out of shape and out
of order, like they were part of a terrifically complicated
moving jigsaw that had an innate sense of where their
own personal little fragment belonged in the whole . . .

. . . And while they dashed about, they made a
sort of music, that came to sound like a song that was
familiar:

I love a starcrossed journey, flying fast and flying slow . . .

sang the little pieces of Puck . . .

But home is where my dreams are, however far I go . . .

They all joined in the chorus, with growing excitement, as the outline of Puck began to appear, Aunt Violet, in her deep baritone as she waved her Spelling Stick like she was conducting an orchestra. Only Theo didn't sing – he was concentrating too hard on his Magic.

Once upon a Galaxy . . .
When dreams will all come true . . .
You'll come home to the fam-i-ly . . .
And we'll be home to you . . .

There was one surprising moment when Puck appeared to be much larger than he actually was . . . until the minuscule pieces of the little robot finally rearranged themselves triumphantly back into the right order, a fork assembling here, a corkscrew there, a cog, a wheel, a wire, a shattered screen, broken helicopter wings, motors, sensors all fitting themselves together quicker and quicker until they were exactly the same shape as Puck himself. He plopped to the ground and blinked open his robot eyes.

Theo let out a great breath and took back his Magic into himself.

'Puck!' cried Mabel. 'You're alive!' And she and Izzabird

and K2 and Theo and Annipeck rushed forward to embrace and make a fuss of the little robot, who was shaking and lopsided, but absolutely the same dear old Puck.

He embraced them back, positively *overcome* by the welcome he received. 'You IS pleased to see me!' he said in delighted surprise. 'I is only a robot but . . .'

'. . . but you're part of the *family*, Puck,' Theo finished the sentence for him.

'You loves me as if I was a Magical Creature!' said Puck in delight. 'Posiquiffly even MORE! To Blink 22 and back again maybe?'

'*To Blink 22 and back again*, Puck,' said K2, hugging the stiff metal body of the robot as hard as he could.

To Blink 22 and
back again, Puck

And then what hugging, and tearful and excited and happy explanations went on about the adventures and perils they had all been through.

Slowly, slowly, Theo reappeared, and as he came back into visibility once more, everyone cheered. 'Ghost Powers! Who'd have thought it? Theo Smith has *Ghost Powers* . . . Well *done*, my boy! We should have a party for you coming into your powers!' boomed Aunt Violet.

Theo Smith has GHOST POWERS!

And although Theo's heart lifted with joy at the admiration in Aunt Violet's voice as she thumped him on the back in friendly congratulation, he was still trembling with the confusion of his emotions: pride, relief, joy, mixed in with a strange sadness, and a guiltiness that he couldn't shake off. He couldn't meet his father's eyes when Daniel enveloped him in a big relieved hug.

'I could not be more proud of you! And your mother would be too!' added Daniel.

Theo's face lifted to Daniel's. 'Really?' he said uncertainly.

'Of *course* your mother would be pleased, Theo!' said Izzabird, valiantly being generous. 'From now on, you grown-ups *have* to keep your promise to Horizabel to teach us about Magic . . .'

The O'Hero-Smith adults solemnly agreed.

We shall see if they keep that promise . . .

'And now,' said Aunt Violet, rubbing her hands together. 'For a slap-up breakfast! I don't know about anyone else, but I'm famished!'

'Me too!' said Annipeck, taking Puck by the hand and leading them all back to the house.

Freya and Daniel and Aunt Trudie took the Magical Creatures they had rescued from Mr Spink's laboratory, to settle them beside the ones they were already keeping in the attic – they would work out how to return them to their own worlds tomorrow. Everyone else went back to their rooms to have showers and get dressed while Aunt Violet and Annipeck made breakfast.

Theo put on his clean clothes, still trembling with excitement, and when the Enchanted Hairdryer had obligingly dried his hair into his old neat self again, he finally got up the courage to open the drawer of his bedside table and take out his mother's letter.

He stood looking at it for a moment.

My father said she'd be proud of me . . . thought Theo.

And then he opened it very quickly before he had a chance to change his mind.

And this is what he read:

Dearest Theo, and dearest Mabel,

I am writing this for you *to open first, Theo, because you are the eldest, and I am hoping you will give this to Mabel when she turns thirteen too.*

There is an old secret about my family that I have never told your father.

Something that can come out every couple of generations, and may appear in either you or in Mabel, generally round about the age that you are now.

Don't worry if it never takes place.

But if anything odd ever happens, something you don't quite

Dearest Theo, and dearest Mabel,

I am writing this for you to open first, Theo, because you are the elder, and I am hoping you will give this to Mabel when she turns thirteen too.

There is an old secret about my family that I have never told your father.

Something that can come out every couple of generations, and may appear in either you or in Mabel, generally round about the age you are now.

Don't worry if it never takes place.

But if anything odd ever happens, something you don't quite understand, something that you or Mabel can do that seems strange, and that no-one else can do... Or if ever you or Mabel or your father find yourselves in trouble...

... you need to knock on the door of the House of the O'Heros at the Crossing of the Ways in a funny little village called Soggy-Bottom Marsh-Place. Ask for help. The people there will look after you.

And I will too.

I am always there, Theo and Mabel. You cannot see me, but I am there. Watching over you from a faraway star. You could not be more loved, and if death were not to part us, nothing else could.

Fly high, and fly kindly, wherever you go.

We will meet again, in another world.

Love,

Mum

understand, something that you or Mabel can do that seems strange, and that no one else can do . . .

Or if ever you or Mabel or your father find yourselves in trouble . . .

. . . you need to knock on the door of the House of the O'Heros at the Crossing of the Ways in a funny little village called Soggy-Bottom-Marsh-Place.

Ask for help.

The people there will look after you.

And I will too.

I am always there, Theo and Mabel. You cannot see me, but I am there. Watching over you from a faraway star.

You could not be more loved, and if death were not to part us, nothing else could.

Fly high, and fly kindly, wherever you go.

We will meet again, in another world.

Love, Mum

Theo stood still in shock and delight.

And then he gave a slow smile.

Theo gave a slow smile.

He put the letter back into the drawer, touched his mother's photograph very gently, and ran down the stairs, two at a time, and into the kitchen.

The O'Hero-Smith family was all sitting down at the rather-burnt kitchen table, chattering excitedly.

Aunt Violet's Laying-the-Table-Machine was springing into action, flinging plates into places. Her Automatic-Toast-Butterer was merrily slapping butter on the toast, a little over-enthusiastically. Horizabel's cleaning-up operation had been effective, but had merely returned the O'Hero-Smith kitchen back to its usual chaos. Bits of Aunt Violet's motorbikes lying around in the corners, Aunt Trudie's plants trailing into the sink.

Izzabird was telling them all about the success of their adventure, ending triumphantly, 'You see, Mum! We ARE going to be Starcrossers one day!'

Freya was so pleased Izza was back home, and safe, she forgot how unlikely that was, and she absent-mindedly patted her on the shoulder, smiling. 'Of course you are, Izza . . .'

As Theo sat down and joined them, he asked his father, 'Dad, why, of all the places in the world, did you come *here*, to Soggy-Bottom-Marsh-Place?'

'Well, it's a funny thing,' said Daniel thoughtfully as he sipped his coffee. 'The only reason I applied to be the headteacher of the school here was that your mother promised herself she would come to Soggy-Bottom-Marsh-Place one day, it was such a humorous name for a village . . . and she never did. So when I saw the application for the headteacher post, and we were all so unhappy, it seemed a little like . . . *destiny* telling us how to get a fresh start.' Daniel looked a little embarrassed. 'I mean, I know there's no such thing as Fate, but . . .' He held Freya's hand.

'Thank goodness you *did* come here!' said Freya, smiling and kissing him.

To Daniel's surprise, Theo gave him a big hug.

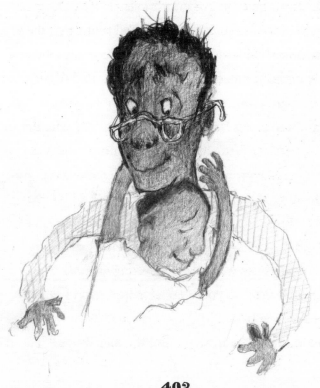

Aunt Violet held her arms wide.

'Breakfast is served!' she bellowed, waving a serving spoon around in the manner of a conjuror, surveying the chaos in front of her with a benevolent smile.

'Here, Theo!' said Izzabird. 'Pass the cornflakes!'

My mother knew! thought Theo, in total, utter joy as he passed the cornflakes.

She wouldn't have been surprised at the Ghost Powers at all!

The Ghost Powers came from *her*!

Their coming to Soggy-Bottom-Marsh-Place wasn't even an accident, not even destiny . . . *she* had sent them there.

Theo looked around the chattering, clattering, mess of Puck spilling honey all over the table as he tried to help by spooning it out with his corkscrew attachment, the noisy argument Izzabird was having with Freya about whether or not they should start the flying lessons immediately, *now*, or tomorrow, Mabel feeding Clueless under the table, Aunt Trudie pouring milk into her tea with what looked like a mini watering can, Annipeck tucking into her second breakfast of the day with gusto, Aunt Violet explaining loudly to Daniel her wonderful moves against Mr Spink's agents, K2 listening to Puck telling stories from Everest's childhood.

A year ago the chaos, the noise, the *mess* of it all would

have got on Theo's nerves.

Now he suddenly found it comfortingly familiar.

It was OK to be happy. His mother *wanted* them to be happy.

Theo ate his cornflakes with a happy grin.

For his heart was lighter than it had been in five long years.

She had sent them *home*.

Epilogue

Last night I went to the House of the O'Hero-Smiths again . . .

Not in person, of course, because those tricksome aunts have closed all the Which Ways that lead there so clam-fast shut that even the skinniest of spirits could not slip through the cracks. So I visited the house through *another* sort of Which Way, one that never closes, the ever-open Which Way of a memory in my dreams, and as I hovered right above it in the dream of my memory, it was as if I saw that house for the very . . . first . . . time.

Three female Witches, living in the house all together, in itself you've already mixed yourself a powerful charm with that. *Five* Magical children, and everybody knows the power of the number Five. Because, yes, Izza will get her Gift. Mabel too, though I couldn't tell you what.

The entire beastly Magical family walking and sleeping and eating in a house absolutely soaked in Magic, dripping with Spellcraft, bathed in Starcrossing, for thousands and thousands and thousands of years, for it is a house that is situated right bang slap in the middle of an Ancient Crossing of the Ways, where the creatures of Magic have been passing through on the way to Anywhere-in-the-

Universe since the very beginnings of recorded time.

Ghosts in the airing cupboard, whispering in those children's ears. Creeping out of the woodwork, rustling in the wall spaces.

As I tossed and turned in my sleep, I was going through that house again, picking over cushions, opening the doors, lifting up the floorboards, searching, searching for the pieces of the Atlas. And as I looked, behind me there were footsteps. And suddenly I could see them, smell them, hear them, all around me. Hoofprints of unicorns, glowing on the hall floor, the bright ring of snowbear claws, going down the stairs, the handprints of long-dead Wizards glowing on the bannister, the manifold historical impressions of the thousands and thousands and thousands of Magical Creatures that had made their way through that house, on their way to different, or kinder reaches of the universe, using the power of the Ancestor's Atlas Gift.

And they left behind them the memory of their breath, the touch of their scales, the dust, the motes and twigs of their Magical natures that had soaked into the wood, up into the ceiling, down into the floor, and even now those beastly Magical children were absorbing that Magic as they ran barefoot up the stairs, eating that dust, mixed up with their suppers, breathing it in out, in out, and goodness knows what they were digesting as they swallowed it down, what supernatural powers were incubating inside them in the bewitching cauldron of Spellcraft and Starcrossing that the House had become.

What were the chances, in that ignorant, backward backwater of a planet on a disregarded arm of an out-of-the-way galaxy, of TWO of those children already being bestowed with truly extraordinary Gifts? One, K2's Atlas Gift, that hadn't been seen for thousands of years, a Gift so powerful that it was the sole reason for the UG's iron rule over the entire Universe.

That was bad enough.

But then, the second Gift, Annipeck's Magic-That-Works-On-Plastic, was an entirely new Gift that *I* had certainly never come across before, and *I* have wandered about a bit through the Which Way Starcrosses of our shiningly beautiful Worlds. And now a third Gift, equally special, Theo's Ghost Powers. Powers that were supposedly mythical. Powers that allowed their wielder not just to be invisible, but to be GHOST-LIKE, wafting their Magic into corners and workings where other Magic couldn't . . .

It can't have been a coincidence. There was something about *that* house, *that* combination of people, *these* historical and present Magical influences, that together were bringing out truly extraordinary Gifts in these children. And these were just the Gifts I knew about.

What about the ones I *didn't*?

Suddenly I knew with utmost dreaded certainty that *all* of the children had dangerous Gifts, and the things you know about are always less dangerous than the things you don't. The children swam before me in my mind's eye, lit up with their auras.

Grey for K2. Well, *that* made sense, the Atlas Gift was an Air Gift (but far paler than it ought to be for a Gift as strong as his, and that made me uneasy).

Theo's bright as the shiniest gold (Earth).

Izzabird's redder than the fiercest blood (Fire).

Mabel's green as the darkest emerald sea (Water).

It was all making a horrible kind of sense. I mean, what good-luck and bad-luck stars had brought those children together and given those children the Gifts of all Four Corners?

And the last child, the baby, Annipeck. It made sense for her peculiar Gift to be an Aether Gift, because all the Corners were represented by her older siblings, and there was a dreadful patterning going on here. But now I came to think of it . . . *her aura was invisible.* It was definitely there, she had an aura, of course she did, even though I couldn't see it, or smell it, or hear the bright ring of my echoes on its edge.

It was all very strange.

What were Mabel's and Izzabird's Gifts going to be?

What I know now, is, we are all racing against time.

For I cannot protect the O'Hero-Smiths forever.

SHE and the Universal Government now know about their existence.

And something worse has happened. Blunderbore contained a Glitch.

The Glitch was caused by K2 holding the Utchimabug while his Atlas was being uploaded. A clever idea of K2's, for the Glitch meant that he kept his own Gift – but it also meant that Blunderbore's version of the Atlas was already going wrong.

So like many clever ideas, there were unforeseen consequences.

Blunderbore was connected to Vorcxix's own computer version of the Atlas, which is connected to the twenty-four Atlases of the Universal Government . . .

So, slowly, slowly, like a creeping virus, things are beginning to go wrong with those Atlases . . .

A tick has become a tear, a tear has become a rip . . .

And the rip is spreading. And soon my OWN Atlas had a Glitch. And the copies of the Atlases.

So now the Twelve Bounty Hunters, SHE herself, as well as Vorcxix the Vile, are all going to be concentrating the might of their powers on getting their hands on the Child-With-The-Atlas-Gift.

K2 is the only person who can draw a new Atlas, that doesn't have a Glitch.

So the O'Hero-Smith family is in more danger than ever.

And as for me, I have so many questions, and not enough answers.

What is Everest doing with the Infinity Clock? I need to get my hands on that slippery Hero.

And why does Vorcxix want it too?

The Universe is in peril.

And I have a nasty feeling, deep in my orphan's bones, that my Quest is going to lead me back to my own past as well as the Universe's future.

I do not want to go there.

But I must.

Once upon a Galaxy

I fly through the Which Way portals,
a million miles or so,
But home is where my dreams are, however far I go . . .
For forever as I star-walk
I'm dreaming as I roam
That I see in every footprint
My family and my home . . .

Once upon a Galaxy
When dreams will all come true
You'll come home to the family
And we'll be home to you . . .

I love a starcrossed journey, flying fast and flying slow
But home is where my dreams are, however far I go.

Love is always
worth it

Cressida Cowell was the 2019-2022
Waterstones Children's Laureate. She is the
author and illustrator of the bestselling
The Wizards of Once book series as well as
How to Train Your Dragon, which has been
translated into forty-two languages, sold
over 14 million books worldwide, and is an
award-winning DreamWorks film series, and
a TV series on Netflix and CBBC.

Which Way Round the Galaxy is the second
adventure in Cressida's out-of-this-world
new series.

ACKNOWLEDGEMENTS

A whole team of people have helped
me write this book.

Thank you to my wonderful editors,
Ruth Alltimes and Naomi Greenwood, and
my magnificent agents, Veronique Baxter
and Caroline Walsh.

A special big thanks to my brilliant designer,
Samuel Perrett, and to my incredible Publicity
and Marketing team, Rebecca Logan,
Camilla Leask and Naomi Berwin.

And to everyone at Hachette Children's Group,
Hilary Murray Hill, Katy Cattell, Katie Maxwell,
Sarah Farmer, Inka Roszkowska, Laura Pritchard,
Bhavini Jolapara, Nicola Goode, Katherine Fox and
the Sales team, Tracy Phillips and the Rights Team.

To the freelancers:
Genevieve Herr
Sally Critchlow
Anna Bowles
Lisa Davis

As Waterstones Children's Laureate until
very recently, I want to say a wider thank you
to all the book-y world heroes: librarians, booksellers,
literacy organisations, teachers, journalists and
book advocates online. Every child has the right
to read for the joy of it, because reading is magic,
and magic is for everyone.

And most important of all . . .

Simon, Maisie, Clemmie and Xanny
The Best Family in the World
Because . . . True Love and Beyond,
and Family really is Everything.

Because a family should be built on
KINDNESS
and kindness has no limits

Discover the Magic of Cressida Cowell

visit
www.cressidacowell.co.uk
to find out all about her books,
events, and lots more!

/CressidaCowellBooks
@CressidaCowellAuthor
@CressidaCowell
CressidaCowell

Read the
amazing
HOW TO TRAIN YOUR
DRAGON
series

DISCOVER THE NO.1 BESTSELLING WIZARDS OF ONCE SERIES

Also available in audio, read by the award-winning actor David Tennant

Watch Out for the final book in the Which Way adventures...

Which Way to the FUTURE